THE CIRCLE-A KILLINGS

THE
CIRCLE-A KILLINGS

SEAN HEARY

Copyright © 2020 Sean Heary

The moral right of the author has been asserted.

Apart from any fair dealing for the purposes of research or private study, or criticism or review, as permitted under the Copyright, Designs and Patents Act 1988, this publication may only be reproduced, stored or transmitted, in any form or by any means, with the prior permission in writing of the publishers, or in the case of reprographic reproduction in accordance with the terms of licences issued by the Copyright Licensing Agency. Enquiries concerning reproduction outside those terms should be sent to the publishers.

This is a work of fiction. Names, characters, businesses, places, events and incidents are either the products of the author's imagination or used in a fictitious manner. Any resemblance to actual persons, living or dead, or actual events is purely coincidental.

Matador
9 Priory Business Park,
Wistow Road, Kibworth Beauchamp,
Leicestershire. LE8 0RX
Tel: 0116 279 2299
Email: books@troubador.co.uk
Web: www.troubador.co.uk/matador
Twitter: @matadorbooks

ISBN 978 1838593 827
British Library Cataloguing in Publication Data.
A catalogue record for this book is available from the British Library.

Printed and bound in Great Britain by 4edge Limited
Typeset in 11pt Minion Pro by Troubador Publishing Ltd, Leicester, UK

Matador is an imprint of Troubador Publishing Ltd

For Sibone

PROLOGUE

Even before Prince Siegfried and Odette ascended to Heaven, billionaire financier Charles Edge was on his feet in his grand tier box at Covent Garden holding out his wife's sable stole. The opening night of *Swan Lake* had been awe-inspiring, but Edge had no time to express his appreciation. He needed to get back to the Ritz.

"Slow down, Charles," his Texas trophy wife pleaded, as they hurried along the empty Opera House corridor. Dressed in a tight black beaded gown and six-inch heels, Samantha was not dressed for speed.

Edge eased up. "Wear something more sensible next time."

"*You* picked the dress, Charles."

"But not the shoes." Edge was never at fault.

"Besides, what's the hurry? They can't start without you."

"Damn right they can't," Edge said, helping his wife through the door onto Bow Street.

There was a nip in the air courtesy of the clear winter night sky. "Is that our limo?" Samantha asked, hugging her stole around her bare shoulders.

Parked in front of the theatre was a silver Rolls-Royce Phantom. Donning his cap, the Ritz Hotel's chauffeur climbed out and with a beckoning smile opened the back door.

Sensing he was being rushed, Edge planted his feet on the swept pavement and lit an Al Capone cigarillo.

"What *now*, Charles?"

"I decide when I'm ready. Not a bum in a rented suit."

Samantha tutted. "For Christ's sake. I'm freezing my tits off and he's parked in a no-standing zone."

"That's his problem."

"Goodness gracious, Charles. Why are you always so small-minded?"

"You don't get it, do you?"

"What? Because you're the nineteenth richest man on the planet you think—"

"Sixteenth."

"And that makes you a better person than our driver, who didn't start life with a Yale education and a red sports car, paid for by his industrialist father?"

Edge scoffed. "You've got to be kidding. That bozo wouldn't have a job if it wasn't for me. And you'd still be working at Hooters."

Tears swelling in her eyes, Samantha climbed into the Rolls.

Unrepentant, Edge refused to move. Puffing on his cigarillo, he gazed absently across Bow Street at the former magistrates' court, famous for prosecuting Oscar Wilde.

"Driver. Take me back to the hotel, please."

"Yes, Mrs Edge." The chauffeur nodded from the pavement, but stayed put.

"Now," Samantha said, slamming the door.

The chauffeur, a serious-faced man in his early sixties, knew who signed the cheques. Ignoring the big-breasted blonde in the back seat, he coughed into his hand to attract the financier's attention. But Edge was frozen in place, his cigarillo held motionless short of his open mouth.

Curious, the driver traced Edge's gaze to the building across the street. Nothing. Then without warning a thunderous crack. The chauffeur's head shot back to his fare, who was lying in a pool of blood on the pavement.

Keeping an eye on the old magistrates' court, the driver scrambled toward Edge and checked his pulse. None. "Get back inside," he yelled to the theatregoers percolating out of the Opera House exit onto the forecourt. "There's a shooter on the roof."

At first the patrons stood and stared, unsure what the uniformed man was saying and why he was pointing to the building across the street. Then, noticing the bloodied body lying at the chauffeur's feet, they darted back inside like field rabbits taking fright.

On the rooftop, a lone gunman, face hidden under an oversized hoodie, dissembled his Nemesis Arms Vanquish sniper rifle and shoved it into a backpack. He glanced down at his victim as he stood before the stone parapet balustrade, shaking a can of red paint. Then, with the flare of a street artist, he sprayed an anarchist's circle-A monogram and #16 along the top railing.

From below came the sound of approaching sirens. Recent terrorist activity had London on high alert; police response times were down to a handful of minutes. But the sniper appeared unconcerned. Recovering the .308 Winchester shell, he shouldered his backpack, descended the stairs and disappeared into Covent Garden Tube station.

1

Rossi gazed admiringly at the intelligent young faces as he entered the Runcie Lecture Room. Dressed in jeans, a patterned blue shirt, a brown vest and a tawny tweed jacket, he was style personified. A shake of his head as he stepped behind the lectern. Three weeks into the Lent term and he was still unsure what he was doing in Cambridge. The day following Rossi's triumphant return from Moscow, Cardinal Santo Capelli, the dean of the Sacred College of Cardinals, invited him to his Vatican office for what Rossi assumed would be a celebratory cup of Darjeeling tea. What happened next happened quickly.

The bespectacled, white-haired cardinal ordered Rossi to take a short sabbatical, to go get his shipshape life back in order. Rossi smelt sacrificial lamb on the spit.

Within a week, the cardinal had bumped him off to Cambridge University with a stack of well-prepared notes under his arm, and a Faculty of Divinity library card in his wallet that read: Lorenzo Rossi, Visiting Academic, Vatican History.

Liam Cleary, the professor of the History of Christianity, accepted Rossi's appointment under duress, protesting that the inspector general was not suitably qualified for such an undertaking.

Expecting Rossi to play to a half-empty house, Cleary booked his freshman into what he'd dubbed an *off-West End* seminar room. But, when word got out that *Tatler* magazine had voted Lorenzo Rossi one of Rome's most eligible bachelors for the last four years running, the class roll filled fast. Juggling classroom schedules, Cleary moved Rossi's production to the larger, more prestigious Runcie Room in the Faculty of Divinity's basement. The bow-shaped, light-wood-panelled theatre with curved white laminated tables and blue fabric retractable seating was cosy with a cabaret atmosphere. This suited Rossi as he liked to put on a show.

The auditorium lights dimmed and the students leant forward, engaged. Grinning to himself, Rossi took a step to the side. In silence, he scrolled through images of Martin Luther, John Calvin, Huldrych Zwingli, Thomas Cranmer and John Knox.

"Hands up if you haven't heard of the Protestant Reformation," Rossi said, looking about.

A young Chinese man slouched in his seat at the back raised his hand.

"Then you've wandered into the wrong music hall. If I were you, I'd escape while there's time – unless you've come for a snooze."

Laughter.

"Whether the Reformation was right or wrong I don't intend covering today," Rossi continued, holding up his hand to quieten the audience. "It would take far too long and end in the police being called." Pause. "But I am prepared, as a good Catholic, to concede the Reformation is understandable within its historical context – greed, abuse, and corruption in the Church." Rossi paused to a sea of nodding heads then started up again. "Or were the Protestants of the day too heavy-handed? Was their solution an overkill of biblical proportions? What do you think? Right up there with the East–West Schism of 1054?"

Rossi didn't like to lecture; it wasn't his way. He preferred a conversation. A hot debate. As he'd expected, his provocative comments had elicited the desired response. Everybody spoke at once: a cacophony of discord.

"Or perhaps motivated by self-interest?" Rossi said, pointing to an attentive blue-eyed girl in the third row. "A touch of King Henry VIII?" he added, singling out an arty-looking young man off to the side.

The audience wasn't having it. "Bollocks," an angelic voice called out from the back.

Rossi turned to the next slide: a painting of the austere sixteenth-century Bishop of Rome, Pope Pius V, with the words "Counter-Reformation" splashed across his forehead.

Good-natured booing came from a third of the crowd.

"Sorry." Rossi held up his hands. "I'm used to preaching to the converted. I keep forgetting I'm in England. All those years working inside the Vatican can twist one's sense of humour," he said, with a wicked grin. "The truth is the Protestant Reformation led to the Catholic Reformation. A period of Catholic revival and resurgence. Some historians argue that, if it had not been for Martin Luther, the power and influence of the Church would have diminished over the centuries."

"Which Church?" came a salvo of voices.

"The one true Church," Rossi said, with an inward smile, as he ran his fingers through his short spiky black hair. Without warning, his heart ached. Memories of Cathy hacking off his thick wavy mane in a Moscow safe house flooded in.

As Rossi spoke on the Council of Trent, a tall man in his early thirties entered the theatre through the door to the left of the floor-level stage. Out of place in his Ermenegildo Zegna suit and groomed eyebrows, Rossi's gaze followed him as he moved lightly up the sloping side aisle. Rossi paused as the man seated himself at the back. *Lawrence?* He couldn't be sure. The room was dim, and the man's face was hidden behind a cello set upright on the seat in front of him. Rossi had seen his share of Lawrences and Cathys since arriving in England. But none as convincing.

At the end of the fifty-minute lecture, Rossi peered up at Lawrence's double. A chorus of young ladies fluttered forward as Rossi removed his microphone and gathered up his notes. He made his excuses and wriggled free of all but one: a braless girl in a tight maroon-coloured sweater.

The girl – more like a woman, Rossi thought: midtwenties – introduced herself as Natasha, a third-year student studying theology and religion. With unblinking eyes, she confessed she was behind in her studies and in desperate need of a private tutor. A tutor the height and build of Rossi.

"Professor," she said, preferring her made-up title over his first name, Lorenzo, which he'd suggested his students call him, "perhaps we can discuss my predicament at the Fez Club this evening?"

"I'm not sure that's appropriate," Rossi said, scanning the room for Lawrence. Gone.

Settling for an invitation to Fisher House – the Cambridge University Catholic Chaplaincy where Rossi was being accommodated at the request of the Vatican for the duration of his secondment – Natasha headed off.

Following her at a safe distance into the brightly lit corridor, Rossi expected to find Lawrence lurking in one of the dark recesses. *Not there.*

As he ascended to street level, Rossi couldn't help but ponder how vulnerable the young students were to the larger-than-life Camrbidge pedagogues. *Or was it the other way around?* He wasn't about to find out. Rossi was determined to complete his term of penance, for whatever crime the Vatican had decided he was guilty of, and return to his job as the inspector general of the Corps of Gendarmerie of Vatican City.

Rossi exited the building through the four-storey rotunda and stood in the faculty's imposing forecourt, scanning the area for Lawrence. *Why come all this way to disappear?*

Peering up at the rows of floor-to-ceiling windows a smile came to Rossi's face. Before leaving Rome, Rossi had studied a satellite image of Cambridge on Google Maps. As he homed in on the Faculty of Divinity from above, he'd got the impression an adjustable spanner had inspired the building's design. The rotunda, from which a wedge-shaped section had been cut out to form the forecourt entrance, reminded him of the spanner's head, and a row of narrow, south-facing terraces the handle. But now he wasn't so sure. *Pac-man. Definitely Pac-Man*, he decided.

Rubbing the back of his neck, Rossi had one final look for Cathy's Moscow station novice. Still no Lawrence. "I'm going crazy," he murmured to himself, opening his umbrella and heading off across the River Cam towards Fisher House.

2

Dressed in a brown cotton trench coat with a green umbrella hanging from his arm, Rossi stood at the window of his Fisher House room staring out at the weather. He'd seldom ventured out since arriving in Cambridge on account of his depressed state of mind following his bust-up with Cathy. When he woke this morning, he decided the moping around must stop. He'd heard from a fellow music-lover on staff about a stall on Market Hill boasting an extensive catalogue of LP records. His colleague had seen an original pressing of Bizet's *Carmen* with Maria Callas while browsing last week. Good condition, but a little pricey.

With a shrug of determination Rossi donned his pork-pie hat and headed out on foot, scouring the deep doorways and the lunchtime crowd on Rose Crescent for Lawrence. By the time he arrived at the open-air market with its multicoloured striped canvas stalls the rain had stopped and the sky offered signs of hope. As spears of sun burst through the clouds, he shook the water off his umbrella and closed it. Strolling around the glistening cobblestone square, in no hurry, he was convinced CIA Special Agent Lawrence no longer existed. Well, at least not in Cambridge. *Why would he?* He was still in Moscow counting body parts. It was just another cruel joke his once reliable mind had played on him since Cathy slammed the door in his face.

For a short while, Rossi lost himself in a rack of classical music.

"You looking for something in particular?" a big Jamaican fella asked, in an East End accent.

"I like that. Who is it?" Rossi said, nodding at the LP playing on the turntable, not wanting to show his hand. "Pavarotti?"

"Close – Mario Lanza."

Rossi let out a laugh. "Pavarotti's the only name I know. No, wait, I lie. Maria Kelly. Saw the movie."

"You mean Callas. I've got just what you're looking for." The Jamaican flicked through one of a dozen handmade LP boxes set side by side along the counter.

"I only mentioned I saw the movie."

"Found it. Brings tears to my eyes. The original three-LP box set. Rare as hen's teeth."

"Bizet: *Carmen*." Rossi examined the cover and then removed the first record. He tilted it from side to side, checking for scratches. "I had a girlfriend named Carmen once," Rossi lied.

"Good omen, sir."

"She ran off with my best friend." Pause. "How much?"

The Jamaican ran a discreet eye over Rossi, his gaze resting for a split second on Rossi's Tag Heuer Grand Carrera. "For a gentleman with your appreciation of fine music – one-fifty."

Rossi smiled and shook his head. "One hundred?"

"Box set; first press; cover in mint condition; not a scratch on it." The Jamaican rattled on, taking the recording back from Rossi. "In fact, I think I'll keep it and give it to my mother for her birthday."

Five minutes later, and £150 lighter, Rossi entered an establishment on Trinity Street with a plastic bag brimming full of Valencia oranges, and the Callas box set wrapped in butchers' paper. The pub was quiet. In-between lunch and dinner.

"A double Laphroaig, *signora*," Rossi called over as he set the oranges on the floor and Maria Callas on the bar.

"Right you are, sir," a dark-haired Irish lass said, gazing past Rossi at an intriguing-looking woman who had just entered from the street.

"I assume this is yours?" the lady said, handing Rossi an orange she'd picked up near the entrance.

"You following me, *signora*?" Rossi asked, looking down at his shopping bag, which was lying on its side.

The newcomer frowned at Rossi then said, "Are you really expecting me to respond to such a discourteous question?"

It was Rossi's turn to be dumbstruck. He had noticed the lady on Rose Crescent and twice in the market square.

She was too interesting to miss: heroin chic, tall and slim with translucent skin, and long mousy-brown hair. He had assumed she was with Lawrence, but now he wasn't so sure. "Forgive me," he said, colouring. "I've confused you with someone else."

"A stalker, it would seem."

"I'm not that lucky," Rossi said, offering her a drink.

"Too early for me."

"A coffee?"

The lady leant in. "How's your memory?"

"They tell me it's rather good."

She whispered an address in Knightsbridge, London. "Don't write it down. Special Agent Lawrence is expecting you. Tomorrow evening. Six o'clock sharp. Come alone and make sure you're not followed."

Before Rossi could protest, the lady had gone.

3

The following afternoon was dull but dry. Rossi caught the 4:10 from Cambridge railway station to London King's Cross, arriving smack on five. As he descended the underground stairs, Rossi wondered what Lawrence wanted and why all the cloak and dagger. It was not social.

As the south-west-bound Piccadilly Line train pulled up, Rossi's eyes peeled left and right. Although he couldn't imagine being tailed, he knew it was possible. So, out of an abundance of caution, he launched a one-man dry-cleaning run. Countersurveillance tradecraft Cathy had taught him in Moscow. Rossi stood on the platform as though waiting for someone. Then, as the doors closed, he sprung on board. Rossi stood near the exit and then alighted the train at Earl's Court, three stops past Knightsbridge. It was 5:20 by the time he flagged down a black cab. The taxi took him back in the direction he had just travelled and dropped him alongside the Victoria and Albert Museum. As if out walking the dog, he strolled the perimeter of the world-famous museum of decorative arts and design before doubling back and criss-crossing his way to Ennismore Garden Mews in Knightsbridge, a short dead-end cobblestoned lane.

Rossi strained his eyes, checking the numbers. The three-storey terrace house was at the very end, with a view back down the street. He glanced over his shoulder as he approached and rang the bell. The magnetic lock released. Lawrence was already descending the stairs as Rossi entered.

"Sorry about all the drama," Lawrence said, stepping around four pairs of black leather shoes. "We're in the middle of a live operation."

"And you need me to stay out of the way? I'm all for that, Paul."

They embraced like old friends. Although they had only known each other for a short time, their common experience in Russia had forever bonded them.

"Come up. There are people I'd like you to meet."

Rossi followed Lawrence up the narrow, polished staircase, fearful of the responses to his unasked questions.

Entering the barn-sized living room, the answer to question one became plain. *No Cathy.* Instead, three shoeless men sat with straight backs on a white-leather U-shaped sofa set, in what Rossi could only describe as the "white room", drinking Jim Beam. *CIA stiffs*, Rossi thought.

The room had little furniture and four white walls. White rugs covered the high-gloss laminated white floor. And two spherical opaque glass pendants hung from the white ceiling. In the far corner stood a Steinway grand piano – white. The only thing that wasn't white were the agents' expensive suits and the colour of their probing eyes.

"Where's John?" Rossi asked, gesturing to the piano.

The four CIA operatives exchanged puzzled glances.

Rossi turned to Lawrence for help. "The white room, the white Steinway, *imagine all the people living life in peace…*" More blank looks. "Never mind," Rossi said with a mirthless grin.

Lawrence made the introductions: Cleveland Jefferson, a tall barrel-chested Afro-American with a short Afro fade; Ethan Rosenthal, a squat, strong New Yorker with curly brown hair; and Alfonzo Riccardo, a tall muscular Pennsylvanian with shiny olive skin and thinning dark hair. Rossi figured they were all in their early forties and had worked together for some time.

No warm handshakes, only appraising nods. Suits of various shades of dark blue. Blazers tapered and slender. Fashionable ties, white shirts, top button still fastened. Rossi sensed the outfits were new and not their usual attire. *Muscleheads dressed up as Armani models.*

"Bourbon?" Jefferson offered, holding up a half-empty bottle of Jim Beam.

A slight cringe. "Not my drink," Rossi said, having already decided he didn't like his new pals and wanted nothing to do with what they were selling.

Lawrence planted his knees on the sofa and reached over the back. "Laphroaig?" he offered, holding up an unopened bottle of Rossi's favourite Scotch.

"I'm honoured, Paul," Rossi said, kicking off his shoes, figuring it would be boorish not to show his socks like his hosts.

A much-needed silence as Lawrence poured Rossi a generous measure.

Rossi took a long sip, set his crystal glass on the coffee table, and sat on the sofa opposite Lawrence. Jefferson sat between Rosenthal and Riccardo on Rossi's right.

"Well, Inspector General," Lawrence said, "you must be curious."

"Beyond imagination," Rossi quipped, not intending to make it easy.

"Charles Edge," Rosenthal said, leaning forward to catch Rossi's eyes. "Does the name mean anything to you?"

"Robber baron."

"Someone blew his brains out last week."

"Not me. I have an alibi."

"Edge was the third billionaire murdered in the last sixty days. Jeremy Crisp was the first and Rudolf Legg the second. Starting to see a pattern?"

"If you think it's the Russians, Cathy's your man."

Rosenthal took a pull on his bourbon, catching an ice cube in his mouth. "The Russkis are way down the leader board," he mumbled.

"Anarchists," Lawrence broke in.

"When you say anarchists, Paul, what group of morons are you referring to?" Rossi asked. "Supporters of the flawed political philosophy, or hooligans out for a bloody good time?"

"They're the same in my book, Inspector General," Rosenthal continued, barely moving his lips. "Wouldn't you agree?"

Rossi swirled his glass and said nothing. He'd decided he'd had enough of the three wise men. Determined to show it, he leant back and studied the all-white frameless painting hanging on the far wall, visible only through the artist's non-original use of texture.

After a long respite, Lawrence motioned with a slight flick of the head for his colleagues to leave the room. One by one they drifted off. Rosenthal, the last to move, took the bottle of Jim Beam with him.

"Sorry about that," Lawrence said. "My fault. They think playing the tough guy gives them the upper hand."

"I'm willing to listen, Paul. But warm me up first."

With the Jim Beam gone, Lawrence drained his glass and poured himself a Scotch.

Rossi sat forward. "So, neither God nor master: anarchist?"

"If we can believe the shooter's claim of responsibility," Lawrence said, removing three large colour photographs from a manila folder and handing them to Rossi.

At first blush they appeared to be random snaps of graffiti, sprayed in red paint on various surfaces. The circle-A was unmistakable to Rossi – a symbol for anarchy. But the # sign followed by a two-digit number wasn't so obvious.

"These are images from the sniper's shooting locations," Lawrence continued. "Forensics give a high probability that the cat scratchings at all three sites are by the same hand."

"Good to know. And the weapon?"

"Ballistic fingerprints confirm the same weapon was used in each of the killings."

"Conclusion: one shooter?"

Lawrence nodded.

There was a long silence as Rossi once more studied the images. "And the numbers. They must mean something. A list of some sort?"

"Go to the top of the class, Lorenzo. It's the victim's ranking on the *Forbes* billionaires list."

"That's a hell of a line-up. Over 2,000 and counting. The shooter needs to pick up his pace if he's going to get through that lot." Laughter. "Assuming I'm not a suspect, what do you want from me?"

"You've heard of the Cambridge Experientialists?"

"Not in this lifetime."

"They're a group of politically minded Cambridge students who believe all forms of government are harmful and unnecessary. Anarchists, in short. Led by Percival Benbow. The CIA's prime suspect. More commonly known as Kiss My Arse Percy. The thirty-two-year-old son of a peer of the realm. A typical silver spooner with no real-life experience. Bored with his privileged life so he figures he'll mess up someone else's."

"Why single out this lot? As far as I'm aware none of the murders have taken place in Cambridgeshire."

"CIA intelligence. And lots of it."

Rossi nodded as if he understood what was on offer. But he said nothing, preferring to hear it in Lawrence's words.

"We need someone, if not inside, then close enough to the Experientialists to know what they're up to." Lawrence threw back a mouthful of Scotch. "Operation Bright Star."

"Undercover?" Rossi smirked over his glass.

"No. You're too well known. Just need you to keep your ear to the ground. Act the tourist. Ask questions – get involved."

4

Rossi didn't say yes or no. He told them he needed time. There was no doubt in his mind: he owed the Americans big. But he couldn't help thinking his new friends had set the price of squaring the ledger too high.

Arriving back at Fisher House, he went straight through to the terrace, a courtyard bordered by a cluster of old medieval houses, renovated and added to over the centuries now forming the chaplaincy. Standing amongst the potted plants and bare vines, Rossi sucked in the damp earthy air as he gazed thoughtfully up at the lifeless sky.

Reaching into his mac, Rossi pulled out the fat celebratory cigar Lawrence had offered him in London with his cognac. Only there was nothing to celebrate. He hadn't agreed to Bright Star. He was not "on board", as the Americans had put it. His reptilian brain was screaming no. You don't need more shit in your life. Still, he had taken the cigar and a box of cedar matches on the way out. Just in case he cheered up on his circuitous route home.

Nearby a spayed church bell gently chimed twelve times. Rossi chewed the cap off the cigar and spat it behind a bush. Striking a match, he rotated the end of the Cohiba Nicaragua over the tip of the flame then blew on the end, checking it was lit. As he drew, he thought of Cathy. She would know what to do. But how could he phone her after what she had said to his mother? Sure, she was right, but that was not the point. Besides, Lawrence had laid down the law. Top secret; keep your mouth shut. Tell no one, which he assumed included Cathy.

A light drizzle. Not enough to send him inside. Oddly, it took the rain to remind Rossi he was in England. Home of crappy weather and James Bond. *Are the Brits in on this?* Strange, he hadn't asked. If not, another bloody good reason to stay well enough away.

Rossi puffed on his Cohiba and blew a stream of thick blue smoke into the heavy night air. *Anarchism – an impractical political philosophy. Why bother?* Another puff and a smoke ring before snuffing the cigar out in the sand bin by the back door.

If you had to – why not Marxism? he thought, ascending the narrow wooden stairway to his chamber.

His tiny attic room with a gable dormer window overlooking the courtyard was at the end of a long corridor with rows of doors on either side. All closed. A slither of yellow light from under his door brought a puzzled expression to his face. Did he leave the light on? He hadn't noticed from the garden. Turning the key, Rossi pushed down on the handle. *Impossible.* Bolted from the inside. Rossi put an ear to the solid oak door and tapped with the knuckle of his index finger. Bare feet on the rug-covered floor. He stepped aside as the brass bolt clunked back and the door flung open.

"That's all I need," Rossi said in an intense whisper, bundling the girl back into the room under the frosted glass ceiling light.

She wore only panties and short pink socks. Rossi recognised her as the cheeky undergrad from his lectures. A Russian name. Olga, Svetlana, Natasha? *Natasha*, he decided.

Gathering up her clothes, he slung them into her arms. "Get dressed."

"You *told* me to come," she protested with a coquettish smile.

Rossi detected a hint of an accent, and her body was older than her girlish face. He now figured she was about thirty. "Not naked and not after ten," he said, shaking the rain from his hat and setting it on top of the four-drawer commode.

Dropping her clothes back on the floor, the girl sat on the edge of the narrow servant's bed and crossed her arms. "You seemed to know what you wanted yesterday, Professor."

"Why are you here, Natasha?" Rossi asked, hanging his damp mackintosh on the back of the door. "Who put you up to this?"

"What peculiar questions."

Rossi cast an eye around the room. The writing desk standing in the dormer window alcove was as he had left it. The Victorian walnut commode next to the door and the narrow single-door wardrobe on the other side, both closed. Nothing seemed out of place. "Who sent you?" Rossi repeated.

"You're reading too much into this, Professor." Natasha stretched out on the bed with her hands behind her head, breasts thrust out. "Now come sit beside me."

Grabbing Natasha's lean, sinewy arm, Rossi yanked her to her feet. "Enough of this nonsense. Get dressed and go."

Breaking free, Natasha seized Rossi's pork-pie hat and set it on her head. Before the mirror hanging above the commode, she twisted handfuls of her long black hair and tucked it underneath. "It suits me, don't you think?" she said, twirling round the room.

That's when Rossi saw it. The circle-A monogram tattooed on the back of her right shoulder. Was there a connection? He needed to find out.

"Like Annie Hall," Rossi said, with an approving nod. "Now, get dressed and I'll find you a drink."

Crouched down in front of the commode, Rossi yanked open the sticky bottom drawer and removed two tumblers and a bottle of Laphroaig. As he rose, he snuck a peek to check if Natasha was dressing.

She was.

He wiped the glasses with a clean T-shirt and poured a good two fingers in each. "I've only got tap water," Rossi said, motioning to the electric kettle.

"Straight is fine," Natasha said, sucking in as she buttoned her Levi's.

"If I recall, Natasha," Rossi said, handing her a glass, "you're reading theology, religion and philosophy?"

"You know your students, Professor."

Rossi pulled the high-backed chair away from the writing desk, reversed it, and straddled it, shielding himself from his amorous intruder, who was now seated opposite on the edge of the bed.

"How are you enjoying Cambridge?"

"A right royal bore until you came along."

Rossi liked the way Natasha smiled as she spoke: with bright, alert eyes showing her natural white teeth and full red lips.

"Seems an odd choice if you're going all out for a good time," Rossi suggested.

Natasha held out her empty glass. "It's part of my journey of discovery. Experience is the source of knowledge."

"I can understand that." Rossi stretched over and topped up her glass, returning the bottle to the floor by his feet. "Interesting stuff. Religion is a large part of who we are. The foundation of our civilisation and culture."

"That's changing."

"Perhaps." Rossi paused, searching for the right words so as not to appear anxious. "That was a hell of an introduction. Can't say I wasn't flattered. Who wouldn't be?"

"I rarely lose control like that." A long sip. "In fact, it's the first time. I've been watching too much weird shit on the internet. I'll hate myself in the morning."

Rossi gave an empathetic nod. He seriously disliked the internet. He reckoned more bad came from it than good. "Tell me something about yourself, Natasha. Where are you from? And where are you heading?"

"Too deep for a first date, Professor," Natasha quipped, draining her second glass.

Rossi glance at his watch. "And too late, besides." Thumping the cork back into the bottle, Rossi rose from the chair, picked up Natasha's coat from off the bed and held it open.

"You kicking me out?"

"Afraid so." Rossi shrugged. "I've got a big day tomorrow. I'll show you out."

5

The next morning, on his way to breakfast, Rossi bumped into the head chaplain on the second-floor landing. "*Buongiorno*, Monsignor Baker," Rossi said, squeezing past.

The short, ruddy-faced cleric latched onto Rossi's elbow. "That young lady last night. I trust I did the right thing?"

Locking her in my room naked? "*Sì, grazie.*"

"She said you'd insisted on her waiting. It was late and Mrs Tarbottom was locking up. I had to put her somewhere." The monsignor paused, his soft permanent smile in need of reassurance. "Such an honest face. And an active member of the Catholic Women's League."

"Purity and virtue incarnated," Rossi murmured almost to himself as he continued down the stairs.

"You're late this morning, Inspector General," the eighty-year-old housekeeper said, as Rossi entered the empty dining room.

"Had trouble falling asleep."

"Full English, sir?" Mrs Tarbottom teased, knowing his tastes were more continental.

Rossi grinned. "With a double serving of black pudding."

Plucking a copy of the *Cambridge News* from the magazine rack on the windowsill, he laid it on a table with his phone. Then at the buffet situated under the kitchen serving hatch Rossi loaded his plate with two crisp-crust bread rolls, a portion of Irish butter and a small bowl of thick-cut orange marmalade. As he did every morning.

"Your double espresso, Inspector General," the housekeeper said, finding a spot on the table under the opened daily.

Rossi looked up. "You've lived in Cambridge long, Mrs Tarbottom?"

"All my life, sir." Being an old lady who likes to natter, Mrs Tarbottom pulled up a chair and sat down. "God's own country."

"*Sì, è bellissimo.*" A pause as Rossi broke apart one of the bread rolls and smothered it in butter and jam. He wanted to appear unrehearsed and spontaneous. Difficult for a man who'd been a policeman all his life. "On the train to London the other day I saw a huge chateau…"

"What we English call a country house."

"Near Foxton." Rossi had done his homework.

"That would be the ancestral home of Henry Benbow, the 8th Earl of Melba. Real landed gentry, sir."

Rossi sipped his coffee. "Is the estate open to the public?"

"It is, sir. But only during the week. Lord Melba has a townhouse in London. He comes up most weekends hunting. Likes to have the place to himself."

"Big family?"

"*Me*, sir?"

A chuckle. "Henry Benbow."

"Lord Melba? He's a widower, sir. Wife passed not two years ago. Drowned in the estate's Tsar Fountain."

"Any heirs or successors? A crown prince or two?"

"An only son – Lord Percy." A suck of her teeth. "A professional student of sorts."

"Good work if you can get it," Rossi said, popping another piece of bread roll into his mouth.

"He's doing a PhD in Russian," the old lady went on, as she brushed table crumbs into her open palm. "I read it in the *Woman's Weekly*."

"Slavonic studies, perhaps?" Rossi recalled Lawrence had mentioned it.

"It could be for when he takes over the running of his father's business. Lord Melba has gold mines in Siberia." She hesitated then added, "Or was that Serbia?"

Another piece of the puzzle? Rossi thought. It would explain the CIA's interest. The common thread. Seems they haven't finished with the Russians. The old-new evil empire. Albeit minus the wizard. He's dead. Assassinated together with half the ruling class. He needed to speak to

Lawrence again. Better still, Cathy. No one knows Russia like Cathy.

Mrs Tarbottom glanced at her watch. "Good heavens, is that the time?" She rose from her chair and continued clearing the tables.

Also mindful of the hour, Rossi checked the internet on his phone. There was a tour bus to Melba House departing in forty-five minutes and returning a full hour before his late-afternoon tutorial. Dirty dishes in hand, Rossi followed the housekeeper back to the kitchen, then went upstairs and changed.

Ten minutes later, Rossi scurried through the maze of dark corridors, slipping into his mackintosh as he went.

"Inspector General," came a faint voice from behind.

No time. Acting as if he hadn't heard, Rossi kept going.

"Inspector General Rossi," the voice repeated, only louder and impossible to ignore.

Rossi skidded to a halt on the polished wooden floor. "Monsignor."

"I forgot to tell you," the head chaplain said, sheepishly stroking one of his bushy eyebrows with his finger, "a young lady came to see you last night. Didn't leave her name."

"Do you mean Natasha?" Rossi asked, with a perplexed expression on his face. "We discussed her earlier."

"No! Someone else. Tall, with an intelligent face. Found her in the library. Not sure who let her in. Perhaps Mrs Tarbottom knows?"

Cathy? Rossi felt his heart skip a beat. "Did she leave a message? What did she say?"

"Nothing, other than she was just passing. Catch you another time, or words to that effect."

"That's a pity," Rossi said, wanting to punch the wall. Besides longing to see Cathy, he was desperate for her advice. She knew more about the shady world of international espionage than most. And he trusted her judgement. She could have helped him decide whether to cooperate with the CIA or run for the hills. Were the three murders really a threat to mankind, as the three wise men avowed, or merely an attempt at levelling the playing field? Global wealth concentrated in the hands of those who write the rules. Rossi understood the argument. He agreed; society needed to address the imbalance before the revolution started.

"Where are you off to in such a hurry, Inspector General?"

"A lightning tour of Melba House. Thought I'd see how the one per cent live."

"No, no. We can't have that," the monsignor remonstrated.

"Why?" Rossi smirked, waiting for the punchline.

"Lord Melba's organised a pheasant shoot for tomorrow. Come as my guest."

Rossi stopped checking his watch. "You *know* the Earl of Melba?"

"After Eton we came up to Cambridge together – read the classics. We've been friends ever since."

Although dead keen, Rossi tried not to show it. "Do you think His Lordship will mind?"

"He'll be delighted. You're a big celebrity in this part of the British Empire, Lorenzo. Someone to flaunt before friends."

"I don't know about that," Rossi protested. "But if you're sure?"

"Agreed, then." The monsignor beamed, seemingly pleased with himself. "Let's say seven for breakfast?"

As Rossi marched back to his room, he couldn't help but think how serendipitous the morning had turned out. A chance to make the acquaintance of the prime suspect's clique, while getting to tick the my-favourite-pastime box.

Rossi had grown up in a sprawling farmhouse in Tuscany surrounded by vineyards and olive groves. When he and his five brothers weren't pruning, picking or pressing olives, they loved to hunt wild boar in the neighbouring Mediterranean woods. A passion sadly neglected since his appointment as head of the Corps of Gendarmerie of Vatican City.

Sure, pheasant shooting wasn't the same as stalking wild boar, but beggars can't be choosers, Rossi thought, unlocking his door.

6

They set off under a light drizzle in Monsignor Baker's 1953 Morris Minor playing Beethoven on the eight-track stereo. The drive to Melba House through flat agricultural land would have been humdrum if not for the sage-green Morris's ill-fitted wipers and malfunctioning demister. Even with Rossi wiping the condensation off the windscreen with his handkerchief every few minutes, the monsignor couldn't see more than three car lengths beyond the bonnet. Driving at half the speed limit, the sleepy Saturday morning traffic on the single carriageway soon built behind them.

Rossi looked relieved when, an hour after leaving Fisher House, they turned off the main road. Driving through woodlands, they came to a wrought-iron gate with grandiose gateposts mounted with a pair of Talbot hounds. The light rain that had tormented them had ceased, and the sky lightened.

Soon brown fields and hedgerows replaced the beech trees. They came to a substantial stone arch topped with three sculptured eagles: the estate's main entrance. An old bow-legged man appeared from within the gatehouse.

The monsignor wound down his window. "Good morning, Paddy. We're not late, are we?"

"Top of the morning to you, sirs," the gateman said, tipping his cap, "You're not the last, Monsignor. But best you hurry or risk missing out on the sloe gin. You'll need it today. There's a chill in the air."

They drove for a short while along a white gravel road through parkland. No buildings in sight. Then, over a rise, the landscape opened before them and a prodigy house of the grandest scale filled the horizon. An Elizabethan palace of silver-grey mullion windows waxy with the low winter sun. Ornamental chimney pots dominated the roofline. And at the end of the long avenue, in the centre of the circular driveway, a large Henry Moore bronze around which the all-male shooting party, dressed in neutral greens and browns, milled about sipping sloe gin to improve their aim. Jackets, breeks, chequered twill shirts with game-theme ties, and tweed flat caps. Rossi couldn't help but make a comparison to the Russian ruling class he'd encountered last month while recovering the Concordat. *Give me the British Establishment over the New Russians any day*, he thought.

The monsignor parked the bulbous Morris amongst the crescent of sleek dark-coloured Rolls-Royces, Bentleys and Range Rovers. He then climbed out and opened the boot. Feeling lucky to be alive, Rossi crossed himself and followed.

Leaning on the car, they replaced their city shoes for wellingtons.

An orange Lamborghini Aventador growled as it swaggered up the driveway, broadcasting the arrival of Lord Melba's last guest. Close behind, two long-bearded Chechens in a black Mercedes G-Wagon.

Disapproving heads turned as the Lamborghini's scissor doors opened vertically, and a man wearing plus fours with long pink shooting socks climbed out.

"Gospodin Zhukov," Lord Melba called out, as he hobbled towards his flamboyant new business associate. "You found us all right?"

They hugged like old friends, or perhaps two pickpockets.

"My dear Lord Melba," Zhukov said with a heavy Russian accent, placing his hand on his heart, "please forgive my lateness. Some senile old fool in a superannuated car caused a traffic jam going back miles in both directions."

"That would be you," Rossi murmured to the monsignor.

The monsignor smirked and motioned towards the Lamborghini. "All the good that did him. Stuck in first gear all the way."

Lord Melba ran his eyes over the group. He counted in his head: eight guns, the gamekeeper, half a dozen beaters, same number of pickers-up and dogs. "All present," he declared, with a loud clap of his hands. "We can start."

They made introductions, Rossi and Zhukov the only new faces. As far as Rossi could tell, the guns were all old guard: old money. The Russian being the exception. Shiny-new, rich, brash and lacking the breeding only time could provide. *The odd man out*, Rossi thought.

"Gentlemen, can I have your attention?" Lord Melba, known for his loquacity, announced in his most aristocratic voice. "Some good news. I won't be joining you in the field today. Thus, you all stand a chance." He held up his walking stick. "An old war injury is playing up, I'm afraid."

"Which war? First or second?" quipped a voice from the side.

"The Napoleonic Wars, more likely," added a second.

After the chuckling and snorting subsided, Lord Melba continued. "Hence, I've asked Lord Percy to deputise for me today." Lord Melba pointed his cane at a young man with brushed back wavy brown hair standing with the gamekeeper.

Murmurs of approval flowed through the guns. Lord Percy was a popular figure amongst the Cambridgeshire elite. Young, vibrant and one of their own.

Rossi stared open-mouthed as Lord Percy stepped forward and joined his father. *A person of interest? Prime suspect?* Rossi knew appearance counts for nothing. But Lord Percy a serial killer? Not likely. *What is Lawrence thinking?*

"Listen up," Lord Percy bellowed, pausing until he had everyone's attention. "For the benefit of all, not just our newcomers, I'll run through the local rules, signals and safety."

Briefing completed, a draw for peg numbers was made and instructions for moving about from drive to drive given. "Questions?" No questions. "Then we're set," Benbow the younger declared. "And please remember only shoot when you can see the sky behind you. We don't want any mishaps."

"Success!" Lord Melba called out, as the guns climbed into three identical bronze-green Land Rover Defenders. "I'll see you back at the lodge for lunch."

They drove along a narrow farm track for a quarter of an hour. On one side, thick scrub; on the other, undulated arable land divided by hedgerows into fields. In the distance, down a rolling hill and back up again, mature woodlands stocked to the treetops with pheasants and partridges. All part of the 8,000-acre Melba estate.

The Land Rovers pulled over next to a four-foot-high drystone wall. The hunting party piled out, grabbed their equipment and headed off through a wooden sheep gate.

Shotgun broken, barrel pointing earthward, and a full cartridge bag over his shoulder, Rossi followed the other guns into the field. Half a mile north he could see the gamekeeper and the beaters, with two – no, three – dogs, entering the woods.

"On your pegs, gentlemen," Lord Percy directed. "We're live on the sound of the gamekeeper's horn."

"Some help needed," Zhukov hollered, waving his draw ticket in the air. "Where's peg eight?"

Again, disapproving glances in the direction of the new money. Shooting etiquette prescribes that noise be kept to a minimum before drives. No point in alerting the birds. Seems no one had told Zhukov.

"Far end of the line," Lord Percy replied, pointing west. "On the other side of the rise."

"Follow me," Monsignor Baker called out. "I'm next to you on seven, Mr Zhukov. But we must be quick about it. The pegs are set thirty yards apart, so it's a full furlong."

At the start of the line on peg one, Rossi loaded his shotgun. A salute acknowledging Lord Percy, drawn on his left. Rossi was pleased with himself. He couldn't imagine a more inconspicuous way of making the acquaintance of the Cambridge Experientialists' chief agitator. *If that's what he was.*

When the horn sounded, Rossi slipped on his ear defenders and readied himself to meet the birds. He stole a glance west. Then did a double take. Peg two was now vacant. Percy had slipped away unnoticed. *Shooting captain's duties?*

First came the songbirds. Then the pheasants, bursting into the sky above the woodlands, wings swirling and gaining height. Rossi's persisting rumination about anarchists vanished. *The perfect flush*, he thought. Birds flying high, spread across the line.

Gun down, Rossi picked his target. Two birds coming together. Eyes locked on the bird on the left, Rossi shifted his weight and mounted his gun. Shotgun butt in his shoulder and comb against his face, Rossi fired. The bird fell. Without taking his gun from his shoulder, he again pulled the trigger. The second bird dropped. Clean kill. An impressive left and right.

"Oh, I say," a picker-up murmured with admiration as Rossi reloaded.

The birds kept coming and Rossi kept firing. Then the

gamekeeper filled his lungs and blew his horn. With the end of the first drive the countryside fell silent.

Rossi removed his ear defenders. "Eight pheasants and a partridge, if I've counted right," he said to the picker-up.

"Jolly well done, Inspector General."

They sent the dogs first. Moments later the pickers-up followed.

Rossi unloaded and resleeved his shotgun. As he gathered up his spent cartridges, he glanced along the line, searching for the next drive. The guns moved west, disappearing behind the curved contour of the hill. Slowly at first, then in a rush.

A commotion ahead. Something was wrong. Something had happened on the other side of the rise. *Monsignor Baker's had a heart attack*, sprung to Rossi's mind. Shotgun slung over his shoulder, he hurried to join the others 250 yards away.

From on top of the rise, Rossi spotted between pairs of legs Monsignor Baker kneeling in the damp grass. From where Rossi stood it appeared as if he was administering the last rites. *But to whom?*

"Where's the captain, for Christ's sake?" one veteran asked, looking about.

At that instant, Lord Percy came belting down the hill accompanied by the two Chechens, who had been waiting in the G-Wagon under instructions.

"What's happened?" Percy screamed.

In silence, one by one, the guns turned and peeled away. The face was a bloody mess, but the knee-high pink socks were unmistakable. Gospodin Zhukov.

Rossi stole a furtive glance at the future Earl Melba.

Did he look flustered, guilty? *Was it him?*

"What beastly luck," Lord Percy moaned, as if suggesting it was an accident.

But no one was fooled. The neat entry wound to the back of the skull was conclusive. Rossi surmised: big calibre ammunition; full metal jacket; soft lead core. The bullet had mushroomed out and expanded on its journey through the brain, slamming the front of the skull like a sledgehammer. A sniper's bullet.

"Did anyone see what happened?" Rossi asked, his gaze starting on the monsignor, then drifting up towards the drystone wall from where he figured the killer had fired the shot.

"Nothing," the monsignor said, his tone apologetic. "When the gamekeeper's horn sounded, I unloaded my gun. Then, when I turned to congratulate Mr Zhukov, he was already down."

Reloading his shotgun, Rossi scrambled up the damp slippery slope in his wellingtons, scaled the low wall and stood in the middle of the gravel track. Three hundred yards east, he could see the roof of the first Land Rover. To the west the road fell away sharply, bent left, then disappeared. Empty. Barrel raised, he moved to the opposite side of the road and peered into the thick shrub. Nothing. No trace of the assassin. Other than his calling card – a circle-A monogram and #27 spray painted in red on a firm section of track.

"Call the police!" Rossi said, as he returned a few minutes later. "Inform them there's been a murder."

"Murder?" Lord Percy gasped, shaking his head in disbelief.

7

It wasn't until late afternoon the Morris Minor returned to Fisher House and Monsignor Baker locked it away for the night. When the head chaplain offered some supper in the dining room, Rossi made his excuses. He needed time alone to decide whether he was in or out. Lawrence was expecting a response, pronto. Besides, he had a 500-gram Milano salami, a jar of Castelvetrano olives, a tub of semi-dry cherry tomatoes and half a loaf of yesterday's ciabatta in his room. And, to wash it all down, an unopened bottle of Chianti Classico. Without a doubt, trumping the reheated bubble and squeak the Fisher House kitchen had on offer.

An hour later, mud and blood washed away under a steaming hot shower, Rossi sat at his writing desk, his eyes locked on the iPhone Lawrence had forced on him two days before. *In? Out? In? Out?* repeated in his head, like an over-wound metronome.

Then suddenly, Rossi pulled the phone close and typed. "Sorry for the hiatus. Been a death in the family. Count me out." He hit send.

As Rossi put his glass to his lips, the phone beeped in response. Squinting, he read. "Condolences. Come for supper. The wife would love to see you."

Whose wife? Rossi thought. *Lawrence hasn't got a wife. And the closest thing I had to one bolted.*

Anxious or frustrated – Rossi wasn't sure – he stood and paced the room. As the fog in his head slowly lifted, his Vatican-issued mobile phone played "Seven Spanish Angels". A local number. Most likely a student from his supervisory group. "Hello."

"Professor," came an animated voice down the line.

"Natasha! How did you get my number?" Rossi asked, not expecting a response.

"You're not *pleased* to hear from me, Professor?"

"Quite the contrary," he lied. "How are you?"

"Missing you deeply." Her tone now steamy. "Thought I'd pop round. Show my appreciation for the other night."

"Natasha! Stop!"

"Relax, Professor. I'm messing with you. I'm far too busy studying to make social calls."

Rossi forced a chuckle. "Then what can I do for you?"

"Tomorrow, Sunday roast at the Plough in Fen Ditton – a new start."

Keen to find out more about her, Rossi agreed. Besides, what mischief could Natasha get up to in broad daylight?

"Super!" she said, sounding rather pleased with herself. "I'll pick you up at noon."

"As long as you're not driving a Morris Minor."

"No way. I'm more the wind in your face sort of girl."

"Then I'll see you tomorrow," Rossi said cheerfully, then added, "and this time wear some clothes." Laughter.

Rossi's mood darkened as he rang off. How to answer Lawrence? He was dead against another tango with the CIA floozies. *They dance to a different beat*, he thought, pushing back in his seat, hands locked behind his head. Sure, they helped him recover the Concordat, but he had returned the favour a million times over. President Volkov was dead, along with most of the Russian ruling class. The new Cold War enemy was in chaos, beyond the White House's wildest dreams. Didn't that make them even? All square? Debt paid?

He again opened the super-encrypted CIA phone and keyed: "Sorry, can't do. Busy with funeral arrangements." A smile swept across his face as he imagined Lawrence's reaction.

Some olive oil and salt for the ciabatta would have been nice, Rossi thought, sipping his wine, waiting.

The iPhone beeped a response: "Funerals are best avoided. Come join the living. Go get some fresh air and think about it."

While Rossi appreciated he could interpret Lawrence's message in several ways, he decided to take it literally. *Saturday night. Bound to be a crowd*, he thought, slipping into his coat.

Rossi glanced about as he stepped out onto the street, not sure what to expect. There seemed to be a certain level of knowledge about his movements. Maybe the Americans had borrowed a watcher or two from MI5. He stood for a few minutes, playing with his phone to allow the spooks to organise themselves. Then he followed the foot traffic north, with Market Hill in mind.

After an hour of aimless wandering, Rossi felt foolish. *Why say "go for a walk" if you mean "stay in and read a book"?*

Then, without warning, Rossi felt the slightest tug on his mackintosh as he glimpsed Heroin Chic flash past in the crowd. She'd put something in his pocket. A skilfully executed brush pass. From her pace, Rossi knew not to follow.

Acting nonchalant, Rossi entered the first pub he came to and headed straight to the toilets. Two young men in skinny jeans and paisley shirts, leaning against the far wall, struck a pose as he pushed open a cubicle. Rossi slid his fingers inside his pocket and pulled out an electronic key. Hilton Cambridge printed on the front; 415 scribbled with a blue permanent marker on the back.

Knocking the toilet lid closed with his foot, Rossi sat down and searched his phone for the hotel's address. He could recall passing it on his wanderings but couldn't remember where.

With the route to the Hilton swirling in his head, Rossi flushed the toilet and swung open the cubicle door. "Look after yourselves, boys," he said, keeping a cautious eye on the paisley shirt brigade as he washed his hands.

"Fifty pounds," one of them said.

Rossi wasn't sure what they were selling and wasn't interested in finding out. "Take care," he said, his tone sincere as he tossed the paper towel in the bin and exited.

Rossi scanned the lobby as he shuffled along with the automatic revolving door. Oozing Italian confidence, he glided across the marbled void and summoned the lift. The golden doors opened without a sound. As he inserted his key in the slot on the control panel, he shot a glance towards the reception desk. They paid him no attention as he held his finger on the button and the door closed.

Stepping out of the lift on the fourth, Rossi felt less sanguine. "Do I knock or use the key?" he wondered aloud, glancing about for security cameras as he strode down the long corridor, unbuttoning his mackintosh. All evening he had readied himself for a fireside chat with Heroin Chic. Now he wasn't so sure. As far as he knew, it could be the three wise men standing around a Steinway singing "Canto Della Terra" with Andrea Bocelli.

Out of habit he reached inside his jacket for his pistol. Not there. Relaxing his shoulders, Rossi inserted the electronic key into the lock of the white-lacquered door, turned the handle and stepped inside.

To his left the bathroom, dark and empty. At a standstill, he listened. The clink of a bottle against a glass.

"Come in," came a cold voice.

Rossi's heart pounded like a love-struck schoolboy. It took every bit of self-control to stop himself rushing forward with open arms. "Cathy," he said, his pitch raised a little. "I was wondering where you disappeared to."

"Laphroaig?" she asked, remaining seated at the coffee table squeezed in-between the king-sized bed and the window.

Rossi tossed his mackintosh on the bed and grabbed a glass from on top of the minibar. "Glad to see your fashion sense hasn't changed. Tight tops, short skirts and stiletto boots." She refused to bite. Lowering himself onto the green suede tub chair opposite her, he picked up the bottle.

"How's that dear mother of yours?"

"Convalescing. Thanks for asking," Rossi said, pouring himself a healthy measure.

"It'd take more than the truth to kill that—"

"Cathy! It's not worth it."

"You're not worth it, you shit."

Rossi had never seen her so riled. Even as she argued with his domineering mama, Cathy had kept her cool. Well, at least until the taxi arrived, and the screen door of his childhood home slammed. He had called her every day for two weeks, only stopping when Lawrence whispered in his ear that she'd changed her number.

"I tried to phone. I wanted to apologise. My mama wanted to apologise. But you vanished—"

"Vanished? Aliens vanish. You didn't try hard enough. It was easier to forget about me."

Rossi picked up his glass and went and stood facing her across the room. It was his turn at bat, but he had no appetite for arguing. Particularly with the love of his life. Whatever he said, she'd slap it back twice as hard. Two long sips on his Scotch before breaking the silence. "So why am I here? Bright Star?"

"A chance to resurrect my career, which you destroyed, along with my life, in Moscow." Cathy stopped briefly, then added, "And to catch an anarchist. I thought Lawrence explained everything."

"Why me?"

"Rotten luck. You happened to be in the right place at the wrong time." Pause. "And because I'm being punished. Christ knows, the last thing I want to be doing right now is babysitting you," Cathy said, flicking her long wavy chestnut hair back off her face.

"But I haven't committed."

"Who are you kidding? You're in it up to your neck. Best friends with Lord Percy. First on the scene of Zhukov's slaying. A midnight tryst with the emancipated Natasha—"

"How the *hell* do you know about Natasha?"

Cathy's honey-coloured eyes shot Rossi an accusing look. "You're not denying it, then?"

"Not my fault. I found her in my room after returning from London. A girl unfettered by traditional views of sexual morality." His smile faded as the penny dropped. "She works for you, doesn't she?"

"Not that I'm aware of," Cathy said, her tone slightly more civil, having blown off enough steam to move the Flying Scotsman.

"Who is she, then? I know I'm a catch. But naked in the chaplaincy? That's beyond the pale."

"First I've heard about naked, Mr Rossi. The office normally avoids people like that. Finds them unreliable."

"Bullshit."

"Perhaps, but she's not with me."

"And Heroin Chic?" Rossi asked, returning to his seat.

Cathy looked at Rossi for a long moment. "Ah! You mean the always elegant Agent Harper Rattle." A smirk. "She's somewhere between Lawrence and the three suits in Knightsbridge."

"Is Chief James on board? Or is Washington saving its nickels to invade South America?"

"After Moscow, they chained him to the desk next to mine in Langley."

"What? No more *sparrow graduates* to share his bed? He'd be climbing the wall."

"Maybe Natasha's one?" Cathy said, with a sideways tilt of her head. "You're egotistical enough not to recognise a honey trap when you see one. The Russians have you down as an easy target. A ladies' man with zero self-control."

Rossi ignored Cathy's barbs. "Natasha's a nice girl."

"Yeah. A potential wife? Or maybe you'd prefer Heroin Chic. She seems to have caught your eye too. Though I suspect her arse is too bony for your taste."

"Why are you so angry? What does it matter? It was you who broke off our engagement. Now I'm moving on." Rossi lied. He hadn't moved on. "So, get over it."

A transitory truce before Cathy spoke. "Shall we start? What happened at Melba House?"

Rossi unlocked his phone, opened the photo gallery and handed it to Cathy.

"What sort of spook *are* you?" Cathy said, scrolling through the two dozen images. "All this happened within shouting distance, and you missed everything. Too busy slaughtering endangered wildlife."

"Wildlife? You mean hunting pheasants for the kitchen table. Goes well with savoy cabbage and chestnuts."

Cathy handed Rossi her empty glass. "The killer even had time to paint *War and Peace* on the road not thirty metres from the body."

"Circle-A #27. Not quite *War and Peace*. My guess is the assassin painted it before he fired. The victim's name was Zhukov—"

"Don't bore me with trivia. I have a copy of the preliminary police report."

"Then what do you need me for?"

"Let's make one thing clear from the outset, Enzo. I don't need you for anything. I'd prefer you were a million miles away. But orders are orders."

"Amen. And the CIA? I'm having trouble reading between the lines. What do they want with me?"

"You're the closest thing they've got to a Cambridge insider."

"Christ! That's what Lawrence said. You're all mad. Me, an insider? Haven't they noticed this sign hanging around my neck?" He drew a square on his chest with his index finger. "Vatican Police."

"Sure, it'd be better if you were a long-haired student—"

"I *had* long hair once. You hacked it off in Moscow."

"I saved your life, didn't I? Besides, it's growing back."

"And another thing. Where the hell's British Intelligence?"

"Number 10 decreed the killings none of their business," Cathy said, with a shrug of indifference. "Classified them as serious crimes rather than a matter of national security."

"Bullshit," Rossi snapped.

"Perhaps. But, for now, the Metropolitan Police's Major Investigation Team has accountability."

"The only way that could be true is if your people are withholding intelligence from their British counterparts."

"As always, Enzo, you're being far too dramatic. More likely it's something much more boring, like lack of funding. The British are a shrinking power. Their budget only goes so far. Terrorism, not anarchism, is the magic word for opening the Chancellor of the Exchequer's ever-shrinking coffers. The Brits, and the Americans for that matter, have decided anarchists are a bunch of spoilt white kids in search of their own relevance and pose little threat to national security."

"So how does it work?"

"You carry on as you are. Act curious. Interested in Cambridge life. No need to interrogate anyone. Join clubs."

A moan and a shake of the head. Then he laughed, but Cathy didn't join in.

"What was it you told me when we were on the run in Russia? 'CIA mission success is directly correlated with selecting the least-worst option.'"

"And here we are again."

"Where do you fit in, pray tell?"

Cathy took her time. "It's no longer Cathy. I'm Ashley Clarke."

"Ashley?" Rossi cringed. "What on earth for? Why not Agnes or Arlene? Both equally disagreeable."

"On my next assignment I'll make sure Langley clears my legend with you first. In the meantime, I'm Ashley.

Research fellow, Slavonic Studies. Paid-up member of the Cambridge University Rifle Association. Discipline: Match rifle."

"Which college has been silly enough to put you up?"

"None. The university has given me a special dispensation to skip college life."

"That CIA code for slumming it at the Hilton?"

"I wish," Cathy scoffed. "I've been billeted to a boutique student dig called Fisher House. Move in tomorrow."

A puzzled expression swept over Rossi's face. "Does Bright Star involve the Church?"

"Doubt it. Well, other than you and Carrick Maloney."

"The Massachusetts senator?"

"Who played a key role in securing CIA support for your Russian misadventure."

Rossi held up his glass. "And for that I'm forever grateful."

"More grateful than you think." A teasing pause. "The senator requested and received consent from Cardinal Capelli to enlist you until further notice."

Rossi stretched back in his chair and took a long sip of his Scotch. "So, this whole Cambridge thing's been a smokescreen from day one?"

"Not at all. Langley only assembled the London team after Charles Edge's murder."

"So Cardinal Capelli threw Fisher House in with the deal? Slate clean."

"That was Commandant Waldmann's idea. Sent me to keep an eye on you. He'd heard about our little bust-up. Thought you might slit your wrists."

"Over you?" Scoff. "In your dreams," he said, feeling the happiest he had been in a long time.

"I move in tomorrow. Can you give me a hand?"

"Sorry! Can't do. Sunday roast with Natasha."

"Wasting no time?"

"Business. She's got a circle-A tattooed on her back shoulder. I noticed it when she came to my room."

"Naked."

Rossi smiled, sensing, for as much as she would deny it, Cathy was jealous.

8

Rossi stood on the sunny pavement outside Fisher House waiting for Natasha. It felt wrong to be looking forward to seeing her. Maybe it was Catholic guilt? Or perhaps a betrayal of Cathy? Rossi glanced at his watch. The midday sun reflecting off the sapphire crystal face stung his eyes.

A pistachio-green Vespa screeched to a halt alongside him. The petite rider, wearing jeans and a black leather jacket, raised the visor of her coral-coloured aviator helmet. "Superb weather, and against all odds."

Rossi blinked, taking a few seconds to recognise the pale face of Natasha.

"A harbinger of love, Professor," she said, lifting the Vespa seat and handing him a helmet.

Love? Rossi drew back. "Car trouble?"

"Only to the extent I don't have one."

"Better I drive – or ride. What is it?" Rossi said, squeezing into the helmet.

"Get on."

Throwing his athletic leg over the pillion seat, Rossi planted his hands on her slender waist and said a prayer to Saint Christopher.

They travelled north-east for ten minutes to the picturesque village of Fen Ditton on the River Cam. From there Natasha, proclaiming the Plough her regular summer hangout, lay a course without a false turn.

"There's a super riverside beer garden for warmer weather," she said, leading Rossi up a short flight of stairs to the pub entrance. "But I've booked us a table inside by the window overlooking the garden. Don't let the morning sun fool you. Weather's very changeable this time of year. They're forecasting rain for later on."

Placing their helmets on the floor, they sat down at a chunky wooden table facing each other. Rossi glanced about. Through French doors, Rossi peered out at the vast terrace and the beer garden beyond. Windows with neat small panes set in rectangular glazing bars. An open fire crackled nearby. Huge wooden ceiling beams. "Rustic charm," Rossi said, with a nod of approval.

Natasha insisted on ordering, being the local. Rossi agreed, though he doubted she knew her pastrami from her salami. Without looking at the menu, she chose the roast beef with Yorkshire pudding, goose-fat-roasted potatoes and vegetables. But, when she suggested beer, Rossi put his foot down and asked for the Coonawarra Shiraz.

The small talk continued until their lunch arrived. Rossi needed rhythm to get where he wanted to go. Interruptions would give her time to think; change the subject; recheck her answers.

"Looks delicious. You've done well."

"To our second date," Natasha said, clinking glasses, then taking a long sip on her dark-ruby-coloured wine.

"Natasha, I'm not sure this is a date – is it?"

"Let's not get hung up on words, Professor. Better to enjoy every experience life presents us. I imagine there's nothing worse than looking back in old age and regretting what you didn't do."

"And you're worried I might be one of your regrets?" Rossi said, his tone whimsical.

"Impossible, Professor. You're already falling in love with me."

Rossi raised his shoulders in an awkward little shrug. Though not the answer he'd expected, he bit his lip and resisted giving Natasha gratuitous fatherly advice she'd probably ignore anyway.

"What are you doing here?" he asked.

"The Plough? Cambridge? Earth? The Universe?"

"You choose."

"The Plough. Lunch with my scrumptious professor," she said, cutting her food into tiny mouse-size pieces.

That didn't work, Rossi thought, pouring more wine. "And Cambridge?"

"To change the world." A sharp smirk before popping a tiny piece of turnip into her perfect mouth.

Rossi now had something to work with. "How? In what way?"

"Where to start?" Natasha said, raising her gaze from her plate. "By destroying American capitalism, Chinese communism, Russian totalitarianism, Swedish socialism…" Natasha's voice faded in despair, then started up again. "We must rid the world of its paternalistic systems that benefit the few. Let's knock down the walls that stop migration and freedom of movement on a free planet." A gulp of wine. "Which incidentally *Homo sapiens* had done for 250,000 years until the greedy ruling class descended from Heaven and claimed the lot."

"Big job, but I'm all for it," Rossi said, holding up a clenched fist. "Power to the people."

Natasha shook her head, as if offended. "Not to the people. Fuck no. That implies democracy. I demand freedom. Freedom for the individual. No one telling me what to do."

"But how?" Rossi asked, leaning forward and laying his hand on Natasha's wrist, something Cathy often did when she needed to connect. "How would you do it?"

Natasha's alert grey eyes locked onto Rossi's as if she were trying to read his mind. "That's why I'm here. To find out."

"By reading theology and religion?"

"Building networks of like-minded people. Awakening resistance in those who have stopped thinking for themselves. Creating chaos. I haven't figured it out yet."

Gazing out at a narrowboat sailing upriver – or perhaps down – Rossi took a dreamy sip of his wine, trying to appear less like the policeman he was. "And have you met any like-minded people since arriving?"

"Haven't you heard? Cambridge is a hotbed of social unrest. The world's meeting point for dissidents and armed revolutionists."

Slow down, Rossi told himself. "And not a word on TripAdvisor." They laughed.

The waitress offered dessert. Rossi hadn't finished with Natasha, and he figured she was clever enough to smell a rat if he raised the subject again on their next *date*.

"A cheese platter to share and a double espresso," he said, as the waitress cleared their plates. "Natasha?"

"I'm driving – I'll stick to the wine."

"What do you do in your spare time?" Rossi continued. "Sports? You look like you work out."

Rossi waited patiently for an answer but was met with silence. "Perhaps you're a star of amateur theatre? I know – Amnesty International. There must be something."

"None of the above."

"What sort of answer is that?" Rossi laughed. "A third date's out of the question unless I know something more about you."

"Is that what you coppers call 'plea bargaining', Chief Inspector? Or tightening the screws? I'm never sure."

Rossi smiled with relief as the cheese platter arrived. Convinced he had overcooked it, he sat quietly chewing on a piece of creamy Danish Blue.

Whether concerned about the third date or tired of playing the mystery woman, Natasha after a while said, "I declare book club and CURA – Cambridge University Rifle Association."

Taken aback, Rossi studied her face. Was the disclosure innocent or was she being deliberately careless? "Books I get. But shooting? What on earth for?"

"Match rifle, at distances from 1,000 to 1,200 yards. Good fun, which could turn out to be handy when the revolution starts."

"Politics, religion, church choir?"

Natasha poured the last of the Shiraz into Rossi's glass. "Religion's not my thing."

"Politics. I get the impression you admire Marx – pure Marx."

"Marx was all about the collective. I'm all about the individual."

Rossi chuckled for effect. "In my apartment, when you did your rain dance, I recall you saying 'experience is the source of knowledge'…"

"You must have been paying attention."

"Isn't that experientialism?"

"If you say so."

At this point Rossi hoped Natasha would throw herself on the mercy of the court. Hope died last. After a long pause he heard himself say, *Are you a member of the Cambridge Experientialists?* But nothing came out.

"Well, what do I know?" Rossi said, his tone jocular.

"Now it's my turn at 'truth or dare.'"

"Fire away," Rossi said, figuring resistance would be futile.

"The Concordat."

From Natasha's eyes Rossi knew she had done her homework. Which wasn't difficult given it happened only a month ago and the media coverage had been extensive. "A treaty between the Vatican and a sovereign state on religious matters. They're fairly common."

"Nice try, Professor."

Natasha opened her phone and read aloud an article entitled "Murders Conceal Secret Vatican Nazi Concordat" by Sabine Reich in the *Frankfurter Allgemeine Zeitung*.

"All eyes will be on the Vatican today as it tries once again to explain its relationship with Hitler during World War II. The discovery of an unknown Concordat between the Holy See and the German Reich, dated 1 June 1939, just three months before the start of World War II, is damning.

"In the agreement, signed by Pope Pius XII—"

Rossi seized Natasha's phone and laid it face down on the table. "A forgery minted by the FSB's Active Measures unit at the behest of the late President Volkov. Purpose: to sow discord in Europe and to strengthen the global influence of the Russian Orthodox Church." Pause. "My job was to recover the forgery before it fell into the hands of the Church's enemies."

"You didn't do a very good job then."

"By that measure – I guess not. But we did recover it and prove beyond a doubt it was a fake."

"And in the process you blew up Volkov and his inner circle, including the Russian Patriarch."

"That wasn't us. The official investigation concluded that the bomb used to kill the Russian president was planted by a person or persons unknown."

"Who's us?"

"The Vatican and the CIA."

"And who's Cathy?" Natasha asked, narrowing her eyes in mock jealousy.

"Forget about her," Rossi said firmly. "She's not important."

"Important enough to marry. That little gem also popped up in the search."

Rossi looked around for the waitress. The bill was the only thing that would save him. "It didn't work out. She decided I wasn't Mr Right after all."

"Star CIA Russian analyst attached to the Moscow station."

Rossi drained his glass then started on the water. "How do you know that?"

"Reporting to Station Chief William James and ably assisted by Agent Paul Lawrence. All in the public domain – if you know where to look."

"Langley assigned Agent Doherty to keep me safe while I was in Moscow."

"Where was she when *that* happened?" Natasha asked, squinting at Rossi's scarred earlobe.

Rossi felt the nape of his neck tighten as he recalled lying disorientated on the floor of an upmarket Paris apartment, a pool of blood forming around his head. "This? It's nothing. A hunting accident in Italy," Rossi lied, as an image of a beautiful Russian agent slumped naked against a sofa with a gaping hole in the side of her head shot to mind.

"I couldn't find a photo of her on the internet. Is Ms Doherty pretty?"

"The CIA strongly discourages its agents from advertising themselves on Facebook." Rossi lowered his shoulders, turned his head towards the window, and gazed up at the heavens. "We'd better get going."

Outside, the sky had darkened; threatening rain clouds moved south. Not Vespa weather, they agreed. Rossi motioned for the bill and when he tried to pay Natasha protested. They went Dutch.

"I enjoyed that," Natasha said, threading her arm through Rossi's as they meandered towards the Vespa.

"Me too. We must do it again," Rossi said, staring into the distance at a telephoto lens protruding from the open window of a white Ford Fiesta. *Heroin Chic?*

9

"Home in one piece," Natasha called out over her shoulder, pulling the scooter to a halt inches from Fisher House's front door.

"A little wet, mind you."

"That's the charm of owning a Vespa. It's like a convertible without the parking hassles."

Rossi dismounted, removed his helmet and stowed it. "More like my bicycle, only slower."

"See you tomorrow morning, Professor."

"At my lecture," Rossi clarified, running his fingers through his helmet hair.

Rossi stood on the pavement and waved as she rode off. *Honey trap or not, I need to be careful*, Rossi thought, bounding up the stairs.

"Pleasant day?" Cathy enquired, seated at Rossi's desk with her laptop.

"I'm all for economy, but who gets the bed?"

"Don't go jumping to conclusions. I'm only passing. Monsignor Baker has banished me to a barred cell in the bowels of the adjoining wing."

"Sounds lonely."

"Not at all. I've got two nuns standing guard outside my door, singing 'Ave Maria' day and night."

"You've been found out. And long overdue if you ask me."

"It was my idea," Cathy said, holding out two audio-surveillance bugs in her palm. "These yours?"

"Not that I know of."

"Lawrence had the ferrets in. Swept your room while you gorged yourself on Sunday roast."

Rossi wondered why he was not surprised. Fishing in his pocket, he pulled out his iPhone and turned on the music in case the ferrets had missed something. "And you think it was Natasha?"

"A naked girl in your room?" Cathy's said, glaring at Rossi. "Do you really think you're that irresistible?"

"Maybe the bugs were already there," Rossi said, removing the Laphroaig from the commode drawer. "A drink?"

Cathy gestured with her thumb and index finger for a double. "Then how do you explain the one found inside your laptop?"

Neither spoke as Rossi rinsed two chipped glasses with water from the kettle and dried them on the front of his shirt.

"The bugs are more likely the handy work of the three wise men than Natasha," he finally answered, pouring two generous shots.

"Get your hands out of your pockets, Enzo. It was Lawrence who organised the sweep."

Resting his backside against the desk, he handed Cathy a glass. "From what I saw in London, Lawrence is no d'Artagnan. He might be shacked up with them, but he's definitely his own man."

Choosing not to hear, Cathy held out her glass. "Cheers."

"What are we drinking to?" Rossi asked.

"Mission success."

"I'm not sure I know what that is."

A clink of glasses. "Then to not killing each other until we've saved the world."

"By the by," Rossi said, "I spotted Heroin Chic skulking about in the Plough carpark earlier. What do I make of that?"

"I've already seen her photos. You and Natasha make a cute couple." Pause. "Lawrence is checking the CIA files to establish whether she's a known operative."

Rossi took a pull on his Scotch. "You're wasting your time."

"Perhaps…"

A mobile phone vibrated on the writing desk. Rossi recognised the country code. "Italy."

"That'll be Commandant Waldmann," Cathy said. "He's been calling all afternoon."

"He's misplaced the ostrich feather from his morion helmet again." Rossi grinned, already standing at the commode.

"You better answer it. Maybe the Pope has died."

"*Ciao*, Christian," Rossi said. "Oh, it's you, Cardinal Capelli. I'm sorry. I was expecting Commandant Waldmann."

As Rossi listened in silence, the smile faded from his face. Pulling Cathy gently by the sleeve, she rose from the desk and Rossi took her place. He put his phone on speaker, laid it on the desk and opened his Vatican email account on his laptop. Top of the screen, an email from the cardinal containing two attachments.

"Do you have it?" the cardinal asked, his tone anxious. "Open the files. They're from the Russian president."

Rossi did. The first: a three-page epistle in Cyrillic typed on thick white paper embossed with the Russian presidential seal. The second: a five-page English translation duly stamped and signed by three government *chinovniki*.

"Have you read it, Lorenzo?"

"I'm not that fast, Your Eminence."

"Ambassador Stepanov delivered it this morning. At first, he refused to hand it over, insisting it was for the Pope's eyes only. I had a good mind to send him packing."

"You'd have been within your rights, Your Eminence."

"You finished?" Silence. "No? Then best I summarise. The letter repeats Volkov's claims used to justify the expulsion of our Church from the Russian Federation."

"For instance?" Rossi mumbled, continuing to read.

"Implicating the Vatican in President Volkov's assassination and accusing the Church of proselytising."

"We know when the Russians make outlandish claims they're negotiating. They have something else in mind."

"And look at page three, Lorenzo," the cardinal scoffed, to the sound of his finger tapping on his large mahogany desk. "President Morozov continues to deny it was the Kremlin who forged the Concordat – despite the weight of evidence to the contrary."

"Absolute nonsense. So, let's read between the lines, Your Eminence. What does he want?"

"The letter is full of inaccuracies and lies."

Rossi was no longer listening. He had finished the letter and knew what was coming.

"And the ambassador had the audacity to claim his would-be tsar was offering a path for resolving our conflict peacefully." Pause. "A way for our Church to re-establish its mission in Russia."

"And what would that be, Your Eminence?" Rossi said, feeling sick to the stomach.

"For me to dismiss the head of the Vatican Gendarmerie."

"That would be me, Your Eminence," Rossi said, thinking it peculiar the cardinal didn't mention his name.

The cardinal sighed. "Why should I? You've done nothing wrong. What are you to them?"

"I'm a constant reminder of their defeat."

"And that's a good thing. What they did was pure evil."

"But it doesn't resolve the matter. There are a million Catholics in Russia in need of pastoral care."

"We have to be patient, Lorenzo, and wait for God's timing."

Elbows on the desk, Rossi rested his forehead in the heel of his hands and thought. After a few seconds of silence that seemed like an eternity, Rossi said in a calculating tone, "I'll resign. Give them what they want. God knows after twenty years I need a break."

Cathy gasped. She appreciated the Corps of Gendarmerie of Vatican City was Rossi's life. He knew nothing else.

Rossi listened as Cardinal Capelli remonstrated. But it was too late. Rossi had decided. He would sacrifice himself on the altar of political expediency for the sake of his Church.

***

In London they marched behind their banners. Fifty thousand strong. Trade unions, left-wing politicians, church groups, charities, students and anarchists, all protesting ahead of next week's G20 summit of world leaders. From Embankment to Hyde Park, they strolled along in high spirits with police lining the route.

In a Soho squat, close to where the parade had passed, a group of 200 hard-line anarchists made final preparations for tomorrow's assault on the London Stock Exchange. Germans, French, Dutch, Belgians and Spanish were among their number. They'd arrived in dribs and drabs over the past week to avoid detection by the Met.

"Sorry I'm late," came a woman's voice from down the tunnel leading to the stage area of the disused pole dancing club.

"High time, Natasha," a man, known only as Sparrow, said.

Natasha strode past as if she hadn't heard, stepping over the sleeping bags, backpacks and empty bottles that covered the polished concrete floor. Sparrow, a man about her age and height with spiky blond hair and an annoying face, was not her equal.

"Companions, gather round," Sparrow called out, "Brother Natasha has graced us with her presence."

A muddle of feet as others streamed in from neighbouring rooms and beset the three-foot-high circular stage, half of them high on marijuana, the rest light-headed from inhaling fumes from the red paint used to spray anarchist slogans on every wall.

The windowless hall was lit by five hurricane lamps placed around the edge of the stage. Hung between two dance poles, a giant street map of the Stock Exchange precinct painted on a sheet of beige tent canvas.

With the energy of a rock star, Natasha sprung up onto the stage and strutted about the boards. "Welcome to their nightmare," she bellowed over the clamour of the revolutionists. "Let's bring down the system. No borders, no nations, just people."

"No borders, no nations, just people," the companions parroted in unison.

"Big day tomorrow, brothers," Natasha bellowed, her face menacing, illuminated from below by the lamps on the floor, like Halloween.

"Ooh, ooh, ooh, ooh…" the anarchists chanted in a tribal grunt until Natasha held up her hands for silence.

"Let's go over the plan one final time," she said, testing a laser pointer against the ceiling. "We've got three groups. Black, Red and White. Anyone doesn't know their designated group?" Silence. "Black – you're responsible for terror, destruction of property, and graffiti. Red – you're in charge of the *rough*. You spot a *suit* coming out of the Exchange onto Paternoster Square, give him a whack. Coppers – two whacks." Laughter. "Groups Black and Red – be prepared for a beating and a ride in a paddy wagon. Not necessarily in that order." More laughter. "White – passive disobedience. Head straight to Paternoster Square. Placards, big voices, rotten eggs. Oh, yeah, Whites – no masks."

"Companions," Sparrow called out from the side. "Is everything clear?"

Nods all around.

"Right then. The assembly points. Black, Festival Gardens at the back of St Paul's." Natasha shone the green laser beam at the location on the canvas. "White, Christ Church Greyfriars public garden, here. And, Red, the entrance to the St Paul's Tube station, here."

"Is that clear?" Sparrow again.

More nodding heads.

"Kick off time: 7:30 a.m. For the Reds, that's half past seven in the morning." Hoots of laughter and pushing and shoving. "We hit the suits while the Gestapo still have their snouts in their breakfast troughs."

As Natasha jumped from the stage, Sparrow took her place. "No borders, no nations, just people. No borders, no nations, just people…" he chanted, pumping his fist in the air, as the companions joined in.

10

The arrival of Agent Rattle at the London safe house failed to create the buzz it deserved. The three wise men remained seated on the U-shaped sofa as Lawrence showed her in. It looked as if Cathy had stolen her thunder by sending a rundown of the day's events while Rattle was on the train. It was the smell of four Zinger Burger meals and two large buckets of chicken that convinced them to raise their eyes from the computer screen and acknowledge Rattle's presence.

"About time," Rosenthal said, pushing aside the coffee table clutter. "We'll take it here."

A slow smile came to Rattle's face. "You're welcome."

"That Rossi's a randy bastard," Jefferson said, slapping closed his Mac. "Gives Catherine Doherty the flick and before the sheets are dry he's off shagging some student slut."

Lawrence looked up from his bourbon. "You can tell all that from one photo?"

"Artificial intelligence. You've heard of it, Lawrence? We have computer systems back home that perform visual perception tasks. They're able to predict what a person is thinking from a handful of images."

"So, you must have a match for the *student slut*, then," Agent Rattle said, her voice heavy with sarcasm.

"You know what Rossi calls you, Rattle?" Rosenthal joined in, flashing a toothy smile between motionless lips. "Heroin Chic."

"Better than what we girls call you studs." Pause. "Aphids."

Rosenthal scoffed. "Very clever. But it doesn't make the slightest bit of sense."

"Rubbish. Think about it," Heroin Chic smirked. "Creepy asexually reproduced bugs, devoid of personality. Okay, aphids are green and you're all blue. But you get the point."

Lawrence sniggered. "Sounds about right."

"The student. Did you get a match or not?" Agent Rattle repeated the question.

"Nothing that sets off alarms," Jefferson said, with a mouth full of burger. "Her name is Natasha Nibley. Born in Kazakhstan to a British father and a Russian mother. Father was the Central Asian sales manager for an American tobacco company based in Almaty. Mother's only claim to fame was beauty and long legs. They posted the father back to London when Natasha was five. She's now twenty-nine. It's possible she speaks Russian." A pause. "No police record. No military service. No spy school. Boring. Don't know what Rossi sees in her."

Rattle narrowed her eyes. "And who decided she's a slut?"

Jefferson pointed to his Mac. "It's in Cathy's report."

"Show me."

"Okay, I paraphrased a little," Jefferson said, moving over for Rattle.

Rattle lifted the lid and wiped the grease off the keyboard with a paper napkin. "I'll get through this a lot quicker with a glass in my hand."

By the time Riccardo returned with a fresh crystal glass, Rattle had finished reading. "We ready to start?" he said, pulling the cork from the bourbon with his teeth and pouring Agent Rattle a generous shot.

"So, what's not there?" Lawrence asked, remaining on his feet.

"The GPS tracker," Rattle said. "I attached one to her Vespa while they were eating lunch at the Plough. I tracked the scooter to a canal narrowboat called *Moon Shadow* moored on the River Cam in Cambridge. As of thirty minutes ago it was still parked at Cambridge station."

"The *narrowboat*?" Riccardo asked.

Rattle shot him a sideways glance. "The scooter, Einstein."

"Do we have her mobile phone under surveillance?" Lawrence asked.

Rosenthal nodded, licking chicken off his fingers. "Well, at least the phone she used to call Rossi yesterday evening."

"It's been stationary since lunch." Jefferson took back control of his Mac. "Just below Jesus Loch on the River Cam. Must be the canal narrowboat Rattle mentioned."

In a stoop, Riccardo topped up the glasses. "If she didn't take the phone to Cambridge station, then chances are she knows she's under surveillance."

"Or she forgot it," Rosenthal offered.

A short silence as the men wolfed down the rest of the chicken and washed it down with bourbon.

"Who owns the boat, Rattle?" Riccardo asked.

"It's registered to a British Virgin Islands company. But, if you believe the retired couple on the boat berthed next to *Moon Shadow*, it belongs to Lord Percy. They said a student matching Natasha's description moved in a month ago. She keeps to herself. They also claim to have seen Lord Percy's Aston Martin parked along the embankment road. Apparently, everyone in Cambridgeshire knows it. Kermit-green, sporting personalised number plates: LP 1. Mind you, they've never seen him in the flesh. He's a night owl, from all accounts. Comes and goes when they're asleep."

Lawrence bent down and picked up a burger wrapper off the floor and tossed it into the empty chicken bucket. "If that's true, then Natasha must be one of Lord Percy's Experientialists. Making her also a CIA person of interest."

"What do they want with Rossi?" Jefferson asked. "First they invite him to Melba House to be a witness to an execution, then they send him a naked girl…"

"Naked girl?" Rattle interrupted. "Don't you mean student slut?"

"They're cultivating him?" Rosenthal declared. "But for what?"

Riccardo offered a suggestion. "Rossi's a left-wing Catholic with a bleeding heart. Perhaps he's being groomed as a double agent."

"That'd be a first," Jefferson added.

Lawrence topped up his glass, then flopped down on the sofa away from the others. "They can try, but they won't get far."

"How did the G20 summit protests go today?" Rattle asked, rising from the sofa and moving to the Steinway. "Any excitement?"

"Ho hum from all accounts," Lawrence said. "Last I heard, the more dedicated have made their way out to Stansted to welcome Air Force One."

"Perhaps that's where Natasha has gone to. Show the finger to the president," Riccardo suggested. "Took the train to London from Cambridge station."

Jefferson scoffed. "A train? More likely she rode to London with Lord Percy in his daddy's Rolls."

"Or his Kermit-green Aston Martin," Rattle smirked, lifting the keyboard lid and tickling out a few bars of "Imagine".

11

Rossi and Cathy looked over as the dining room door swung open and Monsignor Baker entered. They saw no risk in taking breakfast together; both were paid-up residents of Fisher House. Besides, the village gossips and the shadow lurkers needed to get used to seeing them together. Two lonely souls a long way from home, a non-romantic relationship of convenience.

"Jolly good," the monsignor said, as he approached. "I see you've already acquainted yourself with our new lodger, Inspector General."

Rossi craned his neck as he looked up. "Yes, just now," he said, realising from the cleric's remark Cathy was not the lady he'd found in the library.

The monsignor pulled out a chair. "May I join you?" he added, as an afterthought.

"*Naturalmente.*"

"How's the room, Ms Clarke?"

"Full of medieval charm, Monsignor," Cathy smiled. "The antique horsehair mattress and the iron grille on the window takes me back to my schooldays."

Mrs Tarbottom entered from the kitchen carrying Rossi's double espresso and set it down on the table. "Would you like something, Ms Clarke?"

"An Americano?" Cathy said, with a questioning smile.

"A shot of espresso poured over hot water," the housekeeper said, her tone cordial. "We have students from all over the world staying here, Ms Clarke. There's not a coffee I can't make. Whether I choose to, well, that's another matter." Laughter.

"Good for you," Cathy said, joining in.

"You haven't forgotten about *me*, Mrs Tarbottom?" the cleric quipped as the housekeeper returned to the kitchen.

A dismissive flick of the hand from the doorway. "Do you think that's possible? My best customer. A pot of Earl Grey coming up."

"Smashing," he said, joining the others at the buffet table.

"Monsignor," Rossi said with a slight hesitation, "the lady who visited me the other night…"

"Yes, I let her into your room."

"No. The other one – in the library."

A slow nod of vague recollection.

"Can you describe her?"

The monsignor screwed up one side of his face. "Petite with black hair?"

"That's the girl you let into my room," Rossi said, in an unconcerned voice.

"Oh. Well, in that case – I can't remember."

Rossi poured himself some orange juice. "Never mind," he said, although he minded a lot. A hell of a lot.

"Too much altar wine," Monsignor Baker mumbled out loud. "Dulls one's memory."

Cathy's jaw dropped, then a chuckle as she caught the cleric's cheeky grin. "Very good, Monsignor."

"It'll come to me, Inspector General."

***

Down in London an overnight threat by a group of neo-Marxists against the London Stock Exchange had compelled the Metropolitan Police to post extra men around the Exchange building and the nearby St Paul's Cathedral.

The morning was dull and threatening. Low clouds drifted across the sky like smoke from a battlefield. "Perfect day for a revolution," Sparrow shouted, marshalling the Whites in the ruins of Christ Church Greyfriars. "Ready, companions? Okay. Forward march."

Like stray cats, they followed Sparrow across the A4, past the watchful eyes of the Gestapo lining Rose Street, and onto Paternoster Square, where they unfurled their banners and chanted, "Dismantle the system. Capitalism doesn't work."

Seated in the portico bordering the square, alfresco diners craned their necks to read the protesters' placards.

"That's a good one," a young man in a fur-trimmed duffle coat exclaimed in his best learnt Etonian accent. "Politicians are like sperm. One in a million turns out to be human." Laughter.

The wisecracking abruptly stopped as the patrons turned their gaze to the sound of stampeding feet. Gasps as thirty masked anarchists charged through Temple Bar Gate onto the square. Helter-skelter, iron rods and baseball bats raised, they upended tables and smashed windows. Screams of terror. Group Black had done its job.

East, near the Underground entrance, Group Red was outnumbered. Police in blue riot helmets had them isolated and surrounded. Each time they tried to break free the police responded with a cloud of pepper spray and a charge of battens. Masks ripped off, blood streaming down their faces, the riot police tossed the outpatients and hooligans into the back of the paddy wagons and shipped them off for processing.

Below ground, Paterson Carlyle's Bentley pulled up alongside the executive lift. Sir Lloyd Starr, chairman of the LSE, stood straight-backed, waiting to escort the billionaire casino mogul through to the trading floor. Personal service on account of Carlyle's forthcoming £6 billion initial public offering. A listing that would value Carlyle Group at £30 billion and Paterson Carlyle's personal stake at £17 billion.

"Good morning, Mr Carlyle," Starr said, thrusting out his soft manicured hand. "Welcome to the London Stock Exchange, founded in 1571," he added, for show.

"Quite a display you're putting on upstairs," the American said.

"I'd shoot the bloody lot, given half a chance."

"I'm with you there. If those morons were left to run the world, we'd still be dancing around Stonehenge in loincloths."

"Yes. Quite so," Sir Lloyd concurred with a nasal giggle. "Shall we go up?"

A nod from Carlyle and the chauffeur drove off.

The executive lift, set apart from the others, was accessible through an unmarked security door, which Sir Lloyd's middle-aged executive assistant held open.

"Welcome to the London Stock Exchange, Mr Carlyle. My name is Michele Wong," she said with a well-practised smile. "This way, please."

Carlyle and Sir Lloyd followed Wong through to the lift landing, which was no bigger than the lift cabin, licensed to carry six. The lift stood waiting, the door locked open by the key dangling from a retractable chain attached to Ms Wong's handbag.

"How's Margaret and the children?" Sir Lloyd asked, as they stepped into the mirror-polished stainless-steel cabin.

"Wife's in the Bahamas with her mother, and the little brats are at boarding school. A man can't ask for more than that." Laughter.

"Room for one more," came an androgynous voice from the garage.

Ms Wong poked her head out from the lift cabin. The car park door was held open by a black boot. "This is a private lift," she said, in cultured Hong Kong English. "The public lift is to your right."

Ignoring Ms Wong's instructions, a policeman in riot gear wearing a blue helmet with the visor lowered pushed open the door and entered. "Security, madam."

"Do you know who this is?" Ms Wong said, with haughty indignation. "Sir Lloyd Starr, chairman of the LSE."

"Do you know what this is?" the policeman retorted, producing a Glock 19 fitted with a silencer from behind his back.

Ms Wong's eyes grew frantic with fright as she fumbled with the key, trying to unlock the lift.

"Hurry, Ms Wong," Sir Lloyd urged, pressing up hard against the lift's back wall next to Carlyle.

The first shot hit Ms Wong in the temple, the second to the chest before she fell.

"*Jesus*," Carlyle said, as Sir Lloyd made the sign of the cross.

Neither approach helped. In quick succession head shots for Carlyle and Sir Lloyd, followed by a body shot as they lay over each other in Ms Wong's blood.

12

Rossi only heard about Carlyle's killing when he returned to Fisher House after his morning lecture. Cathy had spotted him as he chained his bicycle to the railing below her window and was waiting for him in his room. Dressed in a plaid miniskirt and black leggings, she greeted him with her usual grunt.

"Cathy, I get it. You hate me. But given we'll be living in each other's pocket for some time – if you can't do civil, perhaps you can find it in yourself to be professional," Rossi said, pulling his shamrock-green Aran jumper off over his head.

"I'll think about it," Cathy shrugged, flipping open her laptop. "Seen this?"

Rossi flinched and looked away. "Mafia?"

"It's one of ours," Cathy said, handing Rossi her laptop displaying an image of the carnage inside the lift cabin. "London Stock Exchange. Eight-thirty this morning."

"But it's a different modus operandi."

"Three victims. Six slugs. Head and body shots at close range."

Rossi flicked to the next image. "Circle-A #41. Is it possible there are several killers?"

"My gut feeling is it's the same shooter. Changed his MO to suit the circumstances."

"A copycat killing?" Rossi contested. "A psycho in search of love and attention? After all, the media have done an outstanding job shooting their big mouths off about the graffiti tag."

"That's ridiculous, Enzo. It's clear the shooter came looking for Carlyle. The forty-first richest person in the world."

"Could be a run-of-the-mill underworld hit, dressed up as a political assassination. In his line of work, Paterson Carlyle would have had plenty of enemies."

"Let's stick to the obvious until forensics tell us otherwise."

Rossi leant over the desk and opened the window. "And in the meantime?"

"We'd better find out what Natasha and Lord Percy were up to today."

"Lord Percy? Can't help you there," Rossi said, holding up his hands. "Not my responsibility. But I can tell you, Natasha was a no-show for my morning lecture. She messaged me about saving the endangered oxlip population in Hayley Wood."

"I can see that," Cathy quipped. "Lying in front of a forty-tonne CAT, stopping construction on a vital piece of infrastructure she and her grubby dreadlock cave dweller mates deem unnecessary."

Rossi shook his head. "Doesn't seem the type. More likely she was doing a bit of communing with nature. *Shinrin-yoku.*"

"Forest bathing. What's the difference?"

"One's frolicking nude in an enchanted wood while being sketched by Paul Cezanne. The other's active resistance where you risk getting your head kicked in by some union thug."

"Either way, she's a kooky pain in the arse."

"Wouldn't know. But she missed my excellent lecture on the Vatican and the Spanish Civil War." Rossi puffed out his chest. "Received a standing ovation."

"What vanity. Why didn't I notice it before?"

"Because love is blind."

Cathy glowered at Rossi. "As much as I disapprove, you must call her. Find out the real reason she played hooky."

"I could go for a ride along the towpath past *Moon Shadow*. Maybe she's ill."

"Unnecessary and not advisable. Leave that to Heroin Chic." A check of her watch. "I've got a class. Must build those networks."

"Dinner?"

"Already arranged, thank you. I'm off to the Hawks' Club."

Rossi furrowed his brow.

"Cambridge social club for sportswomen and men. I'll be dining with Robert Morton. Captain of the Rifle Association."

"Shall I join you?"

"Members only, old boy," Cathy said in a posh English accent, sounding Canadian.

"Well-cooked English fare with a boy half your age. Not missing much," Rossi said, his tone dry.

A motherly shake of the head. "You're so transparent, Mr Rossi."

"What does that mean?"

"You do jealousy ever so badly," Cathy said, rising from the bed. Then she added before Rossi could respond, "I've got to go. Don't wait up for me."

"So, what am I meant to do in the meantime?" Rossi asked, regarding her with his once-all-powerful sea-green eyes.

"You're the visiting academic of Vatican history, for Heaven's sake! Stay in and grade exam papers."

As the door clicked closed, Rossi reached for his Vatican iPhone and searched for Natasha's number amongst the list of recent calls. Exasperated, he slapped it back on the desk. A realisation, an epiphany. How was it he no longer worked for the Holy See?

As Rossi slipped back into his jumper and headed outside to buy a phone and grab a bite to eat, he was under no illusion what was on his mind. Had Natasha lied? Was she in London playing him for a fool? He needed to find out.

13

Rossi sat at his desk gazing out of the window thinking of Natasha. Since returning with his new phone four hours ago, he had called her a dozen times. Phone off.

Without Cathy to curb his enthusiasm, he decided to go for a walk along the Cam. If he wandered off course past *Moon Shadow*, so be it. What harm could it do? As long as he stayed out of sight.

Dressed in a dark hooded anorak, Rossi stepped onto the pavement. The mildness of the day had long escaped into an unclouded sky. He glanced up at the windows overlooking Fisher House, expecting to catch the smoky gaze of the androgynous Heroin Chic. His eyes peeled left and right. *Are Lawrence's pavement artists out there?* Or do they belong to the three wise men? No one seemed to be able to tell him.

The mooring was five minutes by bicycle along the towpath, or fifteen minutes by foot through Jesus Green.

More options by foot, he thought, setting off north with long strides. A mist blanketed the park, growing thicker as he tramped across the damp open fields towards the river, avoiding the lamps lighting the tree-lined paths.

He cut a lonely figure as he stood stock-still on Jesus Loch footbridge, straining to identify *Moon Shadow* amongst the long line of narrowboats moored on the north bank.

"Professor?" came a voice full of surprise.

Mouth open, Rossi swung around, then froze.

"What are you doing here? It's late."

"Looking for you," Rossi said, unable to come up with a better answer.

Natasha motioned with a flick of the head towards the thumb smudge of light hanging low in the southern sky. "Is the full moon playing with your libido?"

"You weren't in class. And I couldn't sleep. So, I thought I'd go for a stroll. Check everything's okay." While Natasha considered this, Rossi added, "No thought of disturbing you. Plan was to check for signs of life, then back to Fisher House unnoticed."

"That sounds rather creepy, Professor. And, even if it's true, which I doubt given I sent you a message saying I was going to Hayley Wood, I'm a big girl. I can look after myself."

Rossi felt like an idiot. Not because of what she said, but for getting caught. *If Cathy finds out, I'm dead?*

"You're right. It won't happen again. Next time I'll wait for the police to drag the river."

Natasha smiled. "Since you've come all this way…"

"A ten-minute walk."

"I should invite you in. Perhaps some supper," she added, holding up a mini-market bag brimming with groceries.

"Lead the way."

Threading her arm through his, Natasha did just that. Over the bridge, left past the pistachio-green Vespa, over the railing, and down the steep grassy riverbank.

As Rossi stepped on board the fifty-foot, royal-blue stern narrowboat, a horrible thought came to mind. He was sure she'd never mentioned *Moon Shadow*. Why didn't she ask how he knew where to find her? He had no answer.

With apprehension, he descended below deck to the living quarters. Natasha switched on the lights and drew closed the yellow blackout curtains. Rossi's eyes darted about. White painted walls and ceiling, white carpet. The corners of his mouth twitched as he recalled the Knightsbridge safe house. *Same interior decorator*, he thought, moving further in.

The ceiling was tall enough to accommodate Rossi, but the length and width reminded him of a coffin. A slender yellow built-in sofa stretched the entire length of the saloon. Opposite stood a thin wooden coffee table, with two wicker baskets underneath, pushed hard against the cabin wall. Deeper, a solid fuel stove and a box of charcoal. Then a well-equipped galley. Beyond that, Rossi assumed, the bathroom and the stateroom.

Natasha set the groceries down on the counter next to the sink. "Pour yourself a drink, Professor, while I take a shower. Need to wash off the London grime."

Rossi shot her an oblique glance. *Shower, naked, London, anarchist, murder,* flashed through his head. *Where the hell is Hayley Wood?*

"You'll find everything you need in there," Natasha said, pointing to a storage cupboard beneath the steps they had just descended. "Then be a good boy and light the stove. It's freezing in here."

"Aye, aye, Captain." Rossi was already peering into the cupboard. Two shelves. Bottles of spirits on the bottom. Gin, tequila, vodka, Scotch. Two of everything. On the shelf above, snifters and lowball glasses stored upside down. *Wine must be in the galley.* Rossi always felt you could tell a lot about a person by what they drank. And if the bottle of Ardbeg Kelpie Islay Single Malt and Martell Cordon Bleu XO Cognac were any guide, Rossi concluded that Natasha had money and good taste to boot. *Or at least Lord Percy did.*

He poured himself a full measure of Ardbeg, took a long sip, held it in his mouth, then swallowed. Moving back to light the stove, Rossi couldn't help but wonder how many boaters died each year from carbon monoxide poisoning. *Dying in a floating coffin.* Rossi grinned. He felt great. He put it down to the Ardbeg and being with Natasha. The fire caught first attempt. No surprise to Rossi. Throughout his childhood it was his job in winter to light and care for the fire. Rossi considered himself an expert. And he was.

"Thirsty?" Natasha quipped, returning from the shower dressed in white socks, panties and an oversized dusky-pink jumper.

Perched on the yellow sofa playing with his new phone, Rossi glanced down at his empty glass. "I thought I'd wait."

"Was that you who rang a million times today?"

Rossi cringed. "Twenty, maximum." Pause. "I thought I'd get a local number. Wanted you to be the first to know."

"I'm truly honoured." Pause. "You got the fire going all right? Well done, you," she said, crouching down and adjusting the vent.

"What are you drinking?" Rossi asked, setting his glass on the wooden kitchen counter dividing the saloon and the galley.

"Same as you."

Rossi obliged, topped up his own glass while at it, then sat down again.

"What was going on in London – or Hayley Wood – that caused you to miss my most interesting lecture on the Vatican and the Spanish Civil War?"

"Sounds interesting. Sorry I missed it."

A staged silence as Rossi gave Natasha every chance to answer his question.

"Something to eat?" she asked, putting away the groceries.

"What's on offer?"

"Cheese, olives, grapes, chocolate. I was expecting you," she said, with a wink.

"*Fantastico*," Rossi said, pausing. Then in a measured voice added, "You didn't finish telling me about London."

"G20."

"G20 what?"

"Protest, if you must know. I was in London protesting. About what? Fucking everything," Natasha blurted out.

"So, who was it in Hayley Wood saving the endangered oxlip?" Rossi smiled.

"No one. I lied. I've been in London all day."

"But the march was yesterday." Rossi cocked his head, doing his best to appear mixed up.

Natasha crumpled onto the galley floor and sobbed into her small, delicate hands. Kneeling beside her, Rossi stroked her hair, saying nothing, just waiting.

"People died," Natasha eventually said, her voice muffled behind her fingers.

"Who died?" Rossi asked, expecting a cathartic confession in sufficient detail to get the three wise men off his back. But silence.

Natasha drew in several short shaky breaths and wiped her eyes with the palms of her hands. Brushing away Rossi's arm, she rose to her feet and drained her glass.

"Another one?" Rossi asked, still waiting for the revelation.

A nod of her head sent Rossi scurrying over to collect the bottle. He handed Natasha half a glass, hoping to loosen her tongue. In unison they flopped onto the sofa and stared at the same blank wall. They sat apart, as if they were quarrelling lovers.

It was not until her glass was again empty that Natasha spoke. "The march was on Sunday. I was with you."

"That's right," Rossi said, in a subdued tone. "So, what march did *you* attend?"

"None."

Masking his growing impatience, Rossi rose, moved to the galley and washed the grapes in the sink.

A long silence while each waited for the other to speak. Rossi spooned olives into a small, brightly painted Mallorcan bowl while Natasha again topped up their glasses.

"But you—"

"I organised the frigging show," she said. "I didn't take part."

"And which show would that be, Natasha?"

"The anarchists' roadshow at the London Stock Exchange," Natasha growled into her Scotch.

"But there's nothing connecting the anarchists to the killings…" Rossi lied.

"Aside from the anarchist tag scrawled on the wall of the Stock Exchange lift landing. Just like in the other four murders."

"Rubbish. Who told you that?" Rossi said, far quicker than he would have liked.

"A friend."

Fighting back the urge to go on the attack, Rossi bit his tongue and busied himself preparing supper. Opening a galley cupboard, he found a poppy-print serving tray. Upon it he set two small plates; two cake forks; paper napkins; one large compartmentalised plate crammed with salami, cheese and grapes; and the olives.

"Now, where were we?" Rossi asked, setting the tray on the sofa between them as he sat down. "A friend? How many friends do you have? Any chance we can narrow it down?"

"Percy Benbow."

"*Buon Dio.* Not Lord Percy? Couldn't be two."

Natasha nodded and slid an olive into her mouth.

"Well there you go. You're worrying for no reason. He couldn't possibly know."

"His uncle, on his mother's side, is Home Secretary."

God help us. The inbred ruling class strikes again, Rossi thought. "How's it you know His Lordship?"

"He's my filthy-rich cousin." Another pull on her glass. "This is his boat."

"Are you expecting him tonight? I'd love to say hello."

"He rarely visits," Natasha said, stabbing a chunk of cheese with her fork. "When Percy found out I was coming up to Cambridge, he bought *Moon Shadow* to save me from having to slum it in one of those loathsome university colleges. Goes back if I ever finish."

"*Scusami*, I'm missing something, Natasha. How are you connected with the Stock Exchange murders?"

"By the graffiti – not the deed. Murder is not part of our agenda. Someone's trying to hang it on us. The Stock Exchange and the other murders."

"Does Percy or his Home Secretary uncle have any idea who's behind it?"

"They weren't saying. But unquestionably it wasn't us."

"Now I'm double confused," Rossi chuckled, throwing back his head. "Who is *us* in this revolution?"

Natasha sprung to her feet and set down her glass. Popping open a cabinet door tucked away under the saloon side of the kitchen counter, she turned on the stereo.

"Dance with me, Professor." Arms stretched high above her head, she swayed to Sade.

Not a good idea. Rossi knew it. But what the hell. Four glasses of Scotch had blunted his self-control – what little there was of it. Besides, he hadn't finished. There was so much more to learn. He even thought for half a second a peek in her bedroom would be nice. Collapse on the bed too drunk to undress. But he convinced himself that he remained too much of a gentleman for such an unprincipled act.

Natasha wrapped her arms around his neck and drew him close, resting her head on his chest. She was a full head shorter than him. After Cathy, it seemed strange.

Then, without cause, Natasha released Rossi, took a step back and peered into his sea-green eyes. "Do you think I'm bad, Professor?" she slurred.

Rossi half-smiled, unsure of the context. "Most girls are."

"Hold that thought, Professor," Natasha said, staggering towards the galley, pulling on the dregs of the bottle of Ardbeg as she went. "I need a pee."

Ten minutes passed. Rossi turned down the music and listened. Silence. "Natasha," he called out in a loud whisper, tapping on the bathroom door. Empty. Continuing down the corridor, he squinted into the darkness. The stateroom light was off, but he could hear his host moving on the bed. Convinced she was waiting for him naked, Rossi hesitated then carried on. "Natasha," he said softly, pushing on the door. Heart racing, he stepped inside. Rossi smiled broadly as his eyes adjusted to the light. Lying on her back, legs splayed open, was Natasha. Asleep.

14

"You're sure Lord Percy won't mind?" Cathy asked, as the double white doors of the Hawks' Club banged closed behind them.

"He'll be chuffed, Ms Clarke. Someone new to argue with," Robert Morton said, as they descended the three stone steps onto the misty street. "It would be even better if you believe Stanley Kubrick shot the Apollo moon landings in a film studio, or global warming is a hoax."

"Why is that?"

"Percy's a brilliant polemicist. He loves to argue. Particularly half-sloshed before a rowdy crowd."

"Taxi?"

"Gosh no. It's a five-minute walk, maximum," Morton said. With old-fashioned courtesy, he offered Cathy his arm, and without hesitation she took it.

As they approached the arched tunnelled entrance of the Fez Club, two black bouncers in tuxedos standing behind a "private function" sign eyeballed Cathy.

"Good evening. Names please?" a bouncer asked to his clipboard.

Morton, a tall, lean man, with boyish good looks, expressive round hazel eyes and loose locks of curly brown hair, shot the bouncer a frown of surprise, forcing him to look again.

"Sorry, Mr Morton. Didn't recognise you under that hat." A tick and the human wall parted.

Morton led Cathy down the steep narrow stairs. Small and intimate, with roughly glazed walls of earth-toned palettes. Shades of gold, yellow, burnt orange, tan and cream. Red fabric framing the faux *riad* windows. Shards of coloured light from copper steel Moorish lanterns. A bar, a dance floor, scores of nooks and crannies, and a DJ playing progressive rock – not too loud.

"Fez. I get it," Cathy said, glancing about.

Morton dragged her by the hand to a circular alcove that opened onto the dance floor. Seated on a leather sofa and a scattering of ottoman stools set around a Moroccan zellige table strewn with fancy cocktails and a bottle of champagne – a dozen friends.

"Listen up, barflies," Morton trumpeted. "This is my new best friend, Ashley Clarke – research fellow, Slavonic studies, Fisher House."

The oldest amongst them made room for Cathy on the sofa. "*Fisher House.* What did you do to deserve that?"

"You tell me." Cathy shrugged as she stepped delicately between feet.

"I'm your host."

If I didn't know that, Cathy thought, leaning back and looking him over. "Lord Percy?"

"The charmer himself," he said, with a bob of his head and a flowery wave of his arm.

"Of course, you are. I should have realised." They shook hands. "Robert said you wouldn't mind."

"So, what brings you to Cambridge so late in the term? I didn't know they allowed that."

"They don't. That's why I'm banished to Fisher House. Well, that and the Global Peace Initiative's miniscule budget."

"You don't look like a peace advocate."

A winsome smile and a sideways tilt of the head. "No?"

"Budge up, boys and girls," Morton said, squeezing in on the other side of Percy. He looked about. "Where's Balls?"

"He's around somewhere," one girl said with a glum face.

Leaning close to Morton, Percy whispered, "Does she belong to you, Bobby?"

"Good grief, no. Out of my depth there."

"You mind if I have a crack?"

"Snog away." Morton smirked, holding up a beckoning finger to a waiter.

Lord Percy turned to Cathy, appraising her with his chocolate brown eyes. "I'm not buying your story."

"Ashley, you sticking to the Bushmills?" Morton interjected.

Cathy was grateful for the extra seconds. "Never mix your drinks, Robert," she quipped, before fixing her gaze back on Percy Benbow. "I'm not selling. But if I was – what part don't you like?"

"The whole bloody thing. Sounds like a hoax."

"Love this song – 'A Whiter Shade of Pale'. Let's dance, Robert," Cathy said, latching onto her escort's hand and dragging him into the purple haze of the spacious dance floor.

Morton, who had heard their exchange, coloured as Cathy held him close and slow danced. "He does that. Thinks it's clever."

"I know the type."

"Percy's gormless with the ladies. That's half his problem. Otherwise he's a nice guy." Pause. "He'll come around."

Cathy pulled Morton closer and laid her cheek against his. "We don't need him to come around, Robert. We're just fine on our own."

"Blimey." An awkward grin as he glanced over at his best mate.

They danced the next song in silence. Then Cathy steered Morton across the dance floor to the far end of the bar. It was quieter and away from the others. "Tell me more about yourself, Robert. Are you an Experientialist like Lord Percy?"

"Gosh no. None of us are." Pause. "Except Natasha, Percy's muse. He reckons it's all window dressing with her. A green light to wantonness."

Cathy motioned to the barman. He hurried over. "Two large Bushmills, one with a dash of soda."

"We're a mixed bag," Morton continued. "We've got Marxists, communists, contractarians, socialists, anarchists and egalitarians." Morton closed one eye and stared up at the ceiling as if the list was to be found there. "Capitalists, fascists, nationalists and totalitarians need not apply."

"Feminists?"

"Outright discouraged. The club's a ruse. Established by Percy and his highbrow professor chum to lure undergraduates back to their bedrooms. Percy says there's nothing better than a heated debate about political philosophy to get their juices flowing."

Cathy gave off a playful growl. "Robert, that's beneath you."

"It's not a view I prescribe to, Ashley. Just not worth arguing with Percy."

"What's His Lordship in all this? A militant anarchist?"

Morton glanced over at Percy still seated on the sofa. "If he's anything, he's an anti-capitalist. Dead against the culture of greed that has grown out of America since Reagan."

"Ironic coming from the heir to one of the largest fortunes in Britain."

"Not his fault – wouldn't you say?" Morton slurred, six hours of drinking taking its toll. "Besides, he's against greed – not money. American greed. A modern-day religion worshipped by the one per cent and spread to the ignorant masses like the missionaries of the past. 'You too can be rich,' they shout from the mountain top. But most likely not..."

Cathy got the idea. "Does the professor have a name?" she interrupted. "Don't want to go bumping into his cerebral witchery without fair warning."

Morton deflated his lungs through fluttering lips. "Professor Slack. Philosophy Department. Decent fellow. A little randy, but aren't we all? He'll be lurking here tonight, somewhere." Morton glanced about then gestured with his eyes towards a short plump man in a white shirt and red suspenders on the dance floor. The waistband of his baggy blue corduroys sat above his navel. He appeared drunk, rocking to "Thunderstruck" on his headphones while the rest of the crowd swayed to Genesis. "Family friend of the Benbows," Morton continued. "Taught the young Percy to shoot. A celebrity in his day, so I hear. Represented GB in the 300-metre rifle three positions. Won medals. Commonwealth Games or Olympics? Can't remember. It was aeons ago."

A short silence as Cathy studied Slack.

"Anti-capitalist also?"

"And then some," Morton said, steadying himself on the bar.

A slap on the back. "Stand down, soldier," Percy said, with a chuckle. "Don't want you honking all over Ms Clarke."

An exchange of glances and Morton retired to the darkest corner on the sofa and collapsed on the shoulder next to him.

"What's Bobby been saying about me?" Percy asked, leaning into her space.

Cathy rested her fingertips on Percy's bony chest and pushed him away. "I can't see your eyes if you stand so close."

"Well – out with it. What's Loose Lips Morton been telling you?"

"That's rather narcissistic." A scoff. "Other than in passing, why would we be talking about you?"

"Because – not to put too fine a point on it – you're not who you pretend to be," Percy said in jarring Russian.

A tut. "That's a damn hideous accent you've got there," Cathy riposted in faultless Russian. "Not to mention the grammatical error. Are you testing me?"

"You're an American, Ms Clarke. A person who readily turns their back on social injustice and the suffering of others. As I look into your eyes, I see America First with its flexible set of values staring back at me. And your strut and swagger are way over the top for someone purporting to be a global peace advocate."

Cathy checked her watch. "It's late. Say goodnight to Robert for me."

Percy held out his hand. "Where are you going?"

"Off to bed," Cathy said, pushing past.

Standing at the cloakroom, Cathy turned back to face her host who had followed her. "Maybe *I* should be concerned. Who are you afraid of? What secrets are you hiding?"

"A person of my wealth and standing must be wary of strangers, especially when they're as attractive as you."

"I'll take that as a compliment. Goodnight." Cathy buttoned her coat then ascended the stairs alone.

15

Rossi woke with a start. No sense of time or place. Stretching out an arm, he felt for his phone. Not there. He propped himself on one elbow and glanced about the room. His anorak lay in the middle of the floor next to his muddy chukka boots.

"That doesn't happen often," he murmured to himself as he sat up. Still dressed from last night he removed his phone from his anorak and checked the time. Nine-fifteen. Missed breakfast. He sniffed under his armpits and checked his face in the mirror above the commode. A vague recollection of showering before his midnight tryst with Natasha. With a nod of approval, Rossi slipped on his shoes and jacket, and headed out.

Unlocking his bicycle, he was sure he was over the limit. *Perhaps I should walk*, he thought, as he mounted his eighteen-speed and rode off towards the river. The morning was dull and foggy. The fresh air and the site of Natasha's Vespa on Chesterton Road made Rossi feel better. He secured his bicycle to the railing and clambered down the steep grassy embankment, grabbing branches of the yellow willow tree to stop himself slipping. A light burnt in the narrowboat's galley. *Breakfast*, he thought, jumping aboard. And, if he was honest, he was also excited at the prospect of seeing Natasha again.

The stern deck door was unlocked. No surprise. He had no way of securing it when he left early this morning. "*Buongiorno*, Natasha," Rossi called out, descending the steps.

It was freezing below deck. The stove was out: cold to touch. He glanced about. Everything was as he had left it: dishes in the twin-basin sink; food stored; bottles standing on the kitchen counter.

Rossi stopped and listened. Above on Chesterton Road, he could hear the sound of the hydraulic lifting mechanism of a recycling truck emptying the contents of a large yellow cart into its hopper. On the river a cabin cruiser sailed past, sending ripples of waves slapping against the hull. But nothing from the stateroom. Nothing from the bathroom.

He crept forward, not wanting to frighten Natasha. She'd drunk heavily, but nothing a good breakfast couldn't fix. The stateroom door was open and the red blackout curtains drawn closed. Squinting, he peered into the darkness.

"Natasha," Rossi whispered, waiting for his eyes to adjust. Slowly Natasha appeared. She was lying on top of a black silk sheet in the foetal position. Rossi picked up the grey duvet that had fallen on the floor and stooped forward to cover her. Something wasn't right. *This is my fault*, he thought, fumbling for the bedside lamp.

"Jesus," he said, recoiling in horror.

Transfixed with indecision, Rossi stood staring at Natasha's pale face. Naked and hogtied in what Rossi assumed was a bondage ritual gone wrong. Then the sight of one of his neck ties pulled tightly around her bruised neck cleared his head like a dose of smelling salts.

Someone had murdered Natasha. *And I'm the dupe they're going to blame.*

He removed his phone from his anorak to call Cathy. He needed her advice. But the sound of sirens in the distance had him wondering whether it was too late. As creepy as it felt, Rossi snapped photos of Natasha's tiny lifeless body, before scurrying up on deck.

As Rossi beat a swift retreat, skulking along the river to the relative safety of the Jesus Loch footbridge, he saw flashing blue lights appear and disappear through the willow trees that ran along the embankment. He wondered whether the police could trace his abandoned bicycle. *Probably not.*

Rossi had already crossed the river and was racing through Jesus Green by the time the police screeched to a halt on Chesterton Road above *Moon Shadow*.

Still moving, avoiding the security cameras, Rossi called Cathy. Was he overreacting? A nervous chuckle. *Someone's dead.* He'd done nothing wrong. Cathy could call Langley. A quiet word in the ear of MI6 and the whole thing would disappear. Operation Bright Star. Nudge, nudge. Wink, wink.

"Ashley, something important has come up. We need to talk."

"Usual place. Ten minutes," came the answer.

"Have you eaten?"

"No," Cathy said, surprised by the question. "I was up all night chatting with my new friends."

16

The smug look on Rossi's face as he flung open the door wasn't quite what Cathy expected. Holding up two takeaway coffees and a bag of croissants from the French bakery around the corner, he looked calm and collected.

"I thought you had something urgent to discuss," Cathy said. "I cancelled my manicure appointment for a croissant?"

"But I do, *mio amore*. Only let's go somewhere warmer. My radiator's broken." Rossi tapped his earlobe and motioned with his head towards the walls.

Gathering her things, Cathy followed Rossi to the chapel in the new wing of the Fisher House complex.

They stood at the high altar under the reconstruction of the thirteenth-century Cimabue crucifix and listened. The church was empty, lit by natural light streaming through skylights set between exposed wooden beams in the vaulted ceiling.

"What's up there?" Cathy asked.

"It's the mezzanine level for the choir. Stairs are through here."

Rossi set the coffee and croissants on the only table on the entresol and pushed aside the clutter while Cathy grabbed two of the orchestra chairs from near the landing banister.

"You look like shit, Enzo," Cathy said, sitting down. "Couldn't sleep knowing I was out on a date?"

"I visited *Moon Shadow*," Rossi confessed, hanging his anorak over the back of the chair.

"Thought we agreed to leave that to Heroin Chic," Cathy said, her tone displeased.

Seated, Rossi tore open the white patisserie bag and pushed it towards Cathy. "Try one. All-butter croissants that melt in your mouth. Perfect balance between flakiness and chewiness. At least that's what the sign in the window said."

"Don't change the subject."

"Thought I'd walk by and check for signs of life."

"Was there any?"

"Last night." Pause. "But not now."

Cathy threw Rossi a sideway glance. "So, where is she?"

"Dead."

"Dead? Like in dead tired? Dead drunk? What sort of dead?"

"Deceased."

"Damn it, Enzo. It's Moscow all over again. What happened this time?"

Rossi dug into his pocket and pulled out his phone. His pulse quickened as he opened the album containing the thumbnail images of Natasha's bound lifeless body. "This happened," he said, passing her the phone.

"Jesus, Enzo. Was it an accident?"

"How the hell would *I* know?"

Cathy expanded an image. "What's this around her neck?"

"My tie." Silence. "She must have swiped it the night I returned from London and found her in my room."

"Naked."

Rossi took a bite of his croissant and stared into the middle distance trying to avoid Cathy's gaze.

"And the sex stains on the sheets?"

"Not me," Rossi said, his tone desperate. "When I left, she was alive and kicking. Well, perhaps not kicking. She had passed out on the bed."

"Dressed?"

Rossi's gaze dropped to the floor. "More or less."

"You idiot."

"I'm not arguing with you, Cathy. We drank, she passed out, I put another log on the fire, then left."

"No goodnight kiss?"

"Couldn't if I tried. Now can we drop it?"

They spent the next hour debriefing each other. Then, at full tilt, they drafted a report for Lawrence's eyes only. Why Lawrence? Because they smelt a rat, and Special Agent Lawrence was the only one they were sure they could trust. Cathy and Rossi had worked with him in Moscow. His story rang true. He was one of them.

"We need to go to London," Cathy said, pulling a yellow burner phone from her bag and dialling Special Agent Lawrence. It was one of five pay-as-you-go mobiles she had purchased with cash from a back-alley electronics repair shop: all second-hand, all different colours.

As the phone rang, Cathy removed a large brown Kraft paper envelope from her messenger bag and dropped it on the table. "Have a gander at these happy snaps."

Rossi unwound the red string and held open the flap. Inside were twelve digitally enhanced photographs from the Stock Exchange CCTV security video. Leaning forward, his forearms resting on the table, Rossi studied the shots:

- A Bentley pulling up in front of the executive lift entrance.
- Sir Lloyd Starr greeting Carlyle.
- A policeman in riot gear entering the LSE underground carpark via the vehicle ramp.
- A middle-aged Asian woman holding open the door to the executive lift landing.
- Carlyle, Sir Lloyd and the woman entering the lift.
- A boot jammed in the garage door.
- A policeman standing inside the landing with his pistol raised.
- Close up of tactical shooting gloved right hand holding out a pistol.
- Two centimetres of a thin pale wrist between glove and jacket revealing a small dragonfly tattoo.

- Three bodies in lift.
- A policeman spray painting the anarchist tag on the landing wall.
- A policeman exiting the same way he came in.

"Hello," Lawrence answered, continuing a conversation he was having with someone down the line.

"Le Méridien Piccadilly?" she said, in thick Scottish.

"Wrong number, lady."

"I'd like to book a table for Mendeleev in the Longitude bar for seven tonight," Cathy blurted out, hoping Lawrence remembered their boozy night out in Moscow at the avant-garde bar of the same name.

Without another word, Lawrence rang off.

17

Rossi and Cathy entered the Le Méridien on Piccadilly pulling overnight bags. They'd agreed there was little risk if the spooks caught them together. After all, they had been engaged to be married. Under the present circumstances, a relapse was only to be expected. At Fisher House, under the watchful eye of Monsignor Baker, what chance was there for self-expression? Who could begrudge them a night in a flash London hotel? A West End show, supper, then back to crisp white linen and a king-size bed.

"Booking for Clarke," Cathy said, glancing about.

"Welcome to Le Méridien on Piccadilly, Ms Clarke," the receptionist said, removing the guest registration form from the filing cabinet drawer and setting it on the counter for Cathy's signature. "How would you like to pay?"

Cathy handed over a freshly minted Mastercard, payment guaranteed by the US government. Sure, the card would link her to the hotel, but that was only a problem if Lawrence showed up on the radar at the same time. And that would not happen. "Two keys, please."

"Room 1505, Ms Clarke. You'll need the key to operate the lift. Enjoy your stay."

Rossi gazed into Cathy's honey-coloured eyes as they rode in silence to the fifth floor, wishing he could turn back the clock. Presenting Cathy to his mother the way he had was stupid. It was all his fault. He should have better prepared her for her day before the hanging judge.

The bell chimed, and the brushed steel door opened. Cathy led Rossi down the long carpeted corridor. Decorative sconces attached to the dark-brown walls projected ambient light in vertical beams between the rooms.

"After you, Mr Rossi," Cathy said, pushing open the door.

"Not the honeymoon suite," Rossi said, glancing about. Beige walls; brown patterned carpet; a king-sized bed under a sloping ceiling; and a small round rosewood table between a pair of matching armchairs in red wool. Rossi tossed his overcoat and pork-pie hat on top of the all-white bedding and drew closed the black curtains, shutting out the expensive view of Big Ben and Victoria Tower. "But it'll do nicely."

The clock on the TV standing on a mahogany commode read 14:45.

"Make yourself comfortable," Cathy said. "I've got to go out for an hour."

"Shopping?"

"I'll explain when I get back."

***

Fifteen minutes later, Cathy entered the Parcafé on Park Lane. Seated at the window checking her emails was Barbora Novak, the CIA's permanent liaison officer to MI6.

"Am I late?"

Novak jumped out of her chair. "Cathy," she screamed, as they hugged each other. "How wonderful to see you."

"It's been too long."

"And I hear congratulations are in order. Wow! Inspector General Rossi." A gushing giggle. "Are you moving to Rome?"

Cathy and Novak had first met five years ago at the Sherman Kent School in Virginia while training to become CIA analysts. They had been drawn together from day one by a common enemy: the entrenched culture of virulent sexism and male chauvinism at the school. A bond that has lasted to this day.

"Wedding's off, I'm afraid," Cathy confessed, as they ordered cappuccinos and cupcakes at the counter. "Didn't work out."

"What happened, if you don't mind me asking?"

They sat back down at the window, overlooking Hyde Park.

"I met Enzo's mother," Cathy said, raising her eyebrows. "She's nice enough, but the visit to the family home reminded me of what I was signing up for. A husband, dirty nappies, pasta and a big arse."

"Sounds like a mid-life crisis," Novak said, with a shrug.

"I'm thirty, damn it."

"Thirty-three," Novak corrected. "Anyway, only *you* know what's best for you."

"Two cappuccinos," the barista called out, setting them on a tray with the cupcakes.

Cathy grabbed a sugar dispenser while Novak collected the tray.

"Trouble is, I don't know what I want."

"That's not like you, Cathy. But it's always more difficult with matters of the heart. Sacrifice a piece of your freedom for the unknown. And when you've had a difficult childhood like yours, deciding is even more tortuous."

A thoughtful hush as they sipped their coffee and picked at their cupcakes with their forks.

"What are you doing in London, Cathy? I thought after the Russians declared you *persona non grata*; they'd nailed you to the floor in Langley." A mirthful snort.

"They handed me the key last week. Gave me a legend and bought me a ticket to Cambridge."

"England?"

A nod.

"To do what?"

"Not sure. That's the reason I contacted you."

"And some marriage counselling."

"Always appreciated, Barbora."

"And more valuable coming from a woman who's never been on a date without having to pay for it."

"Not true."

"Remember what you used to say about those arseholes at Sherman Kent."

Cathy smiled. "Half wanted me naked and the other half wanted me gone." Laughter.

"With me, it was unanimous. No one wanted me naked – just gone." More laughter. "Now what's the story, morning glory? Out with it. You must have a brief."

A mouthful of cake and a sip of coffee while Cathy chose her words. Regardless of their friendship, they were still both in the spy game and sharing classified information was *verboten*. "The so-called circle-A killings. Which creaky British institution drew the short straw? Who's in charge of the investigation?"

"The Met's Homicide and Serious Crimes Unit."

"To paraphrase the UK government's own web page," Cathy said, phone already open in her palm, "it is MI5's responsibility to protect the UK and its citizens against threats to national security – including actions that undermine parliamentary democracy by political and violent means."

"For now, someone in Downing Street is limiting MI5 to an advisory role. A position Langley is insisting I support."

"How does that make sense? Anarchism is a political philosophy hell-bent on bringing down all forms of government. Sounds like a security risk to me."

"I agree, but…" Novak had no answer.

"And what's the agency's role in all this? Besides staying on the sidelines."

"Limited to NSA cryptology and signal intelligence support."

"*That's it?*" Cathy said, locking eyes with Novak. "No CIA boots on the ground? Four of the five victims are US citizens. All crooks, granted – but since when has that mattered?"

Novak stared back at Cathy, almost apologetically. "It's strange. But I'm used to strange. The story I'm being fed is that there's insufficient intelligence linking the murders to the anarchists—"

"Other than the circle-A monogram."

"But there's been no follow-up claims of responsibility. The circle-A could be a curveball. Send us off on a wild goose chase." Pause. "It would help, Cathy, if you just came out and told me what you know."

Cathy dropped her guard and smiled. "The part of the CIA I work for insist the assassinations are the handy work of the Experientialists, a group of layabout anarchists squatting at Cambridge University. I would have thought someone would have bothered to inform you." A long pause. "You heard of Operation Bright Star?"

"Not a peep. Is that what you're doing here? Working to catch an anarchist?"

"Me and a couple of buddies." A sip of coffee. "What do you know about a safe house in Knightsbridge occupied by three beefy Americans?"

"Nothing. But I can find out."

Another long lull as they finished their cake and mulled over in their minds the many inconsistencies with the agency's norms.

"Seems you've been dropped into a black operation that the US Intelligence Community don't want the British knowing about."

"So much for the US–UK 'special relationship,'" Cathy quipped, scooping the froth from the bottom of her cup with her spoon.

"Have you considered the Brits may be in on this? Perhaps that's the reason Downing Street have MI5 on a short leash?"

Grim faced, Cathy glanced at her watch. "Got to go. I've got somewhere I need to be. Thanks a million, Barbora. You've been a great help."

They stood and hugged.

"Be careful, Cathy. Trust no one. And don't rely on anyone riding to the rescue when the shit hits the fan. Not even your Chief James is going to sacrifice his pension for a girl like you."

***

"Go find Lawrence," Cathy said, writing their room number on the back of one of the electronic keys and slipping it into Rossi's shirt pocket. "If everything's okay, he'll order a Red Russian."

"What's the rush? Afraid to be alone with me? No self-control?"

"Not likely," she answered, shoving him out of the door.

Striding through the lobby, Rossi descended the stairs to the Longitude 0°8 bar. Glancing airily about, he perched himself on a bar stool facing the mirror-backed liquor shelves. Twenty-plus guests scattered about, all seated at tables, nothing out of place. But no Lawrence. *Too early.*

A barman wearing a white shirt, black waistcoat and bow tie placed a bowl of Wasabi Sweet & Spicy bar mix in front of Rossi. "Good evening. What will it be, sir?"

"A calvados and an espresso," Rossi said in his best French accent, avoiding the barman's gaze.

Removing the cheap disposable phone Cathy had given him from his back jeans pocket, he laid it on the bar. His new non-Vatican, non-CIA iPhone was in his writing desk drawer back at Fisher House. Cathy had reminded him he'd used it to phone Natasha. And if, as they suspected, there was a rogue operative inside Bright Star, his phone was blown. With it, they could track him to the ends of the earth.

"Enjoy," the barman said, setting down the drinks.

"*Merci.*" Rossi took a long sip with an eye to the mirror, which afforded him an excellent view of the stairs to the lobby. A scoff as he reflected on how his life had changed. Not so long ago, he was the well-respected head of the Corps of Gendarmerie of Vatican City. Then, by an act of fate, he found himself thrust into the world of international espionage that led to the doorstep of the Kremlin. At first, he felt blessed. It had all been for a reason. He met Cathy, and they planned to marry. Now, two months on, he was out of a job and his relationship with Cathy was in tatters. *Mama? There's got to be more to it.*

Rossi glanced at his watch: 7:05. In the mirror, between six choices of vodka, a big man descended the stairs, a maroon-coloured fedora tilted forward, shading his face from the indefatigable security cameras.

The man slipped out of his coat and sat at the empty bar, two stools down from Rossi. With his back to the CCTV camera, he removed his hat and set it on the bar stool between them.

"Good evening. What'll it be, sir?" The barman asked his well-drilled opening line.

"A Red Russian," Lawrence said, funnelling a handful of bar mix into his mouth.

Rossi slapped a twenty-pound note on to the bar. "*Merci beaucoup. Au revoir.*" As he stood, he rested his hand on the neighbouring bar stool and slipped Cathy's room key under Lawrence's fedora.

"Thank you, sir. Come again."

Dressed in a white hotel bathrobe loosely knotted around her waist, and with her chestnut hair up in a messy bun, Cathy put her eye to the spyhole before opening the door.

"Okay," Rossi drawled, looking her up and down.

"Get in, Enzo, before someone sees you. And *close* your mouth."

As Rossi stepped inside, memories of Moscow came flooding back. "We have fifteen minutes to kill. Any ideas?"

"I'm taking a shower. Don't know about you."

A boyish smile swept across Rossi's unshaven face. "I also missed my shower this morning."

"If you'd stayed in last night, as you were supposed to—"

"We'd be none the wiser."

"True," Cathy said, closing the bathroom door, but not all the way.

"She's coming around," he murmured to himself, already stooped over the minibar.

Above the sound of running water Cathy called out, "There's a bottle of Laphroaig in my messenger bag, if you're desperate."

He was.

Rossi poured himself two fingers and put it on the bedside table. He then kicked off his shoes, turned on the television, jumped onto the bed and made himself comfortable.

As he sipped his Scotch, he flicked through the channels, searching for the UK news. "57 Channels (and Nothing On)" played in his head. US politics and football. "Finally!" Channel 4 broadcasting a summary of today's news: G20 round-up; anarchists battle police on London streets; no one claims responsibility for LSE murders; forty-five-vehicle pile-up on the M3; Manchester youth stabbed…

"Did they mention Natasha?" Cathy asked, rummaging through her garment bag dressed in a pink lace bra and panties set.

Rossi sat up with a start and swung his feet over the edge of the bed facing her. "Still wearing pink?"

"It seems to bring the best out of me," she said, wriggling her backside as she tugged on her jeans.

"*Splendido!*" Rossi said, staring.

Although Lawrence had a key, out of politeness he knocked.

Cathy threw on an olive camisole and peered through the spyhole.

"Hope he hasn't changed into a dress and heels," Rossi quipped, recalling the last time Lawrence visited them at home in Moscow.

"An indiscreet red hat, but no dress," Cathy murmured before opening the door.

As the door clicked shut, Lawrence threw his arms around Cathy. They hadn't seen each other since Moscow. "The all-conquering Moscow gang back together."

"Where's your phone?" Cathy asked.

"Back at the safe house. Where's yours?"

"Ditched it. Taking no risks until I know what we're up against."

"Great to see you again, Paul," Rossi said, already standing at Cathy's side, offering his hand. "And thanks for coming."

"How could I resist? Your partner made it sound so dramatic." Lawrence turned to Cathy. "Is there a real crisis, or are you missing me?"

"Both, Paul. Both." Cathy glanced into the middle distance, reminiscing. "We were the best in Moscow. Shame we're now *persona non grata*."

"Happens when you kill a president." Laughter. "So, what's the crisis?"

"Enzo and I smell betrayal, so we thought it a good idea to compare notes."

"Agreed. But first a drink to lubricate the upper storey." Lawrence tapped his temple with his index finger. "And none of that Scottish moonshine you've taken to drinking."

"There's four miniature bottles of Jim Beam in the bar fridge." A smile. "I've already checked."

Rossi pulled the small round table close to the bed and set the two armchairs opposite as Cathy took Lawrence's coat and hat and tossed them on top of Rossi's.

"A red hat? What were you thinking, Paul?" Cathy laughed.

"It was that or a nylon stocking. Besides, the saleswoman assured me it's maroon."

They sat around the table, Rossi perched on the edge of the bed under the sloping ceiling, sipping their drinks. Waiting for no clear reason, other than indecision about who was running the show.

Rossi looked at Cathy. "Shall I start?"

A nodding of heads.

"Well, Paul. It's like this. Cathy and I have come to the conclusion Operation Bright Star isn't what the three magi are selling. It's more like a black hole fuelled by duplicity, treachery and double-dealing than the Star of Bethlehem guiding us to Jerusalem."

Lawrence threw Cathy an annoyed look. "In English?"

"Something is rotten in the state of Denmark," Cathy said, curling her legs up onto the armchair. "Shakespeare. Is that English enough for you?"

"Which bit don't you like, Inspector General?"

"The whole shooting match, Paul."

"You're seeing things that aren't there," Lawrence said, his tone dismissive. "Cathy, you know how the CIA works. Nothing unusual here. For now, we're following leads."

Sensing Lawrence was not being forthright, Rossi slapped his glass down on the table and sprung to his feet. Opening the minibar, he removed the remaining two bourbons. By the time Rossi sat back down on the bed he had cooled off.

Lawrence smiled, his lips pressed together. With Cathy's gaze boring into him, he turned to her. "I've lost a yard since our Russian tour de force. You'll need to spell it out. What's making you both so nervous?"

"The Cambridge Experientialists, Lord Percy, the sniper, the anarchist's tag, the *Forbes* list." Rossi drew a deep breath. "We've seen nothing that connects the dots. In fact, I'm not sure there *are* any dots."

"We're going where the evidence takes us, Inspector General." Lawrence pushed back in his chair. "If it leads nowhere, we shut it down and move on. What's your point?"

"There's no evidence," Cathy said. "And we're a little concerned we're being used. To what end? Not sure. How well do you know the three wise men?"

Lawrence broke the seals on the bourbons and poured them into his glass. "Are you suggesting they're not who they say they are?"

"Does Chief James know them?" Cathy asked, her tone firmer.

"I didn't ask. Why should I? I do what I'm told and work with whoever I'm given."

"Is there a backstory that goes with this, Paul? How did you get involved?"

Lawrence stared into his glass, where perhaps the answer lay. "After Edge's assassination, Chief James called me. Said he was heading up a top-secret op called Bright Star. Identify and infiltrate the villains. 'British anarchists' was how he described them. Bound and determined to kill as many rich pricks as possible. Didn't mention *Forbes*. Offered me a piece of the action. At the time I was dodging car bombs in Baghdad. So, I said, 'why not?'"

Rossi sat forward, drawing his head closer to Lawrence. "The three wise men, Heroin Chic, and whoever else is lurking in the shadows – what do you know about them?"

"Bugger all," Lawrence blurted out. "Met them the day before you came down from Cambridge. Been playing catch-up ever since." Pause. "What's this all about, Cathy? Never had you down as a conspiracy theorist."

Cathy straightened her legs and rested them on the bed. Rossi threw her a smile, but Cathy's eyes were on Lawrence. "Lorenzo and I smell a crock of shit, and we're trying to figure out whether you're in on it."

Lawrence's pulse quickened. "What the *fuck* are you on about?"

To deflect Lawrence's angry gaze from Cathy, Rossi jumped in. "Don't play dumb with us, Paul. It's time for straight answers. Why have we been recruited to take part in a wild goose chase?"

"That's nonsense."

"Lord Percy and his college chums are not revolutionists. Rather, they're a coven of sexual predators in search of naïve twenty-year-olds."

"I wouldn't know," Lawrence said, throwing up his hands dismissively.

"Not to mention, all murders to date have been professional hits. You agree?"

Lawrence opened his mouth to speak.

"And target identification and whereabouts most likely provided by a state intelligence service," Rossi said, not waiting for a response. "Anarchist involvement is a big fat zero – a smokescreen, a red herring. Shall I go on?"

"Jesus, Cathy." Lawrence drained his glass. "You got any more bourbon?"

"The truth, Paul," Rossi chided.

"Seems you know more than me, Inspector General. I'm not used to asking questions when I receive orders from above." Lawrence glanced about for a drink. Nothing in reach. "Sure, none of this makes sense. But, at my pay grade, it never does. For security reasons, no one *ever* feeds me the whole story. I expect gaps – and gaps we have."

"As long as you're not screwing us, Paul," Cathy said, in a gentler tone. "We need to be able to trust you. Know that we're in this together."

"I swear, Cathy. Straight up. I'm on your side."

"I *bloody* hope so," Rossi said. "Or perhaps you need some time to decide? To be sure. We don't want you ebbing and flowing. Jilting us at the altar the moment the pressure's applied."

"I believe you, Paul," Cathy smiled.

Lawrence locked eyes with Rossi. "You know me, Cathy. I have no agenda but to stop the killings."

"Now we'd better get you back before your three roommates become suspicious."

Lawrence trailed his fingers through his golden blond hair. "Can't do. Got plans. Besides, I made my excuses before I left the safe house. I met a like-minded gentleman on the flight across the pond. We're going dancing tonight."

A shiver of excitement. "I bought a little red dress for the occasion."

"One last question, Paul," Cathy said as she walked Lawrence to the door. "You couldn't say why we don't appear to be working closely with MI5 or MI6 on this? You'd think with London becoming ground zero for the assassinations, and four of the five victims being US citizens, we'd be living in each other's pockets."

Lawrence jutted out his chin as he thought. "You'd think so. But I can't say I paid any attention to it. Too busy doing my job."

"Well, *I* did," Cathy said. "So, I had a coffee earlier with an old friend. She just happens to be the CIA's permanent liaison officer right here in London. Very discreet."

"Not a good idea, Cathy."

"It bowled her over to hear I'm in Cambridge. Funny thing was, she'd never heard of Bright Star or of any undercover agents operating out of a Knightsbridge safe house. Seems we're running a covert op, Paul. Which is fine as long as someone lets me and our British partners in on the secret. It is a *secret*, isn't it, Paul?"

"You know we haven't trusted the British since the War and the Cambridge Five."

"And they don't trust us. That grandiose narcissist Snowden, stealing 58,000 top-secret British security documents, which no doubt ended up in the hands of the Russians and the Chinese, gives them good cause."

Lawrence turned the handle. "It's all politics, Cathy. Nothing to do with me."

"Be careful," Cathy said, watching Lawrence stride away down the passage, unsure whether she could trust him.

The door clicked closed. "The woman in red," Rossi huffed. "Let's hope there are no photos."

"You should try it sometime, Enzo. Bring out your feminine side. God knows it's needed."

18

Rossi slid his hand into the side pocket of his overnight bag and fished out the doorstopper alarm he'd bought at the station. Forcing the thin edge of the wedge under the door, he gave it a tap with the ball of his foot.

"You think it'll help?"

"Buys me some time."

"Before we jump to our death?"

"To pull up my pants," Rossi said, unbuttoning his shirt. "Seems every time I'm under the shower, housekeeping barges in to turn down the bed or change the towels. I swear hotels have cameras in the rooms just for that purpose."

"Now, haven't you changed?"

"What do you mean?"

"In Moscow you couldn't wait to get naked."

"Not for a woman wearing rubber gloves and brandishing a natural-bristle toilet brush."

While Rossi showered, Cathy dialled Chief James on a blue burner. No answer. Voicemail activated, so she rang off. A glance over at the television clock: 20:30. She did a mental calculation. It was nearly four in the afternoon in Langley, Virginia. "He doesn't recognise the number," she murmured to herself, redialling. Voicemail again. This time she left a message, once more in thick Scottish. "Hello *dadaidh*, it's Albina." She left her number.

By the time Rossi reappeared washed and shaved, dressed in black jeans and a white T-shirt, the round table was back against the window. In its place was their supper on a room service trolley, and an open bottle of Barolo.

"What did the chief say?" Rossi asked, removing the stainless-steel plate covers with the flair of a marching band percussionist and storing them on the shelf under the trolley.

"Voicemail."

"Risky?"

Cathy poured the wine. "I was vague."

"Cheers," Rossi said, holding out his Bordeaux glass with a glint of mischief in his eyes.

Cathy knew that gaze. "I'm not sure one room's a good idea, Enzo."

"Nervous? I get that a lot." A smirk. "If you're worried, I can hang a clove of garlic around my neck and soak myself in holy water."

Cathy twirled her spaghetti on her fork as though she hadn't heard.

"Too extreme?" Rossi added, not waiting for her usual snappy retort. "We could sleep with pillows between us. You under the blanket, me on top."

Cathy shot Rossi a guileful smirk as the doorbell chimed. "On top of what?"

"Housekeeping," came a voice from the corridor.

"I told you. They arrive at the most inopportune time," Rossi said, already at the door.

"Your fold-up bed, sir," a uniformed young man announced as the door opened.

Rossi stood stunned, blocking the entrance.

"Put it over there," Cathy said, tugging Rossi out of the way by his sleeve.

"We expecting guests?"

Cathy gathered the loose change from on top of the minibar and tipped the housekeeper. The door clicked closed, then silence. They stared at each other across the room like two gunslingers at high noon.

Forsaken, Rossi moved to the window and peered out through the curtains. A heavy drizzle had turned Westminster into smudges of Monetesque light. "How long are you going to keep this up, Cathy?" he said, speaking to the view. "You're using my mama as an excuse. It wasn't a big deal."

Picking up her wine, Cathy went and sat on the end of the bed. "You're wrong, Enzo. You know why?" Cathy paused, giving Rossi time to think. "Because you're your mother's child. Brought up to believe men chop the wood and women cook and raise children."

Rossi swung around and rested his backside on the windowsill. "But it's not what I believe."

"Cocky shit, Enzo. You simply don't understand modern women."

"You thought differently before."

"Blinded by love. *Grazie*, Mama Rossi for clearing my eyes." Pause. "Let's face it, Enzo, we're not suited to be husband and wife. Best friends maybe. Partners in crime. Lovers. But not husband and wife."

Cathy's frankness horrified Rossi, and his expression showed it.

The blue burner rang and vibrated on the commode. Number blocked. "Hello," Cathy said, again in thick Scottish.

"Albina?" the chief said.

"You've taken up with another woman?"

"Don't know what you're talking about. I haven't been near her."

"I'm beyond listening to your lies. You'll need to convince me," Cathy said, her tone heated. But before she finished, the phone went dead.

Rossi had abandoned his wine and was drinking Scotch. "How's he going to do that from over there?"

"That's his problem."

"And you and me? Our relationship? What's it to be?"

"Pick from the list," Cathy said, pursing her lips and shrugging her shoulders as if it was a *fait accompli*.

"You *know* I don't do the lover thing well. Too old-fashioned. Never been good at sharing. Ask my brothers."

"That leaves friends or partners."

Sullen faced, Rossi emptied his glass in one long gulp.

"Tempting, but no thanks," he said, swooping down and snatching the whisky bottle off the floor. "Scotch?"

"I'll stick with the wine."

A long silence before Rossi motioned to the foldable bed. "It's not long enough?"

"We'll put the mattress on the floor."

"But what about my allergies?"

"Other than rejection, you don't have any," Cathy said, rising and placing her wine glass on the service trolley. "Now get dressed. We're going downstairs to the bar."

19

Lawrence shook off his umbrella under the triangular entryway pediment of a four-storey Georgian townhouse. Discreetly, he scanned the well-lit street. On the pavement four doors down a man in a beanie ground out a cigarette butt. Parked opposite, a hackney carriage with its "for hire" light off. Approaching from the left, a nurse in white shoes carrying flowers. No one showed him any interest. And nor did he expect them to; it was just good tradecraft.

The front door clicked closed as Lawrence jogged up the old wooden stairs covered by a threadbare runner held in place by brass stair rods. Lawrence had taken the attic studio on short-term lease to escape the monotony of the safe house, and to engage in his favourite pastime: cross-dressing. As far as he was aware, amongst his colleagues, Cathy was the only one who knew his secret. He'd opened up to her in Moscow, sensing she'd understand better than most why a 185-centimetre-tall man would have a fondness for wigs, make-up and snazzy dresses. Lawrence was not a woman trapped in a man's body; rather a heterosexual who liked to dress up.

The real estate agent had listed the Central London property as cosy. Which Lawrence later learnt was marketing doublespeak for: you can't swing a dead cat without hitting a wall. There was a fitted kitchen with a stainless-steel gas hob; a refrigerator that could be opened from the sofa bed; and a white lacquer wardrobe and a matching two-drawer dressing table by the wall of the renovated bathroom. A flat-screen television, which he could only view from the kitchen, hung above the sofa bed. "An absolute steal at £2,100 per month," so the fast-talking real estate agent assured him.

Lawrence laid his clothes out on the sofa and undressed. He turned on the TV and then showered for the second time that day.

Applying lashings of moisturiser in front of the mirror attached to the back of the wardrobe door, Lawrence admired his lean muscular body. "Worth every penny," he mumbled to himself, recalling eighteen months of painful laser hair removal treatment. Payoff: silky-smooth legs and the face of a baby.

The television drew Lawrence's gaze. Women's shoes on sale. He made a mental note of the nearest store as he poured a bourbon. The microwave clock showed 21:15. *Need to hurry.*

Seated at the dressing table in black hip-and-buttock padded panties, Lawrence glued silicone breast forms to his bronzed chest, then slipped on a black bra. Rotating on the stool, he freed his legs and pulled on a pair of black pantyhose. "Now for the hair," he said, with growing excitement.

With an eye on the time, Lawrence combed his hair flat, covered it with a nylon cap, then clipped and glued his dark-chocolate, shoulder-length wig in place. He took a long sip of bourbon as he gazed in the mirror. A smile swept over his face. He liked what he saw because he saw what he liked.

A rap on the door. Lawrence looked up from his make-up case with a start. Female voices in the corridor. He listened. A baby screamed. A second, louder rap. Lawrence, already at the door, peered through the spyhole. Two women in their thirties, the shorter carrying a baby.

Slipping on a long ladies' black military coat, Lawrence opened the door, leaving the security chain in place.

"Hi. I'm your neighbour, Wendy, from one floor down," a brunette with a swimmer's build said through the three-inch gap.

"I'm Jesse," Lawrence said, picking the first unisex name that came to mind.

"This is the previous tenant of your flat," the brunette said, gesturing to a spot Lawrence couldn't see. "She's misplaced her baby's immunisation card."

"Sorry to hear," Lawrence said, speaking in a rising and falling pitch.

"She remembers dropping it down the side of the refrigerator. Forgot about it when she moved out last week. Any chance we can check to see whether it's still there?"

Lawrence hesitated. "Wait here. I'll have a look."

Grabbing the throw blanket from the sofa, he laid it on the stripped wood floor beside the refrigerator then dropped on all fours. Dust and two yellow Lego blocks, but nothing else.

"It's not there," Lawrence said, from behind the door, the chain still in place.

"Thanks anyway, Jesse. I'll see you around," the brunette said, her friendly eyes catching Lawrence's through the opening as the door closed.

Lawrence moved back to the dressing table to apply his make-up. Concealer under the eyes and around the nose; a dollop of foundation; a dusting of powder; bronzing to create female contours; eye liner; eye shadow; and mascara. *Now for the lips.*

In the mirror Lawrence saw his iPhone singing and dancing on the kitchen counter next to his keys. He sprung up and answered it. "Hello."

"Did you meet with Cathy?" Chief James asked down the line.

"Yeah. She was with Rossi. Appears as though the wedding's back on."

"It was only a matter of time." A snickering laugh. "At any rate, what did she want?"

"She smells a rat. I couldn't convince her otherwise. Said our target's a gold brick."

"No surprise there. She's a smart lady."

"What do you want me to do?"

"Leave it to me. I'll take care of it," the chief said, ringing off.

20

Rossi burst into his Fisher House room. "You solved it?" he asked, whipping off his dripping wet jacket.

Cathy, seated at the writing desk in a long white T-shirt, loose brown cardigan and black leggings, glanced back over her shoulder. "How was your lecture?"

"Packed house," Rossi replied, preening his wet hair in the mirror. "Nothing like the nineteenth-century unification of Italy and the Papacy's loss of the State of the Church to get the public through the door."

"*I'd* buy a ticket. And *one* for your mother too."

Rossi grabbed the shopping bag full of spy gadgets they'd purchased in London from on top of the wardrobe. "You promised to tidy up," he said, emptying the contents onto the unmade bed. One radio frequency detector, one white noise generator, one camera lens locator and four mobile phone signal-blocking pouches.

"No time for housework," Cathy said, bashing away at the keyboard. "I'm on the verge of a great discovery."

"In that case, I forgive you, Madame Curie. But can you at least stop long enough to give me an update?"

Cathy glanced at her watch. They had taken breakfast on the early morning express back from London. Coffee and a sandwich. Nothing since. "Two-fifteen! No wonder I'm famished. Let's do it over lunch." Pause. "That's if your front-row fan club hasn't already fed you."

"Had several enticing offers, but being a good Catholic I declined," Rossi said, massaging Cathy's neck as he read her screen. "Besides, I prefer my women mature."

"Mature!" Cathy jabbed her elbow into Rossi's rock-hard abdomen. "I'm thirty, for heaven's sake."

"Mature, as in grown up."

Cathy closed her screen and pulled on her stiletto ankle boots. "I'll meet you downstairs. I need to fetch my hat and coat from my room."

Arm in arm under Rossi's green umbrella they strode down Wheeler Street in search of a restaurant where they could talk. The English drizzle had turned to a deluge; drops the size of vanilla jelly beans ricocheting off the pavement, soaking them from beneath. They scurried past Jamie's Italian, crossed over Peas Hill onto Bene't Street, past Zizzi Pizza and Pasta, and continued on until they reached the King's Parade junction.

On the corner was the Cambridge Chop House. Ceiling-to-floor glass windows. Written on a blackboard in the doorway: "classy British comfort".

"This will do," Cathy said, water sloshing in her boots.

They glanced about as they entered. Black ceiling, bespoke lighting, beige walls, rough-sawn ash flooring, and a bar to their right. By then it was almost three. The lunchtime crowd were already back at the office. They sat down at a round table for two by the window with a view to the Corpus Clock.

"You want to know something interesting about that timepiece?" Rossi said, gesturing with a nod towards the large gold-plated disc on the opposite street corner outside the Taylor Library. "It has no hands or numbers."

"Not much of a clock. Stupid idea."

"Stephen Hawking unveiled it on 19 September 2008."

"You've got too much time on your hands, Enzo."

An acknowledging smirk. "I did until you returned."

They ordered a bottle of Chianti Classico and the two-course set lunch. Rossi went with the smoked salmon and shrimp pâté, and calf's liver. Cathy, the broccoli soup and marinated butter steak.

A clink of glasses and a long sip. "How far did you get this morning?" Rossi asked. "You got it solved?"

"No."

"No as in 'not yet'?"

"If you'd prefer."

Silence as the waitress set their starters on the table.

"So, no direct connection between any of the victims other than they're all filthy rich?" Rossi said, spreading pâté onto a slice of toasted baguette and topping it with pickled samphire.

Cathy stirred her soup. "They're all flimflammers known to Lord Percy, if that helps."

"That goes without saying."

"With sanction breaking and illegal arms dealing flowing through their miserable veins."

"Perhaps the Brits are closer to the mark with their serious crimes assessment? An underworld vendetta the US and British governments might be happy to see continue, but not involve themselves in. Let someone else clean the streets. The courts have proved incapable."

"Can't be discounted," Cathy said sipping her wine. "Because for now it's one of the few options that makes sense. And it would explain why we're being fed bull—"

Rossi glanced behind him to see what had made Cathy stop mid-sentence. An elderly barrel-chested man with wiry faded red hair stood with his back to them at the entrance, shaking out his umbrella.

"Is that who I think it is?"

Cathy nodded. "Don't go picking a fight, Enzo. Promise?"

"What the hell is he doing here? Trying to blow our paper-thin cover?" Rossi said, answering his own question.

Not wanting to alert the pavement artists by making a fuss, Cathy stared out at the Corpus Clock as the former Moscow station chief approached.

"Thought I'd surprise you," Chief James said, throwing open his arms.

"Chief." Cathy sprung to her feet and returned his embrace.

Rossi also rose but shook James's hand coolly, as if he was an estranged spouse. "You're the last person we expected to run into up here, Chief," Rossi said, dragging over a chair from the adjoining table. "Where have you flown in from?"

"Flown?" the chief said, his eyes on Cathy as he dropped onto the burgundy leather cushion. "Train from London. That's your best option. One hour."

"You mean to say you were in *London* when I called last night?"

"Flew in with the G20 crowd," the chief smirked. "Bit of extra security, given what's been going on."

Whether Cathy believed him it was difficult to tell. The expression on Rossi's face was more transparent.

"And you didn't contact Cathy? Why? She's like a daughter to you."

"Risk unmasking her? No thanks," the chief said, again to Cathy.

Rossi drew back in his seat. "Yet, here you are? A red flare on the Cambridge front line. Anarchists and assassins every which way you turn." Pause. "Not very discreet, wouldn't you say?"

"I had no choice after Cathy's panic attack."

Rossi smiled. "You mean the vague message sent from a non-traceable burner phone?"

The chief motioned to the waitress, who hurried over.

"Can I bring you something, sir?" the waitress asked, holding open the menu.

"Yes, you can, my lovely," the chief said, with a dirty-old-man's wink. "Double Jack Daniel's. And be quick about it."

Cathy shot the chief an angry glance. "Same old charmer."

"Not good, is it?" the chief concurred. "Since you escaped my gravity, I've grown even more repugnant."

"Now there's a surprise," Rossi mocked.

"Rumour has it, Cathy, you're back in play. Free as a bird," the chief said, turning to taunt Rossi. "Get caught with your fingers in two pies, Inspector General?" Pause. "Oh, I forgot. That title's redundant too – from what I've heard. Just plain Mr Rossi from now on. Correct?"

"Planning to pick on me next, Chief?" Cathy asked. "Or are you going to behave?"

There was a prolonged silence as the waitress set the Tennessee whiskey on the table and topped up the wine glasses. Avoiding the chief's carnal gaze, she gathered up the starter dishes, then turned and walked away.

Cathy held up her glass. "To old friends."

"And honour among thieves," Rossi added, to the clinking of glasses.

The chief took a long pull on his whiskey then emptied his lungs in a single sigh as if he were carrying the weight of the world on his shoulders. "Cathy, what's this all about?"

Cathy clenched her jaw before she spoke. "I was hoping you could tell me."

"With pleasure. But you must steer." A shrug. "Because I don't understand what you're on about."

"Good. My mistake. Sorry for bothering you."

Silence again as the waitress approached, carrying their main course. Cathy's words hung in the air unanswered as the plates were set on the table.

"How's your steak, Cathy?" Rossi asked, doing his best to ignore the chief and the spin he was bursting to release.

"Cooked to perfection. And your liver?"

Rossi kissed the tops of his fingers and tossed them into the air. "*Magnifico*."

"You girls done?" Chief James asked, in a vexing tone.

Cathy stuffed a piece of steak into her mouth and chewed it slowly. "Sure, we're done. Nothing to discuss. Thanks for the visit."

Knocking back the rest of his drink, the chief rose from his seat, then sat down again. "Okay, no more games. I'll tell you what I know."

"That would be a good idea," Cathy said, holding up the chief's empty glass to the waitress.

Rossi leant back in his seat, trying to dodge the bullshit. He knew in the spy game, once trust had gone, truth was rarely spoken. And right now, they didn't trust Chief James. And, in all likelihood, he didn't trust them either.

"Langley's pushing the anarchist line," the chief said, his tone lacking its usual fire, "far beyond what's supported by the intelligence. Why? I don't know. A hunch: bad politics. Maybe it's the truth; maybe it's not. I have no way of knowing."

"Is it possible we're in the middle of a clan war?" Cathy asked. "A war encouraged or even facilitated by the CIA to eliminate powerful tycoons acting against the interests of the United States? Perfect. We sit back and watch criminal surrogates advance US policy objectives without getting blood on our hands."

The chief chuckled. "Doubt it. What business is it of ours to scrub riffraff off the face of the earth?" Pause.

"Mind you, if you floated the idea in Washington, I'm sure you'd find more than a few takers."

As the whiskey arrived a burst of wind and rain sent pedestrians scattering and umbrellas flying on the street. Rossi thought he glimpsed Heroin Chic scurrying towards the churchyard on the opposite side of the road. Wouldn't swear by it.

"Here's our problem, Chief," Rossi said, leaning into his face. "We don't think it's the anarchists. In fact, it's so far off the mark we're wondering what we're doing here. Especially me."

"You and Cathy worked so well together in Moscow. The office figured, why not?"

"Why not? Why?"

"Does it matter? You're here now. Nothing in Rome to go back to. Career finished. Commandant Waldmann the number one candidate to take your job."

Rossi couldn't help but wonder what the chief was playing at. His answers were feeble and unpersuasive. He wasn't trying to appear credible. *Was he signalling?*

"It matters. It matters a lot, Chief," Cathy protested. "I joined the CIA to serve my country. Not a 'deep state' operating outside 'the consent of the governed.'"

Chief James sneered. "Since when have you fallen for conspiracy theories? Too much Fox News with your Breitbart for breakfast? Christ, Cathy, the 'deep state' doesn't exist. Don't go there."

"Connection between the victims," Cathy continued, as if she hadn't heard the chief's warning. "What's the office's position?"

"Filthy-rich crooks."

"Known enemies?"

"The world," the chief said, his tone softening. "Not only the USA."

"Most likely candidates?"

The chief smiled. "I know it's not what you want to hear, but it's the truth all the same, Cathy. The victims have nothing in common other than the size of their bank accounts."

"So, our intelligence services have come up with money as the motive?"

"And who hates money the most – anarchists?"

A tut and a shake of the head. "Give me a break, Chief."

The chief rested his hand on Cathy's. "You know, my father was a New York City detective. He would always say, 'If it looks like a duck and quacks like a duck, it probably is a duck.'"

"And if I tell you we've found nothing to implicate the anarchists? At least not the British variety."

"Keep looking." Chief James emptied his glass, slapped it on the table, and rose. "Now, finish your lunch. I'm due back in London. Need to find Lawrence."

Cathy's gaze shot from her glass to the chief's heavy-lidded eyes. "What's happened to him?"

The chief turned back to the table and rested his hands on the back of his chair. "He disappeared last night after exiting the Le Méridien." Pause. "Tricky to identify the owner of an unregistered mobile phone. But a piece of cake to triangulate the signal – with the right equipment."

Rossi snapped. "We weren't hiding from you. And we certainly didn't expect you to go blowing the whistle on us."

"Second honeymoon, I told them," the chief said, winking at Cathy. "And still no ring. I warned you about Italian men."

21

Upon returning from their late lunch, Rossi and Cathy swept the room for cameras and microphones. Clean. Then, with the mobile phones squeezed inside signal-blocking pouches and the white noise generator set to 5, they sat on Rossi's bed and pored over images Cathy had found on the internet that morning. Images suggesting a close personal relationship between Lord Percy and the five victims.

The winning entry in each category was: Lord Percy congratulating Jeremy Crisp in the Royal Enclosure at Ascot after his horse galloped to victory in the Diamond Jubilee Stakes; Percival Benbow kissing the bride at the extravagant wedding of Rudolf Legg's eldest daughter; Lord Melba, season patron of Covent Garden, and his only son, Lord Percy, greeting Charles Edge at the Royal Ballet's opening night performance of *Romeo and Juliet*;

Lord Percy, sipping champagne with Paterson Carlyle at the grand opening of the Macau Carlyle Hotel Casino; Lord Melba and Russian businessman Gennady Zhukov inspecting an RPG-28 anti-tank rocket launcher at the Army Expo outside Moscow.

"Proof!" they could hear Chief James proclaim.

Not really, they agreed. The photo ops were only to be expected. Self-promotion. Overlapping business interests. Mere confirmation Lord Percy and his father knew all five victims. Circumstantial evidence. Sure, it looked bad, when considered alongside the death of Natasha Nibley – strangled with Rossi's tie. But their guts told them Lord Percy was not the villain the three wise men would have them believe. Still, they decided to keep him on top of the leader's board, not as much out of deference to Chief James as out of a realisation the CIA were holding back information. So, until they could eliminate him as a suspect there he would stay.

With that in mind, they decided Cathy would contact Percy and apologise for the belligerent tone that had crept into her voice during their first encounter. It worked. Male egos being what they are, Lord Percy suggested a re-run at the Fez Club that night. Cathy accepted.

Rossi, preferring not to sit alone, volunteered to walk Monsignor Baker's dog, Peron, a gentle black-and-tan German Shepherd of advanced years. Thought he'd take a stroll down to the river and see whether *Moon Shadow* was still moored below Jesus Loch. And while at it, for a bit of fun, why not check which parts of his abandoned eighteen-speed remained attached to the embankment railing?

The day finished without rain. By the time Rossi reached Jesus Green the evening sky was clear and a new moon was visible through the leafless London plane trees that lined the central avenue dividing the park.

From the footbridge, Rossi saw deck lights burning on *Moon Shadow*. Carrying Peron, he descended the bridge's metal steps to the river. The tow path was muddy. Peron whimpered as Rossi set him down. "Another fifty metres, girl," Rossi pleaded, pulling on the leash.

Approaching the narrowboat, Rossi glimpsed up at his bicycle on top of the steep grassy bank. Well, at least the frame. Wheels, handlebars and seat all gone. Commandeered for a better cause. "Figures," he mumbled to himself.

"What's wrong with your dog?" an attractive young lady in jeans and a dark oversized jumper asked from the deck of *Moon Shadow*.

Stooped over the dog, Rossi looked up with a start. "Old age and bullheadedness."

"Sounds like my father."

"She's refusing to move." Rossi tugged at the leash. "I'm looking after her while my sister's on holiday. Hope I haven't killed her." Pause. "Do you know anything about dogs?"

The woman, who Rossi couldn't help but think resembled Natasha, stepped ashore.

"For starters, she's a he," the woman said, stroking the back of Peron's greying head. "Tired and cold. Nothing more. You'd better bring him aboard."

Rossi fought back a grin, as he slid his hands under Peron's belly and carried him below deck.

"Lay him down by the stove," the young lady said, leading the way.

Moving through the saloon, Rossi felt sick in the stomach. A flashback of Natasha hogtied on the bed made him think. He had lost track of time. *Why have the police released the crime scene?* It's been only two nights.

As Rossi made Peron comfortable by the fire, the woman crouched down next to him. She checked the dog in a way that suggested she knew what she was doing. "Wet nose, alert eyes, breathing." A shrug. "What more could you ask? He needs a rest."

"Thank God! I wouldn't know what to say to my sister."

"I'm Bella, by the way," she said, turning the palm of her outstretched hand downwards, like a princess offering a hand-kiss.

Rossi's mind was not on social etiquette. He wrapped his hand around hers and shook it firmly. "Lorenzo."

"Can I get you something?"

"Scotch?"

"Afraid not."

Rossi's eyes widened. *A religious fanatic*, he thought, although she didn't look like one. "Coffee?"

Bella moved to the galley and switched on the kettle. As she stood under the white fluorescent light, Rossi saw her face clearly for the first time. Long dark-brown hair, an attractive Roman nose, smiling brown eyes, and full lips. He liked what he saw.

"Nice boat," Rossi said, with arms propped on the kitchen counter dividing the saloon from the galley. "Is it yours?"

"My cousin's," she answered, taking a French Press down from the cupboard and scooping two heaped tablespoons of ground coffee into the glass carafe. "He lets me stay here."

Heard that somewhere before. "*Sei fortunato.*" Pause as the kettle screamed in a climax. "More common these days."

"What is?"

"Alternative forms of accommodation. Globalisation and money laundering have sent the cost of housing in the UK through the roof. One of many scandals being ignored by the government."

"My cousin doesn't have that problem," Bella said, rolling her eyes. "This boat's a lark. He bought it to impress the girls. A nice twist on 'come up and see my etchings.'"

Rossi felt he was floating between a hallucination and the real world. There were questions to ground him, but he dared not ask for fear of scaring her away. Was he being played for a fool? Is she *also* claiming Lord Percy as blood?

As the coffee brewed, Bella set a bowl of water down next to Peron.

"How does that work? Wouldn't that cramp his style?"

Bella's gaze lingered on Rossi as if she was unsure what he'd meant. "I'm part of the act, I guess. Besides, Percy only warms them up here. He's got a country house with a million rooms just outside Cambridge – or at least his father has."

"Landed gentry?"

"Earl Melba."

"Does that make you a lady?" Rossi tested.

"Afraid not." A smile. "At least not in peerage."

Bella made herself chamomile tea and then poured the coffee. They sat down next to each other on the long yellow sofa and gazed out of the window at the hypnotic swaying branches of the willow on the water's edge.

Finally, Rossi spoke. "Wasn't there an accident on Jesus Loch a couple of days ago?"

An unnatural lull.

Again Rossi. "I recall reading something in the papers. Didn't pay much attention to it. A student strangled."

"How ghastly," Bella said, her tone not matching the words.

"It was a Russian name – Natasha? Yes, Natasha I think."

Bella gazed at Peron, now on all fours, lapping up the water. "Looks like he's ready to take you home."

Not wanting to overstay his welcome, Rossi reattached Peron's leash and wished Bella a good night.

22

Cathy felt ill at ease seated on the crowded sofa, squeezed between Lord Percy and Morton. Robert was good-humoured enough, whereas Percy made her skin crawl. It was early, so His Lordship was sober, with his mind on being polite and convivial. But Cathy didn't believe in miracles. She was too well versed in the ways of arrogant men to think otherwise. Hypocrisy and duplicity coated his every word.

Percy hoisted a bottle of Veuve Clicquot from the ice bucket standing on the zellige table in front of him. "A glass of fizzy water, Miss Clarke?"

Cathy picked up a champagne flute and held it out.

"What made you change your mind?" Percy asked, pouring too fast.

"Convinced myself I was too hard on you."

"I deserved it. Behaved like an arsehole."

"You're no orphan," Cathy confessed, raising her glass. "To a new start."

Percy appeared pleased with himself as he repeated the toast.

Cathy scanned the room. "I like this place." A nibble on a coconut shrimp. "Are you here often?"

"He lives here," Morton said, rising and squeezing past them.

"Someone's got to make up for your sad arse existence," Percy called out to Morton's back as he cut across the crowded dance floor.

Gazing at Percy, Cathy's eyes narrowed. "Surely, there's more to you than champagne and an avocado salad?"

"Morton's talking bollocks as usual," Percy said, setting his glass on the table and sitting up.

"I'm all for giving you a fair hearing."

"The truth be known, I've dedicated my life to the non-violent struggle against inequality, global warming, nuclear disarmament and everything that's wrong with the world since the Americans replaced Jesus with the greenback."

Cathy wanted to puke. Nevertheless, Percy had provided her with the perfect introduction. "That's a hell of a mouthful—"

"By special request," Morton interrupted, offering Cathy his hand.

Cathy looked up with a start. "Sorry?"

"Your favourite song – 'A Whiter Shade of Pale'. Shall we dance?"

"What choice do I have?" Cathy smiled. "You're next, Percy. So, don't go disappearing on me."

Every spare pair of male eyes was riveted to Cathy's pear-shaped backside as she strutted onto the dance floor dressed in a body-hugging grey sweater dress and tan-coloured suede high-heel ankle boots.

Cathy held Robert close as they danced cheek to cheek. She preferred the shoulder, but with the heels she was his height. *Rattle him a little. Put him on the back foot.* "Sorry for running out on you the other night, Robert."

"Did you?"

"That's why I phoned Lord Percy – to apologise."

"No harm done, I'm sure."

They danced in silence under the purple light. Then the instant Cathy felt Morton under her spell, she set a trap. "To show there's no hard feelings, Robert," Cathy said, tilting her head back to catch Morton's reaction, "perhaps I could invite you, Percy and Natasha for Sunday roast at the Plough. Comes highly recommended."

"With pleasure. Only Natasha's a non-starter," Morton said, without a hint of nerves or discomfort. "They rusticated her on spurious trumped-up charges."

"Sounds painful. But what does it mean?"

"Send down. Expelled. Gone home to mommy."

Gone to God, more likely. Unless Enzo can't tell a stiff from a blow-up doll, Cathy thought, struggling to prevent her whimsical smile transforming into a frown. "Pity. I was looking forward to meeting her."

As the second song finished, Cathy glanced over at Lord Percy. He was flirting with the waitress, who was opening another bottle of champagne. "Thank you,

Robert," Cathy said, leading him by the hand back to the Sultan of Melba's royal cubbyhole.

"My dance!" Percy proclaimed, springing up from the sofa, sending the waitress shuffling backwards into an ottoman stool.

Cathy held out a stiff arm, halting Percy's charge. "Depends on the song. Slow dance or nothing. I'm not wearing a bra."

"Nobody's noticed," Percy smiled. "Now, name a song."

"'One.'"

"As many as you like."

It was Cathy's turn to smile. "I meant 'One' by U2."

"Did you hear the lady, Morton?" Percy motioned with a flick of his head towards the DJ.

A sip of champagne as they waited.

Cathy held Percy at a distance as they danced so she could read his face. "Most requested song of my graduation year. Brings back memories," Cathy lied.

"Boyfriend?"

"Football captain." More lies.

Truth was, Cathy left home at sixteen to escape an abusive father and memories of a loving mother, whom she'd found hanging from the kitchen ceiling one day after school. Days before her seventeenth birthday, while waiting tables on Hollywood Boulevard in LA, Cathy met a Russian businessman, who took her on as a part-time lover. With a roof over her head and time on her hands, Cathy went back to school to make something of her life. Their nine-year arrangement ended when he hit fifty, divorced his wife and moved in with a two-bit actress. But, by then, Cathy was fluent in Russian and had a master's degree in international affairs from Columbia. Qualifications well suited to a career in the CIA.

"The American dream. Lucky you," Lord Percy smirked. "I bet you were prom queen?"

"Not my thing. Just as well. The honour went to a gay couple."

"University?"

"Ivy League," Cathy said, keeping it vague in the unlikely event he had the inclination to trace her.

Percy leant back and gazed into Cathy's eyes. "Then onto the CIA?"

Cathy slid her hand round the back of Percy's neck. Pulling him closer she whispered in his ear, "Would that worry you?"

"Is it true?" he said, again catching her eyes.

"Why on earth would you think that?"

"I've never met an American with unaccented Russian that wasn't CIA. Unless you were born there, which opens up other possibilities. Perhaps you're a sleeper agent under non-official cover making friends in high places? Sitting alone at night waiting for the Kremlin to call?"

"How romantic."

There was a short interlude. Percy seemingly unsure whether he had received an answer; Cathy wondering whether he had asked in jest.

"My mother's a linguist," Cathy added, laying it on thick. "No Hans Christian Andersen at bedtime. She filled my childhood with tales of 'Ruslan and Ludmila' and 'Baba Yaga'. Always in Russian."

"Bravo, Mumsy."

"You've trained the DJ well," Cathy said, as the outro of 'One' transitioned to 'Wonderful Tonight'.

"I'm their best customer."

Cathy smiled and hung her arms around his neck. Emboldened, Percy wrapped his hands around her lower back and pulled her close.

With Percy's mind on her arse, and his guard down, Cathy probed. "Non-violent struggle against everything wrong with the world. You serious?"

"I'm old money. Old world. Old school of thought. My family continue to maintain a strong sense of international responsibility even if England doesn't."

"Nice story. But how does it reconcile with you being the president of the Cambridge Experientialists?" Cathy asked, throwing back her head and laughing. "Leader of a gang of anarchists all obsessed with ripping apart society as we know it."

"Who said anything about anarchism?"

Lawrence and the three wise men, Cathy thought. "Then what are you?"

"We are not experientialists *per se*, and we're certainly not anarchists. I borrowed the word to convey the spirit of who we are. Society is divided. Its citizens operate in echo chambers. Associate with whoever reinforces their view. No room for dissent." Percy stopped dancing. He dropped his arms to his side, hands turned outwards. "Experientialists believe experience is the source of knowledge. We've extended that notion to apply to how we arrive at the truth. Stop believing everything you read or hear. Democracy has mutated into laws to protect the assets of the wealthy. I'm no communist, but the American mantra 'greed is good' has done more to corrupt the system than anarchists could ever imagine doing."

Percy took a break, but Cathy refused to fill the silence. She was hearing exactly what she had come to hear. *Let the Percy freight train roll on.*

"Politicians are dodgy. Business leaders are bilkers. Social media's a platform for racists and bigots. Where are the leaders? Where can the truth be found? Nowhere. The solution is: believe what you experience."

"I get that, Percy," Cathy said, locking gaze with Robert in the distance, who had been watching her all night. But it wasn't infatuation she saw. More like he was scrutinising her. "But that explains nothing about your club."

Cathy followed Lord Percy back to their table, sat down next to him, and screwed up her face as she took a long sip of her champagne. "Miss, can you bring me a double Laphroaig?" she asked the waitress hovering nearby.

"Driven you to drink?" Robert joked, seated on her right.

"Not at all," Cathy said, cuddling up to Percy's side. "He's been saying the most interesting things." Laughter.

Percy's phone lit up on the table under a pile of paper napkins. "Lord Percy," he said, putting on his posh voice. Silence as he listened. "Did you let him onboard?" Again silence. "I'm coming now," Percy said, ringing off.

"Problem?" Robert asked.

"Not at all," Percy said, turning to Cathy. "Sorry. I've got to go. I'll make it up to you next time."

"Sure," Cathy said, her tone agreeable.

"Look after her, Bobby."

"A minute to midnight," Cathy said, checking the time as Percy climbed the stairs to the exit. "There's something very Cinderella-ish about this."

Robert smirked over his glass of champagne. "We'll look for his glass slipper later. In the meantime, let's dance."

23

Cathy had kicked off her boots and was lying on Rossi's bed when he returned from the shared bathroom at the end of the corridor wearing only a towel.

"You're back early," Rossi said, tossing his toiletry bag on his desk. "Did Percy stand you up?"

Cathy swung her legs over the edge of the bed and sat up. Pouting, she fluffed up her hair with her long slender fingers. "Do you think that's possible?"

"Did you forget your bra?"

"It's an old conjurer's trick. Turns men into putty."

"Did it work?"

"What do you think?" Cathy straightened and pulled back her shoulders. "They move like a hypnotist's pendulum. The second Percy's eyes locked onto these beauties I couldn't shut him up."

"Maybe I should try that," Rossi said, adjusting his towel.

"Who's that?" Cathy asked, staring at a grey and white British longhair that had followed Rossi in.

"Duchess. Darted in yesterday with her tail bristly and erect like a bottlebrush, escaping from Mrs Tarbottom's cat-eating vacuum cleaner." A shrug. "Now she's a regular. Likes me, I guess. Can you blame her?"

"But you hate cats."

"Only the type that run about the garden eating the wildlife." Rossi glanced about the room. "None in here."

"Just me."

Rossi removed a pair of boxers from the commode. "Put your hands over your eyes," he said, dropping the towel.

"What the hell's that?" Cathy laughed, peaking at Rossi through her fingers.

"Christmas present from my brother." Rossi struck a pose in a pair of black boxer shorts that had "Warning: May Contain Nuts!" printed across the crotch.

Cathy reached over and switched on the white noise generator. "Is it permissible to talk during the show?"

"Go ahead."

"Did you go past *Moon Shadow*?"

"Better than that. I went on board and met the new tenant. Bella by name. Curiously, she also claims to have Lord Melba's aristocratic blood running through her veins." A shrug. "It's possible as she resembles the deceased."

"Another one of Percy's cousins. Sorry, Enzo, but that makes little sense."

"That's what she told me. Maybe Bella and Natasha were flatmates – or is it floating-home-mates?"

"How did she explain the body in the bed?"

"Didn't ask. Had to play it cool."

Cathy scoffed. "I've seen your cool, mister."

"She swore she had no knowledge of a fatality near Jesus Loch. No drownings, no suicides, no kidnappings, no nothings. *Moon Shadow* was as peaceful as a churchyard."

Cathy sprung to her feet, poured two large Scotches and handed one to Rossi. "Drink up. We need to get creative. Young Robert avowed Natasha took the train home to mommy – seated in first class. Not a diamond white coffin with a luxurious crepe interior in sight."

"I know a dead person when I see one."

"I would hope so."

Clink of glasses, a long sip, then Rossi pulled on his trousers. "How was His Lordship this evening? No fisticuffs?"

"Talkative. As was Morton. The dapper Professor Slack did a no-show."

Opening the top drawer of the commode, Cathy picked out a black sweater and tossed it to Rossi. "Cover yourself."

"You look flustered," Rossi smirked, pulling the fine wool-knit over his muscular chest. "Shall I open the window?"

"I'll survive."

Rossi sat down in the middle of the sagging mattress, the bottle of Scotch within arm's length on the floor. "I don't suppose Morton or Percy were sufficiently forthcoming that you've got it all figured out?"

Dropping her backside onto the head of the bed, Cathy stretched out lengthways, resting her pedicured feet on Rossi's lap.

"Problem is, Enzo, everyone's lying. Regardless of whether they have something to hide. It's a game. Haven't figured out why." A pause. "I thought I could rely on Robert Morton. But his claim Natasha's at home helping mom with the washing-up is a bare-faced lie. And the notion Lord Percy's a lightweight predator also rings false."

"If His Lordship's insignificant, what's his role?" Rossi asked, massaging Cathy's soft slender feet.

"Buggered if I know. He made all the right noises. Almost believable."

Rossi exhaled long and slow. "I feel we're running to stand still. How do we move this forward if we can't rely on the information we're being fed?"

"Without the office's help, we might as well pack up and go home. We need their product. We need someone we can trust."

"Then pick someone," Rossi said. "I can't. Who do you mistrust the least?"

"Chief James and Special Agent Lawrence," Cathy said, ending with a half-smile on one side of her face.

"Not a long list."

Nodding, Cathy continued. "We know nothing about the three wise men – other than they're playing their own game. And as far as I can make out, Heroin Chic's nothing more than the office girl. The local Joes? Impossible to know. The pavement artists…"

The cat purred as she rubbed against Rossi's legs then rose on her hind legs and pawed Rossi's knees.

"She's smitten with you, Enzo."

A smirk. "I have that effect on the ladies."

"Until they meet your mother."

"James or Lawrence?" Rossi pressed.

Cathy glanced at her watch. One a.m. "Bedtime. But first I want to arrange a one-on-one with the chief. Perhaps he'll be more forthcoming if I'm on my own?"

24

Cathy spotted the chief's black Jaguar SUV parked in a side street, as the West Anglia Main Line train pulled into the Bishop's Stortford station. It was lunchtime, but there would be no restaurant. A serving of truth was the only thing on the menu.

Balanced in the aisle, Cathy buttoned up her burgundy trench coat and smoothed her skin-tight jeans over her thighs. Stepping off the train, she glanced up and down the platform as she opened her umbrella to the English drizzle. Using the footbridge, she crossed over the track and stood in the station building scrutinising all alighting passengers as they passed. Satisfied she was not being followed, Cathy criss-crossed her way back towards the Jaguar. The chief might have forgotten his training but she had not.

"Nobody followed you?" the chief asked, in a dull, lifeless voice as she climbed in the front next to him.

"Not a soul."

Chief James hit the accelerator pedal and drove off in silence towards the Bishop's Stortford Golf Club.

"There's a Subway sandwich and a coffee if you're hungry."

"Did you find Lawrence?" Cathy asked, picking up the coffee.

"Got in a fight on the tube and spent the night in a police cell." The chief chuckled, then added. "Did you know he got himself a flat in Chelsea?"

"He might have mentioned it."

"It was Rosenthal's idea. Reckoned he didn't fit in." The chief took a long, thoughtful pull on his Coke then rammed the bottle back in the drink holder between the seats. "Now – you have some questions?"

"Too many to mention. But let's start from where we left off last time." Pause. "What the fuck is going on? I smell a conspiracy, a plot. Okay, you swear you're not part of it, but you sure as hell know who is."

A pulse on the wipers as he peered into the distance. "If I tell you what I'm thinking, and you don't agree, then what?"

"If you're honest with me, Chief, and haven't roamed too far from the light – then we're good."

"Cathy, we're CIA. Trained to follow orders. No matter how repugnant. And, when the orders contradict everything the US stands for, we can only minimise the damage by dragging our feet."

"Rossi and I are ready to help, but only if we know what's going on. Who are we chasing, Chief? It's time to come clean – or we're out."

The chief picked up his Subway, peeled back the paper and ripped off a hunk like a ravenous dog. Three chews, then he washed it down with a mouthful of Coke.

Cathy opened the vehicle door. "Good luck."

"Sit!" the chief barked, pulling her back by her arm.

She shot him a wide-eyed stare but kept quiet.

"You're no orphan, Cathy. I'm also not sure who to trust. The only thing I know for sure is someone's going around shooting people. Why? Don't know. Unlikely because they're rich. Who? Don't know. Professional and well resourced. Rules out long-haired anarchists and lone rangers." Another swig of Coke. "My view? Unofficial, it's state sponsored. But which state? Ours? Maybe. Extrajudicial killings? Also, a maybe. Why do I think that, you ask? The president's a bum and the White House is stacked with neoconservatives—"

Sensing the chief was heading down a rabbit hole, Cathy stepped in. "You trying to cook me, Chief?" she said, wriggling out of her trench coat and winding down the window.

"Sorry," he said, switching off the heater and killing the engine.

"But, Chief, you're a big deal in the agency. How is it you don't know what's going on?"

"It's an investigation, Cathy. No one's claimed responsibility. I wouldn't rely on the paintwork. The circle-A message is too convenient. Besides, in the history of the sport of revolutions, the anarchists aren't known for their finesse. The large majority are pacifists. And those who choose violence are hot-headed and quickly caught.

'Propaganda of the deed' to them is the equivalent of your modern-day terrorist – only on a smaller scale."

Confusion swept across Cathy's face. "So why are we snuggling up to Lord Percy?"

"You already know the answer."

"Percy's no anarchist, Chief. He's 'old school'. Part of the European establishment."

"An old boy's club long past its use-by date."

"That doesn't make him an assassin," Cathy said, furrowing her brow. "Besides, why tell us we're chasing anarchists if we're not?"

"Someone wants us to believe that. Thought it would look more convincing if you believed it too."

"Bullshit! Give me some credit."

"Orders."

"Since when do *you* follow orders?" Pause. "Something scared you. If it's not your pension what is it?"

Through Cathy's open window came a shout. "Fore." Moments later a golf ball rocketed onto the Jag's windscreen, producing a star-shaped crack the size of a saucer on the driver's side.

Cathy smirked and clapped her hands together. "An admonishment from above."

"For what?"

"Spinning half-truths."

From a gap in the briar and bramble, a sporty middle-aged woman appeared, carrying an orange golf umbrella. "You didn't catch the bounce, love?" she asked, through Cathy's open window, shooting Chief James a look of disapproval.

"Sorry," Cathy said, raising the window, laughing. "She thinks you're trying to have your way with me."

"Gave up on that a long time ago."

"Smart move."

"Now, once again, Chief. What's going on? What aren't you telling me?"

Silence as the roving golfer dropped on one knee and peered under the Jaguar.

"See! Even the old lady doesn't trust you."

"Why do you always think I'm hiding something?"

"Because you always are," Cathy said, her tone sharpening. "So out with it."

The chief pushed back in his seat and stretched his legs. "It's possible – only possible – the killings are a misguided attempt to save Europe from itself. Part of some 'deep state' operation. British or American? Can't tell, but both countries have displayed an amazing level of apathy towards finding the killer."

"Evidence."

"None whatsoever. Just a gut feeling, like you. And the fact that White House interference in global affairs is as time-honoured in America as apple pie and the Fourth of July."

"Good enough."

25

Daydreaming of Cathy, Rossi pushed his brand-new bicycle across King's College Bridge on his way back to Fisher House. A stray scaffolding clamp from renovation work at the University's Sidgwick site had shredded his tyre.

"How's Peron?" came an approaching voice.

Rossi looked up to find Bella's intelligent brown eyes locked onto his. "Wet nose and tail wagging, thanks to your generosity."

"I'm glad," Bella said, inspecting the bicycle. "Off to repair your tyre?"

"It can wait. I'm heading home for a cup of tea and scones. Sorely needed after tutoring five child prodigies for two hours. Don't know what's more exhausting. Dull and disinterested, or bright and curious."

"You're a professor?"

Rossi's gaze dropped to the slow-flowing river. "Not quite. I'm a visiting academic lecturing on Vatican history."

"Then a cardinal or bishop?"

"Christ, you like to set the bar high, don't you?" Laughter. "I'm a mere mortal. Someone who knows enough about the Vatican to fill the Lent Term. Besides, I'm too young and curse far too much to be a cardinal." A smirk.

"Fascinating. Maybe we could meet up later? You could impress me by divulging some Vatican secrets."

"Are you free now?"

"What about your tea and scones?"

"Regrettably, I don't drink tea. And scones are better left to the English."

They headed to Fisher House, where Rossi locked his bicycle to the railing under a streetlamp opposite Cathy's window. *Double security*, he thought.

Rossi checked his watch. "It's almost six," he said, "You fancy a pub?"

"I've got quarter past five."

"Six by the time we're seated," Rossi smiled, gazing into the distance towards the unseen river. "What about the Mill?"

Shaking her head, Bella looked up at the overcast sky. "Too miserable by the Cam today. Somewhere cosy out of the rain."

"Then where?"

Bella puffed out her cheeks and closed one eye. "The Eagle's nearby."

"Lead the way," Rossi said, thinking she looked cute.

As it turned out, the Eagle adjoined the Chop House, where Chief James had paid Rossi and Cathy a surprise visit yesterday.

At the pub entrance Rossi stopped and read a blue plaque marking the occasion in 1953 when Crick and Watson first announced the discovery of DNA.

"Why is there no mention of Rosalind Franklin's contribution?" Bella said, reading the sign herself.

Rossi threw Bella a sideways glance. "Who?"

"Another scorned woman of science." Bella led Rossi inside, past a Christmas tree someone had forgotten to take down, through the lounge, and into the RAF bar at the rear.

"What's that?" Rossi asked, gazing up at the graffiti covering the eight-foot-high ceiling.

"A piece of history. During World War II, the bar was a regular haunt of British and American airmen. They used to burn their names and squadron numbers into the ceiling using candles and Zippos. Thank God, the landlords over the years had the common decency to preserve the room as a memorial."

"Then we should have a drink in their honour," Rossi said. "What can I get you?"

Bella sat down at a table against the red brick wall near the wooden L-shaped curved bar. "A pint of ale, and a serve of fish and chips."

The bar was quiet. Rossi scrutinised the faces in the room as he ordered. Students and tourists. No card-carrying communists or anarchists from what he could tell.

Setting the drinks on the table, Rossi sat down facing the door. "Your fish and chips are on the way."

"Cheers," Bella said holding up her glass and taking an elfish sip, like someone not used to drinking.

"So, you're Lord Percy's cousin." Rossi said, his tone whimsical.

"Is that good or bad?"

Rossi smiled and shrugged. "One of many, I assume? A family tree going back to Farmer George?"

"Just me. There *are* no more."

Rossi swirled his Scotch in his glass, held it to his nose and inhaled the earthy aroma. He needed to slow the conversation down. Didn't want to scare her off. "One of my students also claims to be his cousin. Spitting image of you. Never doubted her. But now I'm not so sure."

"It's a running joke in Cambridgeshire."

"What is?"

"All Percy's tarts are called cousins. Adds an air of respectability when he takes them away for a dirty weekend. A variation on the uncle-niece guise."

In silence Rossi studied a painting hanging on the wall of a Lancaster bomber landing in a field.

"By the way, you were right. They found that girl," Bella said, out of the blue. "Seems you knew about the murder before the police. Trust that doesn't mean you're the killer?"

Rossi remained calm. "Which girl?"

"In the Cam near Jesus Loch. Tied up and strangled. Weighed down with a diver's belt."

"That's terrible. Have they identified her?"

"Percy didn't know."

Rossi's brow knotted at the mention of His Lordship's name. "Percy?"

"He's worried about me. Suggested I stay with him until they catch the killer." Again silence. Rossi refused to talk.

"First night back, and this happens. A nuisance more than anything. It's not as though there's a stalker on the prowl – is it?"

"Back from where?"

"Egypt. A six-week-long field trip to the Giza Plateau." Bella's eyes were on the approaching waitress carrying her early dinner. "I'm reading archaeology—"

"Who looked after *Moon Shadow* while you were away?"

"Fish and chips?" the waitress said.

Rossi pointed at Bella.

"Should I bring another plate?"

Screwing up his face, Rossi insisted it was unnecessary.

"You don't like our national dish either?" Bella said, splashing vinegar over her meal.

"I grew up in Tuscany."

"You're a food snob, Lorenzo," Bella mocked, stuffing a piece of fish into her wide mouth.

"And you're a budding archaeologist who drinks chamomile tea. What else is there to know about you? Politics? Tory blue?"

"Save the Planet green."

"Then you're one of Percy's Cambridge Experientialists?"

Bella rose from the table and picked up their empty glasses. "Same again?" she asked, moving to the bar.

Too many dumb questions, Rossi thought, chastising himself as he waited.

"One of my triple-cooked chips is missing," Bella complained, setting a large Scotch in front of Rossi then taking her seat.

"Seagulls."

A group of students entered the room. One of their number, a young Arab with a thin contoured beard, threw Bella an emotionless nod.

"Friends?" Rossi enquired.

"Ex-boyfriend. From Cairo. And his latest inamorata," Bella said, gulping down a mouthful of beer. "She's welcome to him. He's one of Percy's crowd. I should have known better."

"New rich or old money?"

"A detestable PP."

Rossi shot Bella a puzzled look.

"Percy's Predators – also known as the Cambridge Experientialists."

"Are you a member?"

"Part-time victim. Never a member. Experientialism is nonsense. A word game for arrogant twits. 'Experience is the source of knowledge.' Not much of a revelation. Not interested. Nor is Percy for that matter."

A short silence as Rossi let Bella eat. "I seemed to have misjudged Lord Percy. I got the impression he's a true crusader. Devoted to solving world problems. Inequality, poverty, corruption, climate change…"

"He is. A real zealot."

The barman approached with drinks. "Courtesy of the dark-looking gentleman at the bar," he said.

"I should tell him to shove it up his arse, but that would be rude." Laughter.

Continuing to act nonchalant, Rossi glanced about the room. RAF memorabilia covered every inch. Hanging on the walls were black-and-white photographs of aircrews; acrylic paintings of fighter planes; regimental insignia, wings and shoulder patches in glass-fronted frames. Standing on the high mantle-shelf that ran along three sides of the room: logbooks, Air Ministry binoculars, airmen goggles and aircraft parts.

Rossi turned his gaze on Bella. "Such a primitive war – you know what Albert Einstein said? 'I know not with what weapons World War III will be fought, but World War IV will be fought with sticks and stones.' Genius."

"The end of the world as we know it," Bella said, taking a long pull on her third pint.

"Thought you didn't drink."

A cheeky smile. "Only when I'm nervous. Or eating something salty, like now."

"You never answered my question."

A shrug. "Which one? There's been so many?"

"The narrowboat. Who looked after it while you were sunbathing on the Nile?"

"*Curious*, aren't you?" Bella said, with a puzzled expression, then added, "But if you must know – nobody. What for? It's not a horse. Doesn't need feeding."

Taking the hint, Rossi pushed back in his chair and stretched out his arms. *Time to lay on the charm and drink way too much*, he thought. "How was Egypt? Stumble across any undiscovered tombs of lost pharaohs?"

26

On the return train journey from Bishop's Stortford, Cathy mulled over what Chief James had said: "Europe in disarray". *Was Europe the key?* A Europe that for so long had taken peace and prosperity for granted. A Europe that had under-invested in defence. A Europe incapable of protecting itself.

Cathy knew the European project was collapsing, but why? Mass immigration and authoritarianism in Eastern Europe were the main accomplices. But who was stoking the fires of anger and discontent? It was too easy to say Russia. But she couldn't think of a better answer.

"You're back late," Cathy said, seated at Rossi's writing desk with her laptop open.

Rossi flicked the door closed and switched on the white noise generator. "Fish and chips with Bella."

Cathy's eyes narrowed. "Not a chance. You detest deep-fried food."

"She ate. I watched." Rossi paused, waiting for Cathy to butt in with her usual sarcasm. Nothing, so he continued. "Told me everything about Percy. Lot of interesting stuff."

"Everyone has a view on His Lordship. Why is hers any better?"

"Good point."

"Is she attractive?"

"My type, if you know what I mean."

Cathy turned her gaze back to her computer and mumbled, "Moron."

A short silence as Rossi removed his coat and hung it on the door. "She told me the authorities found a body of a woman in the river near Jesus Loch this morning. Can you check she wasn't winding me up?"

A flutter of fingers on the keyboard. "Ah, here it is. Unidentified female in her late twenties. Death viewed as suspicious."

"Then Bella was telling the truth."

Cathy swung around in her chair to face Rossi, now seated on the edge of the bed removing his shoes. "Don't get ahead of yourself, Enzo. It could have been Bella who tossed Natasha overboard."

A shrug. "Claims she was working at a dig somewhere in Egypt. Returned only yesterday."

"How convenient."

"Did you catch up with the chief? Anything useful?"

"He finally conceded that the anarchist line of

enquiry is most likely a red herring. Reckons the killings have something to do with the collapsing European project."

"Why didn't he say so yesterday?"

"Because he's playing politics."

"Or because he's an arsehole."

"Both. Either way, it got me thinking. I've come up with a new theory. But first we'll need to establish a connection between the victims and the emergence of populism as a political force in Europe."

"Wow," Rossi scoffed. "That'll be easy. Just you and me – the Batman and Robin of global espionage."

"More like Wonder Woman and Inspector Clouseau."

Laughing to herself, Cathy sat on the bed close to Rossi, her knee resting on his thigh.

"What are you up to?" Rossi smiled.

"I'm lonely."

"Get a husband."

"Almost had one."

"A good one, from what I heard."

"You heard wrong."

Rossi scoffed. "I've been thinking about that. Here you are, CIA-trained, a master at dealing with conflict, yet you ran away from my mama."

"A formidable force."

"She's seventy-three years old, with a walking stick. You sure you're not using her as an excuse. Afraid of the commitment? Afraid of marriage?"

Cathy rested her head on Rossi's shoulder. "It took you a long time to come up with that."

"Sorry. I rely on what I'm told. Try to avoid psychoanalysing women. Especially crazy ones. It's a game you can't win."

"That's why you're having trouble finding a wife. Relationships are about reading between the lines. If I'm pissed off, it's your job to work out why."

"What utter nonsense. How does that make sense?"

"Who says it has to?"

"I give up. Now tell me what you're thinking."

Cathy undid the top button of her jeans and made herself comfortable. "The killings have nothing to do with Lord Percy. At least not directly."

"He'll be relieved."

"He's European old money. Not interested in everything going pear-shaped."

"Agreed. So why are we chasing him?"

Cathy slapped Rossi on the thigh. "I kept asking myself the same question. Looked for common threads. And that's when I arrived at my new theory."

"Which you keep promising to tell me about."

"The break-up of the European Union."

"That's it. That's your theory?"

"The bud of an idea."

"More like a spore."

"Europe's in disarray. A union that was the biggest ticket in town not so long ago. A union on Russia's border, a union that fast-tracked NATO membership for former Warsaw Pact members, a union—"

"I get it," Rossi said, rising and topping up their glasses. "Brilliant as always, Cathy. But how does murdering a rogues' gallery of seedy businessmen cause the break-up of Europe?"

"More to the point – how does it prevent it? I'm talking about a counter-revolution. A secret war against those plotting the destruction of the EU. A group fighting to stop Europe slipping into chaos."

Rossi paced the room. "You're saying the victims were involved in a conspiracy to raze the European Union?"

"And you know what else I think? The *pièce de résistance*." Cathy paused. "If you want to draw an extra-long bow, perhaps President Volkov was the first victim of this counter-plot. Russia has long sought to thwart European integration. It was Russian money and support that brought a train load of populist, right-wing leaders to power in Europe on the back of the refugee crisis. Leaders threatening to withdraw their countries from the union. Pitting fellow members against one another."

"A refugee crisis caused by the indiscriminate aerial bombing of civilian towns in the Greater Middle East by madmen sponsored and supported by Russia."

"Enzo, it's possible, isn't it? Or am I sounding like a conspiracy theorist under a tin-foil hat?"

"I suppose it's possible – along with a dozen other wacky ideas." Rossi paused. "But, if it's true, it blows a dirty big hole in our Moscow narrative. We staked our reputations on Revealing Light being responsible for Volkov's death."

"I wouldn't worry about reputations, Enzo. If we're right, we'll be heroes all over again."

"Can't remember being a hero the first time round."

Pause. "What's the next step?"

"Determine who the guardian angels are – the protectors of the European dream. No wars. No borders. Prime suspects: state actors, captains of industry, old money, new money, Lord Percy. Pick one of them. All of them."

"My money is on a state actor," Rossi said, his eyes locked on Cathy, seeking a nod of confirmation.

"But which one?"

Resting his backside against the commode, Rossi projected his gaze west towards Washington. "No one needs a strong united Europe more than the US. Particularly now the world's only superpower is soon to be joined by China and a resurgent Russia. America's renewed interest in Europe has come by default."

"A covert operation run by National Security Council hawks?" Cathy took a long thoughtful sip of Scotch. "Wouldn't be the first time."

"Even if you're half right, how do we prove it? It's back to the start. Who do we believe? Who can we trust? And what's Lord Percy's role in all this?"

27

The grandfather clock at the bottom of the stairs struck eleven. Cathy kicked off the duvet and rose slowly. Dressed in a black modal and cream lace chemise nightdress, she stood in the centre of the room with her hands above her head, stretching. Cathy had worked until dawn searching for a link between Volkov, the five victims, and the failing European project. It was an unproductive night with little to show. Slim pickings on the internet, and the CIA files were blocked. "Above her pay grade," she could hear the chief say. Conspiracy popped to mind.

In the early hours, overflowing with anger and disdain, Cathy sent an end-to-end encrypted message to Chief James demanding access to all information – including phone records. If not, she and Rossi would walk. To her surprise, he agreed.

From a large brown suitcase stored under her bed, Cathy removed a black leather document bag and placed it on the commode. A scan of the room. *That'll work*, she thought, folding yesterday's newspaper in half, inserting it into the leather bag and zipping it closed. A glance at her watch. Still time for a shower. Cathy slipped into the white cotton robe she'd liberated from the Le Méridien and headed down the corridor towards the bathroom.

Half an hour later, Cathy was outside Fisher House under a pitch-black sky. Opening her umbrella, she glanced at the faces on the street. A ping on her phone. She read the message. Rossi had bought a coffee maker. *Long overdue.*

Document bag tucked under one arm, Cathy scurried down Pea Hill past the Cambridge Visitor Information Centre. The heavens opened. Cathy's shoes slid on the wet stone pavement as she turned back and went inside. Unfolding a tourist map by the window, Cathy scanned the empty street. Nothing suspicious.

As soon as the shower passed, she stuffed the map into her trench coat pocket and headed west towards Market Hill. Passing a row of food stalls, Cathy stopped at a Venezuelan hut and bought an *arepa* with black bean, mango and avocado sauce. Breakfast. Umbrella hanging from her wrist, Cathy then strolled north to Christ's Pieces. A check of her watch as she bit off a mouthful of *arepa*. *Plenty of time.* Cathy couldn't help think a lap around the city was overkill. But, until she knew who the enemy was, she planned to maintain good tradecraft. Back past the bowling green, picking up the pace. West along Downing

St, with Pembroke College on the left. Now north. Past St Catharine's, approaching King's College. Another check of the time. Great Gate ahead on the left. Porter's Lodge.

"At least she's punctual," Cathy murmured to herself as she tossed the *arepa* wrapping into a litter bin.

Seated on a knee-high stone wall running along the pavement in front of Newton's Apple Tree was Heroin Chic. Her matching CIA document bag leaning on the wall near her feet.

Cathy sat down and placed her bag on top of her compatriot's. As Cathy made a show of unfolding the unruly tourist map, Heroin Chic rose with Cathy's bag in hand and strutted off.

There was a spring in Cathy's step as she took a roundabout route back to Fisher House. It was clear by the weight and bulk of Heroin Chic's document bag that the chief was playing ball. And, if she wasn't mistaken, that was the sound of a memory stick containing phone records in electronic format knocking about in the bottom.

He's back early, she thought, spotting Rossi's new bicycle locked to a rack on the wet pavement. She rushed up to her room, threw off her coat, grabbed her laptop from under her mattress and made her way along the maze of connecting corridors to Rossi's chamber. A turn of the handle. Locked.

Cathy stooped down and scrutinised a notch on the architrave above the skirting board. A strand of her thick chestnut hair poking out from between the door and frame confirmed no one had entered the room in Rossi's absence. She slid her slender fingers deep into her jeans pocket, removed a loose key, unlocked the door and entered.

Seated at Rossi's writing desk, Cathy smiled with anticipation as she glimpsed inside the document bag. Six large plain manila envelopes, and one memory stick. Under the light of the green banker's lamp, she examined the harvest for signs of tampering. Untouched. Slipping the tip of her index finger under the seal, Cathy ripped open the envelopes and emptied the contents on the desk, like a spoilt child opening presents on Christmas morning. A file on each of the five victims, and a thin document on Natasha. "Top Secret" stamped in red on the covers.

Cathy laid out the dossiers in chronological order according to the date of the victims' murder. A quick thumb through. *That's weird*, she thought. The CIA had been tracking all five of the deceased for several years. For a good five minutes she sat frowning at the folders, ruminating about their significance.

"Coffee," she said, glancing at the commode.

It turned out that after breakfast, fed-up with takeaway coffee in paper cups, Rossi had dashed around the corner to Marks & Spencer and purchased a Nespresso machine and a set of white ceramic cups and saucers with faces of Italian ladies painted on the side. Two brunettes, two blondes, a redhead and, no doubt Rossi's favourite, a raven-haired beauty with fair skin.

Cathy made herself a double espresso then sat back at the desk. Sipping her coffee, she read.

"Homework?" Rossi asked, standing in the doorway, a puddle of water forming at his feet.

Cathy spun around on the chair. "You fall in the river?"

"Bike's out of action, so I walked to faculty this morning," Rossi explained, peeling off his soggy coat. "On my way home, the skies opened as I was cutting across the Backs. Had nowhere to hide. God's not happy with me."

"Impure thoughts and urges about Percy's cousin, no doubt."

"*Bellissima* Bella," Rossi smirked, continuing to undress. "She's in my dreams."

"You're pathetic, Enzo."

Dressed in boxers, Rossi stood at Cathy's shoulder. "What's all this then? Top-secret files?"

"A present from the chief," Cathy said, picking up the empty document bag and slapping it into Rossi's crotch. "And put on some clothes. I haven't eaten."

Rossi didn't move. "Anything useful?"

"I've just started. But so far nothing that contradicts what we're thinking…"

"You sound bothered," Rossi said, resting his backside on the desk.

Cathy stroked Rossi's silky muscular thighs. "Why didn't you bring your racing bike with you to Cambridge? I thought you were a mad keen cyclist."

"No hills. Besides, how far can you ride in England before the sky pisses down on you?"

"So why are you still shaving your legs?"

Rossi coloured. "Habit – now can we discuss the files?"

"The data covers several years and includes a smattering of thought-provoking telephone and internet conversations intercepted under FISA authority."

"Isn't that what your intelligence community likes to do?"

"Five businessmen. All subject to long-term CIA surveillance. All murdered. Similar MOs. There's nothing random about that."

A puzzled look on Rossi's face. "We already knew it wasn't random."

"Enzo. You're not listening. The common thread is within these files. Not the *Forbes* list the three wise men would have us believe."

"A deep state conspiracy?"

"Not necessarily," Cathy said, gazing at the reflection of Rossi's athletic back in the window.

"You're losing me."

"The rationale for the killings is in the files, but the assassin could be anyone."

Rossi moved to the commode, opened the bottom drawer and removed a pair of jeans. "So why aren't you reading, if the answer's in the files?"

"Exactly," she said, frowning at his crotch.

"Me? Am I disturbing you?"

"Not if you cover yourself."

28

"What are you playing at?" Jefferson growled, balancing on the edge of the U-shaped sofa, pouring another round of Jim Beam. "You need to pick a side, like your buddy Lawrence here."

James, seated opposite, snatched at his glass and took a gulp. "I had no alternative, I'm telling you."

"Bullshit," Riccardo called out, as he picked at the thick acrylic white paint of the frameless canvas. "You should have lied. Told her someone wiped the files. Russian hackers, Legion of Doom, Lizard Squad – anyone."

"Cathy's smart. Streetwise. You don't lie to her unless you're telling the truth."

"That's crap," Jefferson mumbled. "Trouble is, you think with your cock. That's why Langley yanked you out of Moscow."

The chief sat forward. "Not even close, Ohio. The Russkis booted me. Awarded me the distinguished Lenin 'persona non grata' medal, convinced Washington was behind the Olympisky Stadium explosion. No doubt Human Resources opened my file to your master's shifty eyes, so you already know that."

"Folks, let's turn it down a notch," Rosenthal said, entering the room, wiping his grease stained hands with a rag. "I can hear you from downstairs."

"Then get your hoods off my back."

Rosenthal picked up a glass of bourbon and sat down between the combatants. "We're looking for cooperation, Bill." He paused, allowing time for the proposition to sink in. "We're more or less on the same side. Your job is to identify the assassin, and ours is to take him out. Teamwork."

"Don't see it myself, Ethan. It's not the way I'm used to doing business."

"Times have changed, Bill. The president is dragging the US Intelligence Community kicking and screaming into the modern era. He expects our support. From now on, inter-state strategic competition and global disorder are our great nation's principal security concerns. Not terrorism. Not the Mexicans."

"Ironic, isn't it? Most sane political analysts hang blame for the breakdown in the rules-based world order on those warmongering evangelists in the White House who happened to have our dumb-shit president's ear."

A shrug of the shoulders. "The president gets to choose who he listens to. Whether good advice or bad, it's up to him to decide. That's democracy. It's not for us to set policy or second-guess the will of the American people. We do what we're told, Bill."

"It's William. Not even my mother gets to call me Bill."

"What's in a name?" Rosenthal smiled, then added, "All I'm asking is you rein in your people. They're in Cambridge to be invisible, gather intelligence. Give the American voters the impression we're on top of this. Agent Doherty's brief does not include reading top-secret files."

Chief James sat forward, his faded red hair catching the light. "Cathy's one of the agency's best analysts. Why not use her? What harm could it do?"

"If she's not ideologically aligned…" Rosenthal paused, glowering back at James. "A damn lot."

"What are you running here, Ethan? What aren't you telling me about Bright Star? Where does global disorder feature in all this?"

Rosenthal gazed at Chief James over his Jim Beam as he took a slow sip then said, "For operational purposes, we've briefed you on everything you need to know."

The chief drained his glass, slapped it on the table, and rose. "It's been a pleasure," he said, turning towards the door.

"Where are you going?" Jefferson demanded, like a father to a teenage son.

"You going to ground me?" The chief groped in his pocket, pulled out the safe house key and lobbed it towards Jefferson. "I'm checking out."

"Throwing in the towel?" Rosenthal asked. "Retiring to the golf club?"

"Decamping. Moving closer to the action and away from the stench. You coming, Lawrence?"

Arms crossed, Lawrence gazed down at his bottle-green cashmere socks and said nothing.

Still by the white canvas, Riccardo pulled his mobile from his pocket and speed-dialled. "Watch your back," he said, eyeballing the chief, "there's a killer on the loose."

At the bottom of the staircase, the chief turned his ear to the white room as he put on his black wool overcoat and fedora. Angry voices and frantic activity. A smirk as he picked up his leather travel bag and stepped out into the drizzle. Squinting into the glare from the streetlamps reflecting off the wet cobblestones, he checked the dead-end lane for faces. No one. *The whole of London is eating supper.*

By the time he reached his Jaguar SUV, parked two blocks away, the euphoria of his exit had worn off. "Watch your back" repeated in his head. Walking around the vehicle, he looked for signs of tampering, then peered inside. Nothing. Squatting on the puddled road, he checked the underside of the vehicle. *Difficult to see.*

A shake of the head. "Gun-shy? What's wrong with me?" James murmured. He opened the vehicle with the remote, checked under the driver's seat and climbed in.

The chief clenched his jaw as he turned the ignition. A smile of relief when the engine fired up. He set the GPS for Cambridge: fifty miles via the M11; one hour fifty-five minutes. *Add fifteen minutes for the rain*, he thought, driving off. He'd be in Cambridge by half nine.

An hour and a half later, driving past the village of Ugley Green, the chief took a pull of Jack Daniel's from his hip flask. Ahead, flashing orange lamps fixed to safety barriers. Squinting, he read the roadwork notice. A stretch of the M11 was being resurfaced. He reduced his speed and turned up the radio. "Belle nuit, ô nuit d'amour", from Offenbach's final opera, played. A sense of calm swept over him. He had a purpose: a quick confession, then Cathy to the rescue.

It was a fool's calm. Once again, the chief had been sloppy. Chronic knee pain and the puddled Knightsbridge Road had stopped him from crouching low enough to catch sight of it.

Magnetically attached to the undercarriage of the SUV was a one-kilogram bomb with a timer switch and a tilt fuse. The chief had missed it when he checked. Moments ago, the one-hour delay timer had activated the device. The next bump and the mercury inside the fuse would flow down the glass tube and flood the open electric wires connected to a battery. And boom.

The chief slowed to almost a stop as the SUV dropped onto a half-mile stretch of pitted road base. A honk of a horn from a tailgating Mini encouraged him to speed up.

Chief James pressed down on the accelerator. The SUV bucked and rolled as he sped off. A beat later, a flash of vivid light and a ball of orange flames as the Jaguar launched skywards propelled by a high-velocity shock wave and superheated gas. Doors open, the chief's SUV fell to earth with a thud, landing on top of the impatient Mini that had skidded into the IED's crater.

29

Cathy was resting on top of the bed with ankles crossed when Rossi returned from speaking to Monsignor Baker. "Ironic, isn't it?" she said, her eyes covered by Rossi's pork-pie hat. "The notion of unifying Europe has been around since the fall of Constantinople. And only now, the moment it takes shape, someone wants to destroy it."

Rossi set a bag of takeaway on the floor next to the bed and hung up his coat. "Same thing happened last time."

"What *are* you talking about?" Cathy said from under the hat.

"When Nazi Germany tried to unify Europe."

Cathy propped herself up on one elbow. "You're speaking rubbish again."

"It's true. At the beginning, when things were going swimmingly, Wilhelm II claimed the hand of God was creating a new world order: the United States of Europe under German leadership."

"Sounds like something my president would say." Laughter.

Rossi set the takeaway and two Belgian golden ales on the wooden chair in front of the bed and sat down next to Cathy.

"What do we have?" Cathy asked, sitting up. "Doesn't smell like your usual olives and goat cheese?"

"Pad thai times two," Rossi said, passing Cathy a cardboard takeaway box, chopsticks and a napkin. "Came highly recommended."

"By who?"

"A young lady I met in the restaurant."

"Did she give you her number?"

"She wanted to, but I told her I'm married."

"Did it work?" Cathy asked, holding out her open hand.

Rossi's eyes sunk to the floor as he pulled a business card from his pocket and ripped it in half. "I didn't want to be rude."

"You know your problem, Enzo? You smile back at them when they catch your eyes. It's like an invitation to do evil."

"What am I meant to do?"

"Read the bloody menu."

A long silence as they shovelled pad thai into their mouths and drank their beers.

"Did Monsignor Baker have any old Melba House hunting snaps?" Cathy asked.

"He's got photographs going back to the Battle of Hastings. He promised to dig them out tomorrow. It might be an idea to show them to Bella. She'd know some faces."

"Forget about Bella, Enzo. She's too young for you."

"She's your age."

"I'm different," Cathy said, pulling on her ale.

Rossi threw her a sideway glance. "In what way?"

"In every damn way."

A long chilly silence.

"What have you concluded from reading the files?" Rossi finally asked, motioning towards the writing desk.

"Nothing that shoots a hole in our theory." Another swig. "It's more or less as I figured. All victims were engaged in activities that could be construed as undermining European unity."

"Such as?"

"Where to start," Cathy said, setting her takeaway on the floor. "Your shooting partner Gennady Zhukov, for instance. Spent most of his waking hours flogging Russian-made weapons in the Middle East and Africa to despots hung up on retaining power."

"By bombing their own cities and slaughtering their civilian populations," Rossi said, shaking his head.

"Causing the migrant crisis in Europe, and the rise of populism. Well done, Russia."

"And what about billionaire philanthropist and all-round good guy Charles Edge?" Rossi asked.

"Nicknamed the Russian Laundromat. He cleaned dirty money for the Russian ruling elite, with most of the disinfected cash ending up in London and New York real estate."

"Much-sought-after foreign direct investment. Explains why the leaders of the free world are reluctant to call it out." Pause. "And Paterson Carlyle?"

"Lovely chap," Cathy said, curling her lip. "Specialised in casinos and prostitution. Activities well suited for gathering *Kompromat*."

"For passing onto the Kremlin."

"Who happen to be Carlyle Group's biggest investor. A secret buried behind layers of offshore shell companies, but known to the CIA," Cathy said, switching off the white noise device. "I'm off to bed."

"Shall I walk you?"

"Best you get some sleep. You've got a big day ahead of you."

"Have I? Doing what?"

Cathy stuffed the top-secret CIA files and her laptop into the document bag and opened the door. "Checking holiday snaps with the lovely Bella."

As Cathy sashayed off, Rossi stood in the doorway feeling gloomy and a little dazed, wondering whether to run after her.

He didn't.

30

Rossi entered the dining room carrying his laptop. He sat by the window looking out at a grey, reluctant morning, which seemed to match his mood.

"Good morning, Inspector General," Mrs Tarbottom called out through the serving hatch, "I won't be a min…" Her voice drowned out by the venting of steam from the espresso machine.

Rossi set his laptop on the table and scrolled through the dozen photographs Monsignor Baker had sent him an hour ago. The oldest, according to the prelate's accompanying note, ten years. Other than the shoot he'd attended with the monsignor, Rossi didn't recognise a face.

"Not hungry, Inspector General?" the housekeeper said, setting Rossi's double espresso on the table.

Rossi looked up with a start. "Could eat a horse, but I'm waiting for Ashley."

"You'll be waiting a while, sir. Ms Clarke has already eaten."

"This morning?" Rossi asked, furrowing his brow. "Are you sure?"

"She sat with the monsignor. Quite an appetite – both of them."

"But I checked her room. She wasn't there."

"She wouldn't be, sir." A grin. "She took the Monsignor's car to the Queen Elizabeth Way shooting range."

Rossi's eyes narrowed. "What on earth for?"

"The dining room was empty – I couldn't help but overhear," Mrs Tarbottom said, her tone apologetic.

"Yes?"

"Ms Clarke received a last-minute invitation to try out for the women's four."

"Shooting?"

"Cambridge University's Small-Bore Rifle Club, sir. There's a varsity match against Oxford next week."

A shrug. "I'm on my own then," he said, rising and moving to the buffet table.

"How wonderful, sir. You and Lord Melba," Mrs Tarbottom declared, studying the image Rossi had left open on his laptop. "What a lovely souvenir of your time at Cambridge. And there's young Lord Percy, Sir Thomas Hickey, Mr Pickworth—"

"That's impressive, Mrs Tarbottom," Rossi interrupted, setting his breakfast plate on the table and sitting down. "Is there anyone in Cambridgeshire you *don't* know?"

"Only the Johnny-come-lately types. New money. Foreigners who like to watch re-runs of *To the Manor Born*."

"Wouldn't be too much of that at Melba House, would there?" Rossi flicked to the next image.

A tut. "Lord Melba's an English gentleman, sir."

Rossi wasn't sure what that meant, but it didn't matter. "Who else do you know?" he asked, flicking to the next image. Within thirty minutes, including interruptions and quiet periods as other lodgers competed for Mrs Tarbottom's time, Rossi had an impressive list of names. There were gaps. Gaps he hoped Bella could fill.

***

The shooting range was located under the northern access ramp to the Elizabeth Way bridge that crossed the River Cam just over a mile north of the chaplaincy.

Following Robert Morton's instructions, Cathy entered the twenty-five-yard indoor range through an unlocked door in the middle of the pedestrian underpass. She switched on the lights and glanced about. Concrete floor, white painted walls, girders and columns.

"Is anyone here?" The only answer was the repeating "clip, clip" of vehicles running over the bridge's expansion joints above her head.

The windowless space was musty and damp. Cathy folded her arms as she moved deeper inside. At the shooting position, a row of narrow desks and a scattering of wooden chairs. Against the far wall, transparent plastic drop-down targets hung like PVC strip curtains in a meat packing plant. *I'll wait in the car*, she thought. Then without warning the room went black. Wheeling around,

Cathy caught the silhouette of a woman framed by the door lobbing something inside.

"*I'm* in here," Cathy called out, as the door slammed.

The smell of burning black powder and a visible flame sent Cathy diving behind a metal-covered concrete column. Visions of dynamite and death raced through her mind. Then a flash of light and a deafening bang. For sixty seconds, Cathy lay on the dusty concrete floor with a roar in her ears as the range filled with the smell of smoke and sulphur.

"Bloody firecrackers," Cathy murmured, regaining her senses. Propped up against the column, she covered her mouth and nose with her scarf, pulled out her phone, and switched on the torch. Dabbing the inside of her ears, Cathy checked for blood. There was none.

Through the dust and smoke, Cathy moved to the exit. For a short while, she pounded her fists on the grey metal door and bellowed for help, head throbbing, unable to hear her own voice. No response, so with gaze fixed on her phone, she walked the room searching for a signal. *Not a chance*, she thought, again dabbing her ears for blood.

"I guess I wait," Cathy murmured to herself, setting a chair by the door.

***

Laptop in a messenger bag slung over his shoulder, Rossi walked his two-wheeler to Giuseppe's Bicycle Repair Shop.

At the back of the workshop, Rossi spotted the bicycle mechanic – Giuseppe, he assumed – seated on a stool next to a mountain bike clamped to a work stand.

"*Buongiorno,*" the mechanic said, over the sound of music playing on the radio.

"I phoned."

"From *Toscana*?" the mechanic said, in a sing-song Italian voice. "The man in a hurry."

"*Sì.*" Rossi motioned to his shredded bicycle tyre. "It's possible?"

"For a fellow countryman – fifteen minutes. Five minutes quicker than I take for Her Majesty."

Rossi wandered the shop as Giuseppe fastened his bike to a work stand. He picked up a pair of full-finger cycling gloves and put them on the counter near the cash register.

"IRA," Giuseppe said, nodding at an old silver radio cassette player.

Rossi listened. Black Jaguar F-Pace blown to pieces. Travelling north on the M11 near the village of Ugley Green. Two dead. Names withheld pending notification of relatives. One a foreign national.

"Why the IRA?"

"With the Good Friday Agreement in tatters, it was inevitable. Only a matter of time. It'll get worse before it gets better."

"Let's hope not," Rossi said, his tone cheerless. "Europe's got enough problems already."

The mechanic unclipped the bicycle and rested it against the counter. "Now let's see," he said, pounding away at the cash register.

Ten minutes later, Rossi chained his bicycle to the railing next to Bella's pistachio-green Vespa and bounded down the embankment to *Moon Shadow*.

Spotting him through the open curtains, Bella went on deck and greeted him.

"Sorry I'm late. Repairing the puncture took longer than I thought," Rossi said, taking off his new gloves as he stepped aboard.

"It's Saturday morning. Nothing to be late for."

"You're a girl after my own heart," he said, kissing her on both cheeks.

Below deck was warm. The stove had been burning all night. Rossi stood in the saloon, resting his forearms on the kitchen counter watching Bella prepare coffee.

"What's this about hunting photos, Lorenzo?"

"Research for a book about game shooting in Cambridgeshire." Rossi removed his laptop from his bag. "A friend sent me a series of photos from Melba House. I'd like to identify as many faces as possible."

"Uncle Henry and cousin Percy?" Bella said, setting Rossi's coffee on the counter next to his open laptop, "Are they in on this?"

Rossi produced his most relaxed, honest face. "I want it to be a surprise."

"Give me a look then," Bella said, already standing next to him, her hand resting up on his shoulder.

***

Cathy sprung to her feet and killed the lights, as a key turned in the lock of the grey metal door. She took up a fighting stance as the door swung open with a groan. A dull winter's light drifted in followed by laughter and much-needed fresh air.

Cathy listened for a few seconds. Teenagers carrying equipment. New members receiving instructions. What she'd expected to hear two hours ago.

"I got locked in," she said to a dozen wide-eyed sixth formers as she stepped out from behind the door.

"Who are you?" an instructor asked, appearing from the side.

"Ashley Clarke," Cathy said, holding out her hand.

After a not-so-honest explanation of what had happened, Cathy bid her rescuers farewell and headed back to town to meet Rossi for lunch.

31

"What did Robert Morton say?" Rossi asked, setting two glasses of Sauvignon Blanc on the same table he and Bella had dined at two days earlier.

"You'll have to speak up, Enzo. My ears are still buzzing."

Rossi repeated the question.

"Claimed to know nothing." Cathy said, turning her good ear towards Rossi. "He reckoned it was a prank carried out by the students who rescued me. When I insisted it wasn't, he said he was late for class and rang off."

A clink of glasses and a healthy sip. "But he invited you, didn't he?"

"Apparently not." Cathy paused, waiting for Rossi to remonstrate. Silence, so she continued. "Some arsehole purporting to be Robert Morton, captain of the Cambridge University Rifle Association, phoned after I returned to my room last night. I was half asleep and there was a hell of a racket on the line. Fez Club, I figured at the time. He urged me to try out for the women's four. I agreed."

"Aren't you too old to be chasing medals?" Rossi mocked.

"I was thinking more about infiltrating Percy's inner circle, Mr Rossi. Anyway, he gave me the address and time. I went there this morning – and you know the rest."

"Someone's trying to scare you?"

A nod. "Unless they planned to starve me to death." Laughter.

"You checked the number?"

"It was the landline at the Fez Club all right. From the bar, most likely."

A short-haired waitress in tight jeans and a white T-shirt approached carrying two servings of fish and chips. Cathy made room on the small round table. "I'll fetch the vinegar," the waitress said, smiling at Rossi.

"Who else knew you would be there?" Rossi asked, his eyes following the waitress's round backside as she returned to the kitchen.

"Monsignor Baker," Cathy said, salting her chips. "He lent me the bulbous beast. Mrs Tarbottom, of course…"

"And anyone at the Fez Club in earshot of the caller," Rossi added.

"Suppose." Cathy shrugged as she cut off a piece of the beer-battered cod and jammed it into her wide-open mouth, like a ravenous factory worker after a double shift. Reticent, Rossi looked on, sipping his wine.

"Dig in, Enzo. You promised you would try it. It's scrumptious."

Rossi pulled his plate closer. "I'm building up to it."

"How's Bella?"

"Very nice, thank you."

Cathy pursed her lips and kicked Rossi in the calf with the vamp of her sneaker. "You were such a good Catholic boy when I met you."

"You changed me."

"I prefer the old version."

"Gone. Psychologically damaged. I could have turned to drink and grown a beard. Went for driving you crazy instead." Pause. "And it seems to be working."

Another kick. "Finished? Good. How far did you get with the Melba House photos?"

"All done, for what it's worth." Rossi smirked. "Got chatting with Mrs Tarbottom at breakfast. She knew most of the faces. Then Bella filled in the gaps."

"How many names?"

"Didn't count – fifty, sixty. The list is on my desk. You can check them out tonight."

Cathy glanced at her phone. A sigh. "I'm worried. The chief texted me last night. He sent it to the blue burner I used in London, so I didn't see it until this morning. Said he was on his way to Cambridge with urgent information. He should have contacted me by now."

"Try the bordellos."

"You didn't notice a flashy black SUV near Fisher House during your wanderings?"

Rossi's smirk faded. "What type of SUV?"

"A Jaguar."

"Google 'car bomb on the M11 near Ugley Green,'" Rossi said, waving an index finger at Cathy's phone.

A long silence. "*Must* be a coincidence," Cathy said, flicking through more results. "The chief's indestructible."

"Like the *Titanic*," Rossi said, gathering the empty wine glasses and moving to the bar.

When Rossi returned with two large Laphroaigs, Cathy was on her official CIA phone speaking with Lawrence.

"Get yourself out of there, Paul, and keep your head down," she said, ringing off and picking up her Scotch. "It was the chief all right. Lawrence confirmed it."

"What else did he say?"

Cathy looked up from her glass, a tear running down her cheek. "Nothing. He was at the safe house. I could hear Jefferson and Riccardo in the background."

"To a fallen comrade," Rossi said, holding out his glass.

"To my dear mentor and friend, Chief William James," Cathy added in a murmur, as their glasses touched.

A moment's silence.

"This is getting serious," Rossi said, glancing about the room as if he were expecting someone. "Let's pray we're not next."

"No divine intervention required. The chief had lost his edge. Started trusting the wrong people. We, on the other hand, trust nobody."

"That's called paranoid personality disorder. It's definitely not healthy. Speaking of which, isn't it time we checked out of Fisher House? We're sitting ducks there."

"If we run, they'll hunt us down. For now, it's best to stay put and act dumb."

A smirk. "I can do that."

The waitress cleared the table and offered a selection of desserts. A guilty look as Cathy ordered a slice of limoncello cheesecake and two forks.

Rossi poked at the fish on his plate. "Who did this? The media suspect the New IRA."

"We know *that* isn't true."

"Then who? Perhaps he was murdered because he'd identified the assassin?"

A pensive shake of the head. "No. But he was getting close."

"The Kremlin? Revenge for Moscow?"

"No foreign government, not even the Russians, have the balls or the stupidity to take out a senior CIA operative in such a public show of high theatrics."

Rossi picked up their empty glasses and headed back to the bar as their dessert arrived. The waitress set the cheesecake in the middle of the table, while Cathy again checked her phone.

"Then it's someone within the CIA? Someone who knew his movements. The three wise men?" Rossi said, sitting back at the table with a Laphroaig in each hand.

"I've been thinking about that." Pause. "Don't know the answer."

"Jesus, Cathy."

"It's not as scary as it appears, Enzo. The CIA has too strong a culture for something like this to succeed. Sometimes things go rogue, but they're quickly shut down. Besides, I've never heard of them killing their own. It's just not done."

"Well, that eliminates everyone."

Cathy pulled the cheesecake closer. "Not quite," she said, dipping her fork into the Cornish clotted-cream ice cream.

Rossi's eyes narrowed. "With the chief gone, how the hell are we going to build our case?"

"Brick by brick, starting with Heroin Chic."

"And Lawrence?"

"That depends on him. I'm sure he knows stuff. Whether he's willing to share – only time will tell."

32

Cathy sprang out of Fisher House into a crisp, clear Cambridge morning. Document pouch loosely concealed under her overcoat, she scurried off toward Market Hill like a Girl Scout off to earn a merit badge.

Confident she was being followed, Cathy criss-crossed the market square. The purpose was not to shake off Heroin Chic, rather to corner her for an out-with-it *tête-à-tête*.

At a walk-in hat stall, Cathy donned a brown corduroy fiddler cap. Tucking her hair up under the brim in the small round mirror hanging off the stall's frame, Cathy glimpsed Heroin Chic in the distance.

"It suits you," the moustached Indian stall owner said, wobbling his head as he spoke. "Made from the finest Brisbane Moss fabric."

"I'll take it," Cathy said, holding out a fifty-pound note. "Would you like a bag?" Another wobble of the head.

Cathy adjusted the cap in the mirror. "No. I'll wear it."

Taking her change, Cathy idled back in the direction she had just come. Pausing at every turn to ensure her tail remained attached, she made her way to the Museum of Archaeology and Anthropology.

Five minutes maximum. That's how long Cathy figured she had to set the trap before Heroin Chic came slinking in. She dashed up the stairs, searching for a service room. Difficult in a museum with floor guards and friendly gallery hosts in every space.

Standing on the central atrium balcony in the shadow of a soaring Haida totem pole, Cathy waited for Heroin Chic to arrive. It didn't take long. Cathy stepped back from the railing as her watcher appeared between a marble statue of Buddha Shakyamuni seated in meditation, and a grotesque wooden carving of a mythological creature baring fangs. *Thai*, she thought.

Cathy glanced about. "Bad choice," she murmured to herself. The building was not conducive to a noisy confrontation. *Abort?* Too late. Heroin Chic had spotted her and was heading for the open staircase. Cathy bustled down a dimly lit recess. Dead end. Ladies' toilets on the right. Men's on the left. Opening the door to the ladies', Cathy peered inside. Beige tiles, four aluminium frame cubicles with sand-blasted glass doors, and a matching vanity. Cathy pushed the ladies' door wide open, then scurried into the men's room opposite, holding the door ajar half a centimetre to hear what was going on in the passageway.

As the door to the ladies' clicked closed, Heroin Chic's head snapped right. Grinning, she glanced at the ceiling, then behind. No cameras. Sliding her gloved hand inside her puffer jacket, Heroin Chic pulled out a pistol and slipped the safety catch.

She means business, Cathy thought, pulling out her SIG-Sauer P228. *Two can play this game.* The hunter had become the prey.

Cathy stayed put until she heard the door to the ladies' toilets click closed behind Heroin Chic. Stepping into the passageway, Cathy listened as Heroin Chic flung open the four cubicle doors.

"Where the fuck is she?" Heroin Chic screamed from inside, kicking over the bin.

Taking up a fighting stance in front of the door, Cathy waited for the handle to turn.

The squeak of the latch opening sent Cathy's foot smashing into the lockset. The door hit Heroin Chic like a train, crushing her wrist and sending her crashing to the floor. Pistol raised, Cathy stepped inside, shutting the door with her backside.

"You looking for me?" Cathy said, picking up Heroin Chic's pistol and ejecting the magazine.

"That wasn't very friendly," Heroin Chic said, nursing her arm as she rose to her feet. "Aren't we meant to be on the same side?"

Cathy peered at the tattoo on the inside of Heroin Chic's pale wrist. "A dragonfly! Now where have I seen that before?"

"What do you want?"

"We need to talk. Clarify a few things. Establish who's who in the zoo." Pause. "Let's be civil and do it over lunch."

"Do I get my gun back?"

"Depends on how lunch goes."

Fifteen minutes later, Cathy, under the cover of Ashley Clarke, and Agent Harper Rattle, also known as Heroin Chic, were seated in the RAF bar at Rossi's usual table in front of two pints of ale and two serves of fish and chips.

"Who's your case officer?" Cathy asked, getting straight down to business.

"Don't know." Pause. "It *was* Chief James. Now I'm not sure. Some suit in Langley, I guess."

"You know the chief's dead?"

A nod. "He was coming up to see me."

Trying not to show her surprise, Cathy trained her eyes on Rattle, watching and listening for signs of insincerity. "What on earth for?"

"Sex."

"Sex?" Cathy was angry, though she was not sure at whom: Heroin Chic or the chief. Then again, who was she to judge? Not an angelic past.

"That's what he normally drove up for." Pause. "Mind you, he did say he also needed to see you. Warn you about something. But I took it as an excuse. Unless he was doing you too."

"Phew!" Cathy grimaced. "Not likely."

"You knew him better than anyone, so I hear. With his high libido and a suitcase full of US Intelligence Community-funded erectile dysfunction medication, it's difficult to believe he hadn't tried."

"Of course he tried. Long ago. But he quickly grew tired of rejection and moved on to easier targets."

"Like me?"

A shrug. "If you don't mind me asking, was love involved?"

Heroin Chic threw back her head and laughed. "You must know the answer to that. It was a business arrangement. Eyes wide open. He helped me with my career and I helped him quench his animal urges."

"What's your assignment in Cambridge, Agent Rattle? I never quite understood it. I got the sense you spend most of your day watching me and Rossi."

"Surveillance, messenger girl, odd jobs man, sex slave…"

"Why on earth was Chief James wasting resources following us?" A confused frown. "After all, he chose us. No one forced us on him."

"A smokescreen." A gulp of beer. "I watch Lord Percy. The chief had convinced himself the lord of the manor and the safe house trio were one and the same. In cahoots in some way. Teammates."

Cathy drained her glass and banged it on the table, louder than she intended. "And were they?"

"Never caught them at it."

"Did the chief mention anything about a *black operation*?"

"Bright Star, yes. But nothing about a black op. Why would he?"

"To impress you," Cathy said, her tone hard. "I don't know. Perhaps he talks in his sleep?"

"Our relationship didn't involve sleep." A smirk. "Chief was a kinky old sod. Closets, kitchen tables, bathrooms, chandeliers – no beds."

"He never spouted on about White House neoconservatives or the right-wing evangelicals?"

"No more than anyone else. Didn't like them – didn't trust them."

"Who else didn't he trust, Rattle?"

"Other than the three Green Berets operating out of the London safe house, I couldn't say."

Cathy lost her breath for a short moment, then repeated calmly. "Green Berets?"

"You didn't know?"

"Let me get this clear," Cathy said. "You're telling me the three lugs held up in the Knightsbridge safe house are, in fact, freewheeling US Army Special Forces. And not CIA agents under the control of Langley?"

"That's what Chief James told me. Rosenthal is Colonel James Beasley, US Army Special Forces. I have no reason to doubt him."

"And the other two?"

"Lieutenant John Abbott and Sergeant Tripi. You may know them as Cleveland Jefferson and Alfonzo Riccardo."

Cathy bit her lip, finding it hard to accept the chief had confided in Heroin Chic but not herself. Then again, the chief had a long history of reckless pillow talk.

"Now do I get my weapon back?" Heroin Chic asked, scooping up a dollop of mushy peas with a chip.

"First explain this," Cathy said, opening her document pouch and handing Heroin Chic the photograph of her pale dragonfly-tattooed wrist taken in the private lift landing of the London Stock Exchange on the day of the triple murder. "I'm sure the chief showed you the image, so you've had plenty of time to hone your answer."

"Timing," Heroin Chic said, picking up the two empty glasses and moving to the bar.

Cathy couldn't help but be impressed, peering at Rattle coolly chatting with the strapping barman pouring the pints. *Too cool.*

"Timing," Heroin Chic repeated, setting the glasses on the table and sitting back down.

"Not Photoshopped?"

"No. The image is real enough. That's me. I was there. Followed Natasha to London after Rossi's Sunday roast."

Cathy sat back in her seat, her eyes shifting from side to side as if she expected the three wise men to burst in and take her away.

"But your interpretation is all messed up," Heroin Chic added, with a smug smile.

"I only know what they've told me. If there are alternative facts, let's have them."

Heroin Chic took a sip on her ale then with the side of her hand wiped the creamy moustache off her top lip. Resting her elbows on the table, she leant forward and locked eyes with Cathy. "I came down the car park stairs from Paternoster Square just as Carlyle's limo was driving off. On the far side of the garage I saw Carlyle, Sir Lloyd and an Asian woman entering the executive lift landing through a private door. I thought nothing of it until a policeman in riot gear appeared from the shadows and followed them inside. Half a minute later the cop flew out of the same door and belted up the car park ramp. Didn't look right, so I went over to check. As a precaution, I drew my gun before entering. Three dead. Professional job. Nothing I could do so I hightailed it out of there. That's where that blown-up image is from."

"But why doctor the investigation report?"

"Chief surmised someone was setting a false trail. After the killings, the CCTV footage from the cameras in the lift cabin and the landing area were wiped. They'd been hacked. Then out of nowhere a dozen still images turned up in the file. Including a beauty of me entering the lift landing from the garage – featuring my dragonfly tattoo."

"Who is the someone?"

"The chief wasn't sure – or wasn't saying."

"He knew, otherwise he'd still be alive."

The waitress approached and cleared their plates, returning moments later with the dessert menu. They both declined, agreeing to stick with the ale.

"What's this I hear about you and Rossi?" Heroin Chic asked. "The chief told me the two of you were once an item."

"Ancient history," Cathy said, to her glass. "Finished. Done and dusted."

"You parted on good terms?"

"Best of friends," Cathy said, on the verge of telling Heroin Chic to get stuffed.

"Then you don't mind if I have a crack at him?"

Cathy rolled her eyes and chuckled. "You're not his type. He's mixed-up Catholic."

"So am I. My late father was a Catholic priest."

"And my mother's a saint."

"It's true," Heroin Chic insisted. "He was a C of E vicar, then converted to Catholicism after my birth."

"Rossi's *devoutly* Catholic."

"Never met one that couldn't be broken. They're a pragmatic lot."

"I wouldn't bother with him if I was you." Pause. "Celibate," Cathy added in a whisper. "Saving himself for marriage."

"Sounds like a challenge. He's not *gay*, is he?"

Cathy gestured to the waitress for the bill. "I've got to go."

33

"Don't know whether I believe the bitch," Cathy said, removing her coat and flinging it onto the end of Rossi's bed. "She's strange as hell and bloody difficult to read."

"I know someone like that," Rossi said, seated astride the writing desk chair with his arms resting on the high back.

Cathy's eyes narrowed. "You mean *me*?"

"Strange in what way?"

"For a start, she said she fancies you. Why provoke me?"

"Perhaps it's true."

A sharp puff of air out one side of Cathy's mouth. "She had the cheek to ask whether I'd finished with you."

With an expression of smug satisfaction, Rossi leant back against the desk and stretched his arms high in the air. "And you said, 'Sure thing, he's all yours'?"

"Not likely. Told her you're chaste."

"You didn't say that?"

"Did."

"What the hell for?"

"A bit of fun. Anyway, it's true," Cathy said, pausing until she caught Rossi's gaze. "Isn't it? That's what you told me."

Rossi chuckled. "Not quite. Besides, I'm a little more flexible since leaving the Vatican."

Cathy flopped onto the bed. "What have I missed? Saintliness and godliness are what you offered me."

"There are special rules for you, Cathy."

"Because you live in hope."

A short silence. "Did she tell you anything we didn't already know?"

Cathy kicked off her sneakers. "She reckons the three wise men are Green Berets, not CIA. That bit I believe."

"Explains a few things."

"Maybe not. Langley could have engaged them to take out the assassin—"

"Equally, they could *be* the assassins."

Cathy nodded, then said, "And she professed to being Chief James's concubine. Not something you'd own up to unless you had to."

"He's a certified sociopath," Rossi said, exhaling with a whistle. "They should have left him in Moscow."

"She also claimed the chief had assigned her to watch Lord Percy – not us."

"Thought that was our job?"

"There's a big difference. She's outside in the cold peering through the curtains, while we're seated by the fire drinking Lord Percy's booze."

Images of Natasha and the bottle of Ardbeg they had shared on the narrowboat the night some sick bastard murdered her flashed into Rossi's mind.

Cathy rose and paced the room. "Speaking of booze, be a darling, Enzo, and pour me a Scotch. Then find those snaps of the London Stock Exchange slaying."

Rossi did what he was told. Scotch first, then the photographs.

"Look at the sleeve of the cop in this shot and compare it with the dragonfly tattoo," Cathy said, resting her backside on the writing desk.

Rossi laid the two images side by side. "The jacket linings are different. One's fleece, the other nylon. How did we miss that?"

"I think Heroin Chic was telling the truth."

"Two individuals?"

"Not in the report," Cathy said, already seated on the bed. "Looks as if the tattoo image was added later to confuse us."

Rossi rose from the desk and sat alongside Cathy, thighs touching. "Seems we've landed in the middle of a conspiracy of some sort. What do we do?"

"Depends on which outcome you'd prefer. Turning a blind eye to a handful of murders aimed at keeping Europe safe could be viewed as reasonable to some folks."

Rossi shook his head. "That's a right-wing pretext. Assassinating your political opponents is something evil tyrants do – or am I being naïve?"

"Are we going to stop it or burry our heads in the sand?" Cathy smirked.

"We've got to blow the whistle." Rossi sprung to his feet and topped up his glass. "What's the name again of the congressman who helped us with Russia?"

"Carrick Maloney, the senator from Massachusetts."

"We could contact him."

"Hah! Since when have you trusted politicians, Enzo? Besides, in this age of impunity and party politics, who's prepared to risk the wrath of the president? Wreck their re-election chances for what?" Pause. "Give me the computer. I know what we need."

***

Bowed over Rossi's laptop, Cathy scanned the online sites of the mainstream newspapers searching for a modern-day hero. Someone to shake the foundations of the ivory tower across the pond.

Rossi, who had been speaking on the phone for the last half hour, rang off. "It's all fixed for tomorrow. I didn't even have to play the Pope card."

"Details?"

"The Church of Corpus Christi on Maiden Lane. Between the Covent Garden Market and the Strand. It's ours after morning mass. The church remains open all day, but it's usually empty."

"Christ." Cathy scoffed. "Any other business would have sold these non-performing assets by now and doubled down on biotech."

"That's capitalism for you. Like burning the Amazon. Everything's about money." Pause. "Have you found your Deep Throat?"

"Deep Throat!" Cathy laughed. "That's us, Enzo. We're the secret informants, lurking in the bowels of the earth. I'm looking for a Bob Woodward or Carl Bernstein. Top-flight investigative journalists tough enough to write the story, no matter the cost."

"All semantics. Have you found who you're looking for?"

Cathy smirked, as if about to tell a joke. "Do you remember Sabine Reich from the *Frankfurter Allgemeine Zeitung*?"

"'Murders Conceal Secret Vatican Nazi Concordat'. That Sabine Reich?"

"The same."

"Surely not?"

"She's in London covering the assassinations for the German papers."

"No way!" Rossi protested. "The crap she wrote about the Church…"

"It wasn't crap. Her reporting was accurate. Spot on, in fact. And she was one of the few who followed the story to the end. Including the outcome – not guilty. Just because the public weren't interested in a happy ending, that's not her fault."

"Why are you defending her?"

"Enzo, she's the best person for the job," Cathy said, with spirit. "She's angry with the world and the institutions that control it. Just what we need."

Rossi shrugged. He knew better than to argue with Cathy when she used such a tone. Besides, she was right. "What next?"

"We travel to London on the next train. Set up the meeting from there."

"Le Méridien again?"

"No. Somewhere low key. We'll walk in off the street and pay cash. It's safer if no one knows we're there."

Rossi pulled his overnight bag from under his bed.

"Spare underpants and socks only," Cathy said. "No travel bags. We need to take exceptional precautions. Don't want Heroin Chic thinking we're skipping town."

On the way to her room to change, Cathy took a detour to the ground-floor laundry to borrow one of Monsignor Baker's pressed black neckband shirts and a white dog collar she'd seen hanging on a rack earlier.

Ten minutes later, they exited the side door of Fisher House and strolled arm in arm to the Eagle. Laughing as they entered, they walked straight through the RAF bar, out the back into the beer garden, left down the rear alley, and onto King's Parade, where the taxi they had booked was waiting, engine running.

"Where to, pet?" the driver asked, as they settled low on the back seat.

"Waterbeach railway station."

The taxi travelled six miles north, in the opposite direction of London. They were taking no chances. Cathy had surmised Heroin Chic worked for the three wise men. It wasn't difficult. Why else would they have Fisher House under surveillance?

"Look at that!" the driver said, pulling the taxi to a stop close to the train station entrance. The taxi rank was six vehicles deep, and the evening commute was all but over.

"Could be a slow night," Cathy said, fishing in her bag for her purse.

"Not for me, pet. You're my last fare. I'm off home to run a bath for him indoors."

Cathy smiled, handing the driver twenty pounds and alighting the cab.

Rossi stood in the shadow of the train station and lit a cigar. As soon as the taxi's red tail light faded into the distance, he ground his cigar under his leather-soled Italian shoe and, together with Cathy, climbed into the first taxi in the rank.

"Foxton railway station, please," Cathy said, buckling up behind the driver.

The sixteen-mile journey south took a full half hour. Rossi and Cathy took turns peering out the frosty back window into the darkness, checking whether they were being followed. It was impossible to tell.

By the time they arrived at Foxton station a thick fog had drifted in from the surrounding fields. Cathy stood on the pavement, scanning the horizon for vehicle headlights, while Rossi paid the driver. The brown-brick station building was unstaffed. A middle-aged woman seated near the old fireplace looked up from her knitting as they entered and nodded.

Rossi checked his watch as he read the timetable in a glass frame attached to the wall. "Ten minutes."

They bought two tickets to King's Cross, stopping at all stations, from the machine on the platform, then went back inside. A bearded man in his mid-thirties wearing a flashy padded jacket and hood entered from the street at the same time. He looked Cathy up and down, ignoring Rossi.

Rossi monitored him as they boarded the train. Cathy wasn't so concerned. "Too showy for surveillance," she insisted.

"How far is the hotel from King's Cross?" Rossi asked. "We don't arrive until nine. And we still need to phone Reich."

"You worry too much, Enzo," Cathy said, rubbing his thigh. "I'll have you tucked in by ten-thirty."

Rossi and Cathy were last off the train. The man in the padded jacket had got off at Welwyn North and was long gone. They glanced about looking for an unwelcome reception committee, but there were too many faces.

"Taxi or by foot?" Rossi asked, exiting the station building.

Cathy took Rossi's arm. "All the above," she said, steering him towards the taxi rank.

They took thirty minutes to travel the two miles to their hotel, the last half mile by foot.

"The Waldorf Hilton?" Rossi said, entering the foyer. "Not quite what I expected."

"I got a friend from college to book the room using her card. She's off the radar screen. I'll pay cash when we check out."

"King-size bed?"

"I insisted on it," Cathy said, handing Ashley Clarke's passport to the hotel receptionist. "With an extra-long sofa bed for you."

"Room 218, Ms Clarke. Enjoy your stay."

The instant the door clicked shut, Cathy pulled a burner phone from her pocket to phone Sabine Reich. No answer. As the voicemail activated, Cathy rang off and dialled again.

"Hello," came a woman's voice down the line.

"Sabine Reich?" Cathy said, in a soft tone.

"Yes. Who's this?"

"A whistle-blower with a Pulitzer Prize feature story."

"I'm listening."

"Not on the phone."

34

"I'm going to take a shower," Rossi said, as they returned to their room after a buffet breakfast in the hotel's Homage Restaurant. "Want to share? Save the planet?"

Cathy glanced at her watch. "Tempting, but no time. Barbora Novak texted me. She's got some information for us. I've agreed to meet her in Green Park in twenty minutes."

"Want me to tag along?"

"Not a good idea. Best not to have an audience when you're divulging state secrets."

"Don't be long. Sabine is not likely to hang around if you're late."

"I'll be back in plenty of time," Cathy said, her tone reassuring, pecking Rossi on the cheek as she opened the door.

The morning fog had skulked back to the Thames and a clear sky had presented itself as Cathy stepped out of the Waldorf into a hackney carriage for the fifteen-minute ride west.

Alighting from the taxi in front of Green Park, Cathy lingered a minute or two before entering through Canada Gate with a group of tourists. Seventy metres north, she spotted her Sherman Kent roommate seated on a bench under an ancient lime tree reading a tabloid.

That's not right, Cathy thought, scurrying off the path and taking up a position on the narrow walkway running down the centre of the Canada Memorial. Novak was a diehard tree lover. In all the time she had known her, Cathy had never once seen Novak with a printed copy of a newspaper or magazine. "One tonne of newsprint equals twelve murdered trees," she could hear Novak protest.

Cautiously, Cathy peered out from the centre of the inclined water sculpture. Clear. Deciding the tabloid was nothing more than a prop, she inched forward. Then, above the sound of water cascading down the bronze maple leaves inserted into the sloping red granite surface, Cathy heard heavy footsteps and men yelling.

Cathy watched on in horror as Agents Jefferson and Riccardo – going by Rossi's description – approached Novak from either side. Straining to hear, Cathy turned her ear towards them. An angry exchange.

Folding the newspaper in a theatrical flurry, Novak sprung to her feet and tossed it into the bin. "Out of my way!" Novak said, squeezing past the two titans.

As Jefferson spun her around, Novak glimpsed Cathy's long chestnut hair poking out from the centre of the war memorial. The slightest of nods and a blink of her eyes convinced Cathy to stay put.

With a sense of guilt for having involved her friend, Cathy watched on as Jefferson and Riccardo escorted Novak towards Hyde Park Corner. *They'll interrogate her, then let her go*, Cathy assured herself.

The instant they were out of sight Cathy crept forward to the bench and fished the newspaper from the bin. "The *Daily Mail*?" Cathy mumbled to herself, holding out the paper and shaking it. Nothing. Seated on the bench she flicked through the pages. No circled article or underlined words.

Dismayed, Cathy stood hands on hips gazing west towards the Hyde Park Corner end of the park, half-tempted to run after Novak and demand some answers.

Lobbing the newspaper back into the bin, Cathy checked the time. Rossi was waiting back at the hotel about to head off. As Cathy turned, she did a double take. Jammed between two seat slats was a tightly rolled piece of clean white paper, no bigger than a cigarette. Cathy's mood brightened as she imagined the possibilities. Had Novak put it there?

Knocking the paper loose with her pen, Cathy unrolled and unfolded it. "Bingo," she said, stuffing it in her pocket and hurrying off to flag down a cab.

Back at the Waldorf, Cathy found Rossi washed, shaved and dressed in black.

"Don't you look the part?" she said. "A dog collar short of a priest."

"You know, my father groomed me for the priesthood. Luckily my mama saved me. I'm her favourite, and she expects grandchildren."

"You nervous, Enzo? You've told me that story a hundred times. Perhaps you're confusing me with Bella?"

A sheepish smile suggested she was right.

"Did you pass my regards onto Ms Novak?"

"Didn't have a chance. Not long after I arrived, Jefferson and Riccardo turned up and frogmarched her away."

Rossi waited for Cathy to burst into laughter. She didn't. "You're not joking, are you?"

"But all is not lost." Cathy unfolded Novak's note and handed it to Rossi.

Rossi read:

> Two years ago, our newly elected president, under the spell of the batty evangelistic right, proposed a series of extrajudicial killings to curtail Russia's active measures program aimed at destroying unity in Europe, NATO, and weakening other global institutions put in place to prevent war.
>
> The proposal, codenamed Project Crusade, was studied, then closed down on the grounds it was unethical.
>
> The whisper on the Hill is: the new Messiah and his occultists have kicked off the holy war without congressional knowledge or oversight.
>
> As for the three wise men, no records. They're not ours.

Dumbfounded, Rossi stood open-mouthed in the centre of the room, wondering whether it could all be true. "A programme of extrajudicial killings? If I ever needed a reason to go home to Siena and pick olives – I've got it. Are you buying it?"

"It's the only thing that makes sense."

"We can run it past Sabine later. I'm sure she can use it to great effect."

***

Although she was on time and the church was only 500 metres to the west, Cathy bustled along the Strand at a decent pace out of habit. As she turned from Southampton Street onto Maiden Lane, Cathy glimpsed Corpus Christi on the left. Standing for a short while, she studied the façade and tried to visualise the scene as it would have been in the second half of the nineteenth century, when the church was completed to serve the market workers of nearby Covent Garden.

Entering through the stone archway, Cathy descended three steps to the portico. A statue of the Sacred Heart of Jesus on a pedestal greeted her. A red flame flickered in a sanctuary lamp attached to the wall nearby. She entered the narthex through the door on her right. Dipping her fingers into the holy water stoup, Cathy blessed herself and scanned the space. Not a big church by any stretch of the imagination. A smile came to her face as she pictured Rossi sitting in the mahogany confessional booth that stood against the far wall.

The service had started. At the altar, the priest, wearing a green chasuble and stole with gold embroidery over a white alb, read from the Book of Revelations.

Tiptoeing down the west side aisle, Cathy sat on the third pew from the back and gazed about in awe. Cathy had long since lost her faith but always found peace inside an old church. It gave her a sense of security, shielding her from the evil that lurked outside its large solid doors.

The clerestory of the soaring nave was painted azure blue and covered with golden stars. The ceiling was constructed from planks of dark wood laid on exposed rafters. The nave arcades featured charcoal-grey arched pillars with gold decorative capitals. Small green ceramic tiles filled the spaces. From high above, rays of light streamed through the stained-glass windows colouring the gold and stone chancel and altar. Cathy closed her eyes for a long moment, lost in the church's majesty.

A stirring in the pews cut into Cathy's rumination. Half of the twenty worshipers in attendance rose to their feet, shuffled sideways towards the central aisle, and lined up for Holy Communion. Cathy looked at her watch. Twelve-thirty. A full hour before Rossi was due to hear Sabine Reich's confession.

"The body of Christ," the priest proclaimed, holding up the host.

"Amen," the communicants responded one after another.

As the faithful knelt and prayed, the priest purified the sacred vessel at the credence table on the epistle side of the sanctuary.

Parish announcements? There were none.

"About time," Cathy mumbled to herself, as the Concluding Rites began.

After the blessing, the priest dismissed the assembly. "The Mass is ended; go in peace."

"Thanks be to God," came the congregation's response. Cathy joined in.

The priest kissed the altar, bowed profoundly, then exited the sanctuary. As the faithful drifted out, Cathy perused their faces against a photograph of Sabine Reich concealed in her palm. Not there. Within minutes the church was empty.

Cathy rose from the pew, moved to the confessional and checked for any devices an investigative journalist might plant to help identify a source. Nothing. And there shouldn't have been, as Cathy had not yet informed Reich of the final location of their confluence.

On the street in front of the entrance, Cathy removed a packet of Tic Tacs from her coat pocket and popped one in her mouth, signalling all systems go to Rossi, seated in the window of the Grind espresso bar opposite.

Rossi slipped on his overcoat and exited the café carrying a slim leather briefcase. A casual glance up at the sky as if expecting rain to avoid Cathy's gaze as he crossed to the church.

Lingering at the entrance dressed in an Italian black woollen suit and one of Monsignor Baker's best black shirts, Rossi slid his large hand into his coat pocket, pulled out a dog collar and added it to his livery, completing the charade. *If only my papa could see me now*, Rossi thought, glancing about. Against the far wall of the narthex, he spotted the confessional booth and moved reverently towards it, genuflecting to the tabernacle as he passed the central aisle.

"The diocesan bishop wasn't kidding," he murmured, opening the confessional door and tossing his overcoat onto the oak T-back chair squeezed inside. The church was empty other than a cooing pigeon perched on a roof brace above the high altar.

A guilty smirk as Rossi straightened his collar in the glazed doors of a large wood-framed noticeboard fixed to the back wall. He couldn't help but think the fancy dress was way over the top. When he'd suggested as much to Cathy, she quickly reminded him they were not playing Scopa. Rather, they were committing a crime of mutiny and sedition. "High treason," was how she'd put it. Punishable if caught by a thousand lashes, and a dark cell in a supermax federal prison alongside the worst of the worst.

Inside the Grind espresso bar, Cathy spoke on a burner phone with Sabine Reich, who was waiting for her in the London Transport Museum 400 metres away. "There's been a change of plan. Go to the Church of Corpus Christi on Maiden Lane. I'm in the confessional booth opposite the entrance," Cathy said, ringing off before Sabine had time to complain.

Ten minutes later Sabine descended the steps to the church's portico and flung open the door to the narthex. She charged towards the confessional with an angry frown on her face, convinced the whole thing was a hoax. Sabine stood and listened.

Sensing her hesitance, Rossi shifted in his chair, alerting her of his presence.

"Is someone there?" Sabine whispered, poking her head around the wooden screen that conceals the penitent from public gaze.

Rossi stayed silent, knowing Sabine expected to hear Cathy's voice.

"Am I meant to kneel?" Sabine asked, with a trace of German intonation.

Leaning forward, Rossi held his mouth close to the small mesh-covered opening and in a low voice said, "If you want to hear what I have to say, it would be advisable."

Sabine took half a step back. "Who the hell are you? Where's the lady from the phone?"

"Kneel."

Sabine stooped down and picked up an opaque plastic sleeve Rossi had placed earlier on the kneeler and then knelt. "Why the theatrics?"

"You're in London, reporting on the circle-A killings. Correct?" Rossi said. "I have information that'll light up your story."

"I'm all ears."

"Open the plastic sleeve."

Sabine did. Inside was a facsimile of Chief James's CIA identification card. "Who is he?"

"A senior CIA operative, murdered because he knew too much about the circle-A killings, as the press has dubbed them."

"Was his death reported?"

"His SUV was blown into a million pieces on the M11 three nights ago near Ugley Green. Unfortunately, he was at the wheel at the time."

"I read about it," Sabine said. "But there was no mention of him being CIA. That's news."

"His death is linked to the circle-A killings." Rossi paused for a reaction.

At that moment, Sabine shot a glance behind her. A vase of flowers standing on the high altar had toppled and was lying smashed on the tiled floor. "Is there someone else in the church?" she whispered, glancing nervously about.

"A trapped pigeon," Rossi assured her. In the distance, the faint sound of wings furiously flapping against a windowpane.

A short silence while Sabine regained her composure. "I'm not sure what you're telling me," she finally said.

"Conspiracy at the highest level."

"The queen, the tsar, the prime minister? Which highest level?"

Rossi crossed his arms and sat back in his seat. *A reasonable question.* "The number one tenant of 1600 Pennsylvania Avenue – 'the Chosen One.'"

"*That* highest level," Sabine said, her voice raised an octave.

Rossi stayed silent, waiting for her to catch up. But he needn't have worried.

"You mentioned the circle-A killings. How are the murders linked?"

"Best guess: they're extrajudicial. Carried out by dark forces assembled at the right hand of POTUS to prevent the collapse of the European project. And the CIA agent – they killed him for stumbling on the truth."

"Best guess? Sounds slapdash."

"That's why we're involving you. To shake the White House tree. See what drops out. Together we can arrive at the truth."

"And if we find it? What then?"

"USA go home," Rossi said. "We scream it from on top of the Matterhorn. Tell them straight. The people of Europe are not interested in their mad king's hermetically sealed neoconservative world. Extrajudicial executions are out of style. *Passé*. Europe still believes in humanity, democracy and the rule of law. Shall I write it for you?"

"Slow down, *amico mio*," Sabine said, picking up on Rossi's Italian accent. "You're losing me." Pause. "The purpose of the circle-A killings is to protect Europe. But how?"

"All victims were engaged in activities undermining European unity—"

"For instance?" Sabine asked, scribbling on a notepad.

Rossi shook his head, wondering whether Sabine was up to the job. "Haven't you already checked their backgrounds? You're an investigative journalist, for God's sake."

"Humour me."

"How long have we got?" Rossi paused then continued, not expecting an answer. "For instance, Edge laundered Russian money to fund Eurosceptic parties and politicians. Carlyle's casinos and brothels gathered information on Western leaders for passing onto the Russian security services. Zhukov sold Russian-made arms to despots in the Middle East and Africa. Arms used to bomb civilians resulting in mass migration to Europe… Shall I go on?"

"So, you're saying the black hats are being murdered by the white hats. The goodies killing the baddies. An interesting twist. Have I understood you correctly?"

"That's one way of looking at it."

A chilly gust of wind caught the narthex door and flung it open with a bang. Someone had entered. The click-clicking of high heels on the tiled floor. *Cathy?* Rossi thought. *Or perhaps Lawrence in his red dress?* He peeked out from behind the purple curtain covering the small lattice window in the booth's door. *Of course not.* A young blonde with lots of wild hair, dressed in black woollen culottes, a matching top, grey scarf and beige boots. A rich tourist abandoned by her husband for the day. Or maybe in cahoots with Sabine?

"And what about the anarchists? The circle-A monogram? Who's spinning that version?" Sabine asked, as the lady walked down the centre aisle towards the altar, filming herself with her iPhone on a selfie stick.

"White House right-wing fringe. Threw the press a cut of meat they recognised. You know how it works."

Rossi fell silent as if he had finished.

"That's *it*?" Sabine said, frustration in her voice. "I need more than that to avoid being stonewalled in Washington."

"The lame duck CIA operation is called Bright Star. The president's programme of extrajudicial killings is called Crusade. Say them both within earshot of the president and you're bound to evoke a response."

"Like getting pushed off a station platform into an oncoming express train."

"Sure, there's danger involved. I wouldn't lie to you."

"What else do you have?"

"Ennismore Garden Mews, Knightsbridge. You'll find a safe house occupied by three Green Berets. Find out what you can."

"Names?"

"Cleveland Jefferson, Ethan Rosenthal and Alfonzo Riccardo. All covers."

"Good. It's enough to demonstrate we've infiltrated their defences. It'll embolden the president's innocent peripheral. The White House will leak like an old wooden rowboat."

"Go rattle their cage," Rossi said. "I'll follow your progress with interest."

The narthex door slammed shut as Sabine exited. Cathy followed the *Frankfurter Allgemeine*'s gun journalist at a safe distance until she'd flagged down a black London hackney cab on the Strand and drove off west.

Still seated in the confessional booth waiting for Cathy to collect him, Rossi heard the click-clicking of high heels approaching. "Give me a break," he murmured to himself, pushing the edge of the curtain against the lattice opening.

A tap on the screen. "Father," the lady whispered, kneeling. Another tap. "Father, can you hear my confession?"

Rossi froze, thinking. *If the lady's an imposter, what does it matter?* But if she's in genuine need of absolution for offences committed against God, it would be a travesty to administer the Sacrament of Penance. *The greater good*, Rossi decided, sliding back the wooden window and turning his ear to the mesh-covered opening.

"Bless me, Father, for I have sinned," she read off her iPhone. "This is my first confession."

"Are you a Catholic, my child?"

"I'd like to be."

Rossi rolled his eyes. "Did Sabine Reich send you?"

"I hear voices in my head, Father," the lady said, as if she hadn't heard Rossi's question. "They're telling me to poison my husband."

"What on earth for?"

"He's a womaniser."

"Wouldn't it be better to divorce him and take half his money?"

"Where's the joy in that?"

"I think we're done here, lady," Rossi said, his tone harsh. "Can you please leave so I can lock up?"

The lady's head shot back. "Aren't you meant to help me? I'm a vulnerable woman in need."

"Lady, turn off your camera and go find your sad husband."

Cathy entered the church as the young lady stormed out. "Who was that?" she asked, opening the confessional door.

Rossi put his hand up to shield his eyes from the bright light streaming in through the narthex's large circular window. "A YouTube prankster, I suspect." A roll of the eyes. "Where's Sabine?"

"Long gone."

35

They rode the train past Cambridge to Waterbeach, then took a cab back to the Eagle, from where yesterday's journey had begun. A nip of Scotch in the RAF bar before strolling arm in arm to Fisher House, Rossi hauling a heavy shopping bag full of tapas and wine they'd bought in London.

"Good to be home," Rossi said, mounting the stairs.

"*Home?* You *have* settled in well, haven't you? I thought I detected a hint of a sexy Cambridge accent."

Setting the bag on the hallway floor, Rossi stooped low and plucked the strand of Cathy's hair from between the door and the frame. "No visitors."

Cathy turned the key in the lock and pushed warily on the door. "And no bang either."

"Do you think we're also developing a generalised anxiety disorder to go with our paranoia?" Rossi quipped.

"The threat is real, Enzo. Ask the chief," Cathy said, tossing Rossi's briefcase stuffed with yesterday's lingerie and underwear onto the end of his bed.

"Does that mean I need to check under my bicycle seat every time I throw my leg over?"

"I wouldn't bother."

Rossi set the takeaway on the writing desk then studied the label on the bottle of Chianti Classico. "How about a drop of red to celebrate a successful day?"

"We've earned it."

Coats hanging on the back of the door and shoes kicked into the corner, Rossi opened the wine. Cathy rinsed the glasses, emptying the swill into a ceramic pot of parched soil standing on the windowsill.

Rossi poured as Cathy removed the lids from the tapas.

"We're coming for you, Mr President," Cathy said, holding out her glass.

A clink, two long sips, then silence as Rossi tore apart the crackling baguette and Cathy loaded her paper plate with fried calamari, *pimientos de Padrón*, olives and a slice of tortilla.

Cathy settled on the edge of the bed, balancing her plate on her knee. "Have you prepared your slides for tomorrow's lecture, Enzo?"

"Not yet." Pause. "Here's an idea. *You* could present it for me. It's a subject you know well."

"Stupid arrogant men?"

"Concordats."

"Tomorrow morning?" A long thoughtful sip. "Sorry, I'm busy. I'm meeting Heroin Chic. Got some unanswered questions."

Rossi handed Cathy a piece of baguette topped with *jamón Ibérico*. "Be sure to arm yourself. I don't want to be the last man standing."

Cathy narrowed her eyes. "Because you couldn't live without me?"

"Be difficult," Rossi conceded. Another clink of glasses. "Who'd remind me what an arsehole I am?"

"Dishy Bella?"

A grin and a slow nod of the head. "Yes. I could see that happening with time."

"Moron!" Cathy said, her tone hot.

"Cathy, you're not fair. You know I only have eyes for you."

"Then you need an optometrist. You've got a bad case of strabismus."

A puzzled look.

"Wandering eye."

A dismissive breath. "I'm a single man, Cathy. I must find a mate to propagate before it's too late." Pause. "For my mother's sake."

"By gawking at their arses?" Cathy scoffed. "A sure-fire way of finding a wife."

"I don't get it, Cathy. Not to put too fine a point on it, *you* ditched me. This is of your making."

Cathy set her empty glass on the commode and slipped on her boots. "Let's talk about this when you've grown up."

"You could be waiting a long time."

Before Cathy made it to the door, her phone rang. "This has got to be Lawrence. I gave this burner number to the chief. It's unused."

"Answer it then."

Cathy put the phone on speaker. "Hello."

"Some news from the front. Three things," Lawrence said in an anxious whisper. "One – find Balls. I've heard the name murmured half a dozen times behind closed doors."

"Roger."

"Two – I'm almost certain it was Rosenthal who attached the IED to the underside of the chief's Jag. Ten minutes before the chief told the three wise men to go fuck themselves, Rosenthal returned from outside with dirty hands and wet knees. Like he'd been kneeling in a roadside puddle."

"Roger."

"Three – Agent Rattle's one of us. The chief swore to me she could be trusted. You be the judge."

Cathy waited. Nothing more. "Are you safe, Paul?"

"No. I feel like a dead man walking. If they want to take me out, there's little I can do about it. For now, I'm just waiting."

"Best to keep your mouth shut and act normal."

"Not likely." A chuckle. "I'm out dancing every night to cheer myself up."

"If you must. But do me a favour. Ditch your sexy red dress. Makes you too easy to spot," Cathy said, ringing off.

"How can you be so sure Lawrence is telling the truth?"

"I can't. But there comes a time when you've got to believe someone. Besides, Lawrence told us to find Balls. I've heard that name before. Robert Morton asked after him at the Fez Club."

"You still insist on staying put? Seems we now know as much as what got the chief killed."

"We're at no more risk here than any other cubbyhole. We've just got to be on our guard." Cathy moved about the room, measuring with her outstretched arms the area next to Rossi's bed. "There's plenty of space."

"For what? An indoor spar?"

Cathy tossed Rossi her room key. "Go fetch my mattress. We'll agree something with Mrs Tarbottom in the morning."

36

"You got someone down there?" Cathy joked, snuggled up under Rossi's duvet, her eyes closed.

"Sorry," Rossi grunted, between push-ups. "No gym."

Cathy rolled onto her side and opened one eye. Pitch black. "What's the time?"

"Six-thirty." Groan.

"Don't you hate winter?"

Rossi rotated onto his back. Sit-ups. "I like all seasons."

Flinging back the duvet, Cathy sat up and turned on the bedside lamp. "Coffee?" she asked, stepping over Rossi.

A grunt. "Is that your Gina Lollobrigida look?"

"I didn't want to get caught dashing to the bathroom wearing only panties."

"I can see that."

Cathy pirouetted in her black modal chemise nightdress. "You approve?"

"Can't get enough of it," Rossi said, propped up on his elbow admiring the lace.

Cathy turned on the electric kettle and warmed up the coffee machine. "Now, if you've done with gawking, check the *Frankfurter Allgemeine* site. See if Sabine's posted anything. And put something on."

"Doubt she has," Rossi said, springing to his feet and pulling on his jeans. "She'll wait until she has more of the story. Keep it exclusive as long as she can."

As the kettle boiled, Cathy warmed the espresso cups over the steam rising from the spout. "Blonde, brunette or redhead?"

"Raven with half a sugar."

"Anything online?" Cathy asked, raising her voice above the whirling of the coffee maker.

"Just her previous article, challenging the accepted view of the involvement of the anarchists."

Cathy set Rossi's coffee on the desk, kissed him on the top of the head, and sat on the bed.

"You're in a good mood this morning," Rossi said, reading the *La Gazzetta dello Sport*.

"And why not? We're almost done here."

Rossi shot Cathy a sideways glance. "How d'you figure that?"

"Now that we're aware of the extrajudicial killings, we know what to look for. And with Sabine Reich putting the right royal shits up the president's inner circle it won't take long for the good ship Crusade to spring a leak. A damn big leak, as the career hangers-on run for cover." Cathy paused, as if she had made her point, then added, "Next step is to smoke out Balls – and for that I have a plan."

"Happy to hear that. Does it involve torture or seduction?"

A grin and a nod. "Seduction – starting with Robert Morton. I need to get into his room and plant a bug. Hear the real narrative. Not the babblings of an upper-class boob."

"Can I watch?"

"No time. You've got a lecture to give. After which you must do a little romancing of your own."

"Bella?"

"She knows more than she's letting on."

Rossi sniffed under his armpit. "I need a shower."

"I'm first."

"How long will you be?"

"By the time you return with croissants and fresh orange juice, I'll have washed my hair."

Rossi motioned beyond the window with his eyes. "Out there on my own? What if I'm killed?"

"I'll eat downstairs."

37

After Rossi left Fisher House for his lecture, Cathy messaged Heroin Chic requesting audio-surveillance support. Plan agreed, Cathy then phoned Robert Morton. She reminded him of their dinner at the Hawk's Club and how he'd boasted the famed English novelist E. M. Forster had lived in his King's College room at the turn of the twentieth century.

Proclaiming *A Passage to India* the greatest work of literature of all time, Cathy declared her intention to come pay homage. They agreed lunch. Her treat. Scotch eggs, salad and pickles.

Two hours later, Cathy headed up to Market Hill with a packed lunch generously prepared by Mrs Tarbottom.

As Cathy wandered purposely amongst the market crowd searching for a present for Morton, Heroin Chic brushed past, artfully dropping two VOX voice activated transmitters into Cathy's open bag.

"How much for Jeremy Fisher?" Cathy pointed towards the corner of the top shelf behind the owner.

"You have an excellent eye, if you don't mind me saying. An original Jeremy Fisher doll complete with mackintosh and shiny galoshes," the owner said, supporting the small of her back with her free hand as she reached up. "Exactly as Beatrix Potter intended."

"How much?" Cathy repeated, examining the seams with the tops of her thumbs.

"Fifty pounds," the lady said, in a bold voice.

Cathy held out two twenty-pound notes.

"Here! Don't go waving it about, miss," the lady said, with a painful expression, "you'll have everyone wanting a discount."

Five minutes later, Cathy stood gazing across the lawn in the front court of King's College at the statue of Henry VI as she listened to the head porter's instructions.

"Is it true that E. M. Forster once lived at King's College?" Cathy asked.

"He did indeed, Ms Clarke."

"At Bodley's Court?"

A chuckle. "Did young Morton tell you that?"

Cathy smirked.

Dressed in tight jeans and a burgundy trench coat, with a bulky leather tote bag slung over her shoulder, Cathy followed the path along the Keynes Building, past the Old Provost's Lodge, until arriving at Bodley's Court. Two steps at a time, she ascended the T-staircase to the top floor and found Robert Morton's room.

Cathy slid her hand inside her bag, checked her handgun was in place, then pulled out Jeremy Fisher. She rapped loudly on the door.

"It's not locked," came the call from within.

"Robert, how I've missed you," Cathy said, throwing open her arms. "Come here and give me a hug."

Morton did, kissing her on both cheeks.

It was obvious from the smell he'd had a few beers to calm his young nerves. "This is for you," Cathy said, fighting back a smile, imagining Morton tearing at the guiltless amphibian like a rabid dog, searching for a hidden camera.

"How sweet. Thank you." Another hug.

"There are shadows because there are hills," Cathy said.

Confusion swept over Morton's face. "Where?"

"It's my favourite line from *A Room with a View*," Cathy said, standing at the mullioned window gazing out at King's College Bridge.

"Can I get you a beer, Ashley?"

Cathy pulled a large bottle of single malt and a small soda water from her bag. "Two glasses would be better."

"Coming up," Morton saluted, disappearing into the bedroom.

Cathy glanced about the seven-sided sitting room, looking for a place to hide a not-so-small VOX bug with its chunky nine-volt battery. A Japanese paper lantern pendant hung from the centre of the curved vaulted ceiling. *First place he'd look.* A disused stone fireplace permanently closed off with an iron screen. *Tricky.* A mantlepiece bestrewn with photographs and greeting cards. *Not likely.* A blue wall-to-wall carpet covering the uneven floor. *Stick out like dog's balls.* A cluttered writing desk and a comfortable chair. *He'd have to be blind.* A coffee table in front of a three-seater sofa. *Too obvious.* An upright piano dotted with more keepsakes. *Maybe.*

Cathy ran her fingers along the keyboard. Tuned, but a section was muted. "You didn't tell me you played the piano, Robert."

"No virtuoso," Morton said, standing in the bedroom doorway drying a glass with an old Princess Diana souvenir tea towel. "But I can bash out a tune."

Cathy picked up a framed photograph from on top of the piano. "Your family?"

"Mother, stepfather and half-sister. If you can call that a family?"

"Your mother looks a little Spanish?"

"A lot in fact. Her parents emigrated to Canada from Cuba when she was five."

"I thought all Cubans lived in Florida."

"Most. But not mine." Pause. "My mother's not welcome there. She's related to the late El Comandante."

"Holy Moses, Robert," Cathy said, with a sideways glance. "You're not a revolutionist, are you?"

A cheeky grin. "Do I look like one?"

Another photo. "Lord Melba, Percy and Professor Slack. Who's the lady? She's gorgeous."

Squinting, bottle of scotch in hand, Morton moved closer. "Percy's cousin, Bella."

"Not Natasha?"

"Who's Natasha? Morton asked, removing the foil wrapper from the single malt and pulling the cork.

"I thought you said…" Cathy balked. "Never mind."

"You promised me Scotch eggs and pickles."

"All in good time, Robert," she said, distracted by the trove of souvenirs and keepsakes before her eyes. Cathy picked up a birthday card, opened it, and read it aloud. "Happy Birthday, Bobby. Onward Christian soldiers, marching as to war. B."

"It's a song," Morton blurted out, as if the words had a hidden meaning.

"Who's B?" Cathy caught Morton's gaze. "Not the elusive Mr Balls?"

Morton winced as he poured two healthy shots. "You don't know him," he said, adding a splash of soda to his glass.

Another framed photograph. But Cathy didn't need to ask who they were. Professor Slack, Lord Percy, Morton and a fourth man. "Isn't that the US president's son-in-law?"

Beaming, Morton handed Cathy her drink.

"You move in elite circles, Robert."

"A chance meeting," Morton giggled. "I didn't even know who he was at the time."

A clink of glasses. "To Edward Morgan Forster and his journey to India," Cathy said, taking a sip, barely wetting her lips.

Morton took a gulp. Then another.

"Are you all right, Robert?" Cathy asked, setting the lunch on the coffee table. "You seem a little nervous."

"Never been better."

As Cathy shook and splashed the honey vinegar dressing over the salad, Morton fetched two plates and cutlery from his bedroom.

"Homemade?"

"Compliments of Mrs Tarbottom, the housekeeper at Fisher House," Cathy said, scooping salad onto his plate and topping it with an egg.

"Jolly nice," Morton declared, taking a bite. "Well done, Mrs Tarbottom."

"You're an all-rounder, Robert?" Cathy motioned towards a golf set standing near the writing desk.

"Cricket and shooting are more my scene. The golf clubs belong to a friend. It's a stupid game. You play all day without breaking a sweat."

"A good walk spoilt – who said that?"

"Lord Percy," Morton said, straight-faced.

For an hour they sat on the sofa eating, drinking, and chatting about Forster.

"You should hang his photograph on the wall," Cathy said, topping up his glass. "Impress your lady friends."

Slumped on the sofa, Morton turned his head towards Cathy. "I'll do it tomorrow."

Cathy sat up. "You're not falling asleep on me, Robert?"

"Not at all," Morton slurred, his chin resting on his chest.

Pivoting on the sofa, Cathy threw a leg over Morton and straddled his thighs. "Good," she said, pulling off his white, long-sleeve T-shirt.

Eyes rolling in his head, Morton yanked off Cathy's pullover.

"Robert, before I can show you my magnificent breasts, you must tell me the truth about the rifle range. Why did you make that call from the Fez Club?"

Robert looked up, opened mouthed, as Cathy dangled her breasts an inch above his flickering eyes. "Olivia made me do it."

"Olivia?" Cathy said, pinning Morton's groping hands to the sofa.

"She's one of the Experientialist's pussycats. She was worried Percy was taking a fancy to you. There's already enough competition amongst the girls without someone of your dimensions throwing their car keys in the ring."

"I'll take that as a compliment," Cathy smiled, releasing his wrists.

Face smothered between her warm heavy breasts, Morton flung his arms behind Cathy's back and fumbled with her bra band, searching for the hook fastening.

"Ouch," Cathy said, reaching back and capturing Morton's hand. Her thick chestnut hair was caught in the solid gold prongs of his clunky ruby ring.

"I'm not very good at this, am I?"

Cathy fought back a smile. "On the contrary, Robert. You're a tiger."

"Stuck fast, I'm afraid," Morton apologised, the ring wedged against his knuckle. "A family heirloom. Doesn't come off."

The threat of biting off his finger did the trick. The instant they relaxed, Morton's hand fell free and he resumed his search for the troublesome clasp.

"Let me help you," Cathy said, releasing the clip and allowing her bra to drop onto Morton's benumbed face. "You like?"

Morton tipped backwards as he looked up, mumbling something. Cathy smirked. With the gore of her bra resting on his nose and a triangular cup covering each eye, he reminded her of a big-eyed bug.

"Robert?"

No answer.

"Robert," Cathy repeated, slipping back into her bra and pullover.

Morton's cheeks were flushed. Cathy gave him a nudge. She felt his pulse. He had fallen into a deep sleep. The dyeless, powdered flunitrazepam she had added to his club soda back at Fisher House had done the trick.

Smoke alarm, wall socket or light switch? Cathy thought, glancing about. Whichever provided sufficient space to accommodate the bug and battery. Rifling through her bag, Cathy pulled out the two audio transmitters and a compact zipper case containing an electrician's tool set.

Behind the piano, Cathy spotted an unused plug socket with a switch. She snapped photos of the polished ebony upright before pulling it away from the wall. Removing a small slotted screwdriver from the tool case, she detached the socket cover and peered inside. "Perfect," she mumbled to herself, tucking the bug into the hollow.

The piano hard against the wall, Cathy checked the image on her smartphone. Satisfied everything was back the way she'd found it, she hurried to the bedroom to install the second bug. No mucking around. A few taps with the hammer and chisel to deepen the hole. *That should do it.*

Sweeping up the brick chippings and blowing away the dust that had fallen onto the skirting, Cathy rose and examined her handiwork.

Back in the sitting room, Cathy searched Morton's work desk. She snapped photos of anything of interest, which was not much. The laptop was password-secured. Cathy turned it over. Nothing written on the back. A check of the drawers. Nothing resembling a password. Lying next to it, Morton's mobile phone. Also locked. Old model – no fingerprint scanner.

A hunch. A tuned, partially muted piano. Cathy cleared the keepsakes from the top, lifted the lid and peered inside. Jackpot. A paper bag containing wads of large-denomination banknotes. Cathy estimated £40,000. *Enough to fund a small revolution*, she thought.

Morton stirred. Cathy shot him an anxious glance. But she need not have worried. After murmuring something imperceptible, he settled back to sleep.

The cash reposed back on the piano's hammers, Cathy lowered the lid and returned the framed photographs and cards to the top, again matching the image on her phone.

"Unless Robert is packing a radio frequency detector, I think we're good," she murmured to herself, speed-dialling Heroin Chic on a burner.

"How's the weather?" Cathy whispered down the line.
"Perfect."

"And now?" Cathy asked a moment later, standing by Morton's neatly made, queen-sized bed.

"Clear," Heroin Chic confirmed, ringing off.

Cathy glanced at her watch. The flunitrazepam dose was small for a man of Morton's size. Before he became coherent, she had one task remaining. To leave Morton with the unmistakable impression they had attempted sex.

Stripping down to her pink panties, Cathy straddled her naked host and peppered his cheeks with kisses. "Robert, Robert," she said, shaking him. "Don't go falling asleep on me."

Morton blinked his red eyes as he woke. "I've embarrassed myself, haven't I?" he slurred, in a dry whisper.

"It happens, Robert," Cathy sympathised, leaning over him, brushing her breasts against his lips.

Seemingly keen to rescue his reputation, Morton wrapped his arms around Cathy and pulled her towards him.

Morton was an attractive man so Cathy went with the flow. Stretching out on top of him, she ran her hand behind his head and kissed him. "Oh, Robert," she moaned, writhing on top of him in fake ecstasy.

But Morton had gone limp. His eyes fluttered on his expressionless face.

"Robert?" A slap on each cheek. Nothing. He had fallen back to sleep.

After pouring the remaining Scotch down the basin in the bedroom, Cathy cradled the bottle in Morton's forearm and gathered the evidence in her bag. Then, for effect, she covered his manhood with a spare pair of pink panties she had brought with her for that purpose.

A photo of Morton for the record, and she was gone.

38

Tired of her cramped Fisher House residence, Cathy dialled Rossi as she strode along the Gatehouse archway. "Enzo, it's me," she said, nodding to a porter as she exited through the lodge's double brass doors onto King's Parade. "You free?"

"Just finished a tutorial. I'm on my way back. Is there a problem?"

"Fisher House," Cathy said. "It feels like a prison. I'm going stir crazy staring at the four walls day and night. I need a break."

"That's what I've been *saying*. Let's find a safe house with a decent kitchen and a big bed."

"I meant let's go for a drink."

"Thought you'd been at it all afternoon."

"I was working," Cathy said, in a high tone. "It was

Morton doing the drinking. You know how intimidating I can be when playing the vamp." Laughter.

Seated at their usual table in the RAF bar, Cathy opened the photo album on her phone and passed it to Rossi. "Morton's family. Mother, stepfather and half-sister."

"Nice."

"Young Morton's maternal grandparents emigrated to Canada from Cuba in the 1970s. His grandmother has the distinction of being a distant cousin of *El Caballo*."

"Castro? That's certainly a good dinner party story. But where's the relevance?"

"Revolutionary blood runs through Morton's veins."

"I didn't know insurgency was a genetic disorder."

"Being rocked to sleep with Soviet Red Army songs and tales of the incredible feats of Che Guevara. It would scar you for life."

"Shades of Aldous Huxley's sleep-teaching?"

A nod as Cathy took back the phone and flicked to the next image. "Do you recognise anyone in this little ensemble?"

"Lord Percy, his father and the dishy Bella. The clown," Rossi said, pointing to a dumpy man wearing a white shirt, suspenders, and red-and-yellow-striped pants, "I've seen about on campus. Hard to miss. Who is he?"

"That's Professor Slack."

"The headbanger from the Fez Club? Percy's shooting instructor? The co-founder of the infamous Cambridge Experientialists?"

"And who said heavy drinking shrinks the brain?" Cathy held up her empty glass for a refill. "Your memory's fine."

While Rossi stood at the bar, the waitress approached. "Fish and chips?" she asked, already familiar with Cathy's order.

"Perhaps something different," Cathy said, reading the menu. "How's the steak and ale pie?"

"Best in England – so they say."

"Two times, with mash."

"*Ciao, signorina*," Rossi smiled, returning from the bar with the drinks.

"Back again," the waitress replied, adjusting the thin headband in her short dark hair.

"Can't keep away. Love those fish and chips."

"Sit down and stop making a fool of yourself, Enzo," Cathy quipped, as the waitress turned and left.

Rossi continued working through the photographs as Cathy described the day's events. With Heroin Chic listening to Morton's every word, it was only a matter of time. One false, incriminating word and they would be all over him.

"What happens if we've got the wrong man?" Rossi asked, not looking up from the screen.

"We haven't." Cathy leant forward and found the image of Morton with the president's son-in-law. "This might help convince you."

"Is he an idiot?" Rossi said, shooting Cathy a puzzled look. "This was on display for all to see?"

"Maybe he was trying to impress me?"

"With his stupidity?"

The waitress arrived with steak pies and set them on the table.

"What? No fish and chips?" Rossi said, in a flirting tone.

"You've already exceeded your limit for the month, Enzo," the waitress smirked with a wink.

Cathy shook her head. "Did *she* just call you Enzo? I thought the diminutive was for family members, close friends and lovers only?"

Rossi produced a sheepish smile. "She caught me at a weak moment."

"Her number?" Cathy said, holding out her hand.

Rossi searched his wallet, removed a scrap of paper and handed it to Cathy.

"Call me, Enzo," Cathy mocked, resting an index finger on her lips.

"It's not my fault." Gulp. "She put it in my hand. I couldn't just throw it away – could I?"

"You're pathetic, Lorenzo."

Rossi stared into his Laphroaig for a short while then changed the subject. "I take it Morton didn't identify Balls?"

"I tried but came up empty." Pause. "You're seeing Bella later, aren't you? Maybe you can ask her…"

"Without raising her suspicion?" Rossi puffed out his upper lip as he thought. "I doubt it."

As they ate, Cathy took back her phone and googled Sabine Reich, *Frankfurter Allgemeine Zeitung*. "No new postings," Cathy mumbled.

"Perhaps we should arrange a meeting," Rossi said. "Update her?"

"Let's wait and see if Morton talks in his sleep."

Cathy's phone rang. Blocked number. *Heroin Chic*, she thought. No doubt phoning to report Morton was up and about. "Hello."

"Weather's turned bad," Heroin Chic said. "All souls lost. Captain went down with the ship. We need to discuss funeral arrangements. Jeremy's house at six."

"Bugger," Cathy said, ringing off.

"A setback?"

"I sacrificed a pair of my best pink panties for nothing."

Rossi gazed over his glass at Cathy, waiting for a translation.

"Morton's dead."

39

Rossi stood on the Jesus Loch footbridge, gazing at *Moon Shadow* through the rising mist. Wispy white condensation rose from the boat's chimney flue. The blackout curtains were drawn closed, though a slither of light escaped from the edge of the stateroom window. Bella was expecting Rossi, but with Morton's death he was uneasy about what awaited him.

He ambled down Chesterton Road, scrutinising the shadows and the faces in the houses overlooking the river. Ahead of him the pistachio-green Vespa. He couldn't help but think of Natasha: another casualty of the "greater good".

Right hand in his overcoat pocket covering his Heckler & Koch pistol, he bounced down the steep grassy riverbank and boarded *Moon Shadow*. He rapped on the cabin door. Silence, so he turned the handle. Unlocked.

"Bella?" he called out, opening the door and descending the steps. "Bella?" he repeated.

"I'm in the shower."

"Shall I come back?"

Holding a towel to her breasts, Bella poked her head out into the corridor and caught Rossi's gaze. "Don't be silly. Pour yourself a drink and get comfortable. I'll be with you in a minute."

"I thought this was a dry boat?"

"Who told you that?"

"You did. When we first met."

"Oh yeah. I remember." An embarrassed chuckle. "I lied. What can I say? You were a complete stranger. A maniac, for all I knew." More laughter as the bathroom door clicked shut.

Rossi removed his overcoat and hat, hung them by the door, and moved to the galley in search of a drink. He opened the refrigerator. Milk and mineral water. *No thanks.* A warm bottle of champagne on the counter. *Pass.* He flung open the overhead cupboards. Glasses.

"*Naturalmente,*" Rossi murmured to himself, heading back to the cupboard next to the stairs where Natasha had stored her liquor. *Not there.* The expensive bottles of spirits and the shelving were gone; replaced by a shabby blue suitcase, a crate full of Egyptian copperware glinting like a pirate's treasure chest, a spanking new hookah with a green glass base, and a set of golf clubs.

As Rossi closed the cupboard door, he couldn't help but wonder why the sudden interest in golf. First Morton, now Bella.

Turning his ear towards the bathroom, he held his breath and listened. The sound of water running off Bella's back. Heart racing, he coerced the black and red Titleist golf bag into the open. Pulling his phone from his inside jacket pocket, he opened the image Cathy had taken in Morton's King's College room. As far as he could make out it was the same set. Another glance behind, and the rattle of a bath towel pulled from the rack. Frantically, Rossi snapped photographs from every perspective, returned the golf bag to the way he found it and shoved it back under the stairs. Done.

Keyed up, Rossi scurried back to the galley and poured himself a glass of water.

"Did you find the Scotch?" Bella asked, standing in the passageway wrapped in a white towel scarcely covering her backside. Whether aimed at arousing or distracting him, Rossi wasn't sure. Either way, it was working.

"No luck," Rossi said, looking her up and down.

With one hand at her chest holding up her towel, Bella moved to the cupboard under the saloon side of the dividing counter and released the magnetic door catch with her foot. "Down here."

The same cupboard Natasha kept her audio system, Rossi thought, as he squeezed past Bella, who was heading down the passageway towards the bedroom.

"Not bad for a dry vessel," Rossi called out, peering into the cabinet full of top-shelf booze. "Get you something?"

"Vodka and tonic. There's lime in the fridge and ice in the freezer. A highball glass if it's not too much trouble."

As Bella dressed, Rossi felt conflicted. His gut feeling was Bella and the bag had nothing to do with what was going on. But, then again, with beautiful ladies he was often wrong.

"That's better," Bella said, appearing from the passageway dressed in jeans and a brown off-the-shoulder Bardot jumper. "I wasn't sure you'd turn up so I went for a run."

"Why?"

Bella shot Rossi a sideways glance. "Because jogging improves cardiovascular health and burns calories. Ask your doctor if you don't believe me."

"I meant, why did you think I wouldn't come? I said I would."

Bella hesitated. "You're a busy man, Lorenzo." Pause. "And I'm a social butterfly with too much time on my hands."

"True," Rossi laughed, passing her the vodka and tonic. *Or perhaps you thought I'd be busy with Morton's death?*

"Either way," a clink of glasses, "I'm glad you're here."

"The pleasure's all mine," Rossi said, pulling his earlobe to prevent his eyes wandering to the opened mail tucked between a fourteen-piece kitchen knife set and the cabin wall.

Bella put down her glass. "Hope you're hungry," she said, opening the refrigerator door and removing a bunch of green asparagus, a packet of smoked salmon, and a small bottle of cream.

"Absolutely," Rossi lied.

"Good – you can help, then. But first, turn on some music. Choose something I like."

Rossi glanced about the saloon. "Where?"

Bella pointed to the sofa. "Lift the third cushion."

Rossi did. In the storage compartment under the seat, a large black boombox and a stack of CDs. "Don't tell me – you inherited this piece of nostalgia from your grandmother?"

"Close."

Rossi flicked through the disks. "Any genre as long as it's electronic?" Laughter. "Kraftwerk seems like a safe bet given you've got every one of their albums," Rossi said, inserting *The Man-Machine*.

"Perfect. Now come here." Bella handed him a bamboo cutting board and two shallots. "Finely chopped."

Rossi couldn't help but smile. Lunging for a knife, he knocked over the heavy wooden block, causing the mail to scatter on the counter.

"Sorry," he said, glancing at the address as he gathered up the letters. *Isabella Bats. P.O. Box 86G Cambridge, CB1.*

"What's so interesting?" Bella asked, watching Rossi's eyes.

"Bats. An old English name?" Rossi enquired, cursing himself for not being more patient.

"We've traced the family name back to before the Norman Conquest."

Rossi clumsily peeled and chopped the shallots. His large hands not suited to such a delicate task. "Bats – like in cricket bats and balls? Did I pronounce it correctly?"

"Like a true Englishman."

"Is that your nickname then?"

"Bats?" Bella asked, with raised eyebrows. "Hardly a nickname if it's my name."

"I meant balls."

To Rossi's relief, she pulled a face as if to say: you idiot.

Bella placed the asparagus on the chopping board in front of Rossi. "One-inch pieces cut diagonally. And no blood."

"I *can* cook, Bella."

"I keep forgetting you're a bachelor. Normally it's the married men chasing me."

Rossi was certain he wasn't doing any chasing. Still, he kept quiet. "Just shows how little we know about each other."

"Grab the big saucepan for the fettuccini." Bella pointed to the cupboard under the gas hob. "And the steamer for the asparagus."

Filling both pots with water, Rossi set them on the hob and turned the burners on full. "Anything else?"

"After you refresh my glass, I think you're done. Galley's excessively small for two."

"How many Bats are there in the UK?" Rossi asked, mixing another vodka and tonic. To him it was inconceivable Bella was the person Lawrence had overheard the three wise men discussing at the safe house.

"Down to one."

"No brothers, sisters, mad uncles, flirtatious aunts?"

"Just me, I'm afraid. I take the family name to the grave." Bella dropped the fettuccini into the boiling water. "Unless I have a child out of wedlock."

"Sport?"

Bella stood on one leg and extended the other high behind her body in arabesque. "Ballet."

"Nothing more active?"

"You know nothing about ballet, do you?"

"How hard can it be?" Rossi smirked, pulling the coffee table closer to the yellow sofa.

"There are place mats, cutlery and napkins in the wicker basket."

As Rossi set the table and changed one Kraftwerk album for another, Bella plated up.

They ate and chatted about nothing consequential. Neither mentioned Morton, golf or Balls. It was eleven o'clock before Rossi tore himself free from Bella's grip, insisting he needed to return to Fisher House to prepare for tomorrow. Prepare what, he didn't explain. A hug and a kiss and Rossi scurried off across Jesus Green back to Cathy.

40

Not wanting to alert his nosey neighbour, Lawrence removed his high heels before ascending the stairs. Safely inside, Lawrence switched on the television and poured himself a flute of champagne from the bottle he had open earlier. Backside resting against the kitchen bench, he scanned the channels searching for CNN.

A rap on the door. "I'll shoot her," Lawrence breathed, turning down the sound.

Another rap. Lawrence's weight on the ancient oaks betrayed him as he tiptoed towards the door.

"Jesse. It's me, Wendy – your downstairs neighbour." With a broad attractive smile, she held up a bottle of champagne wrapped in clear cellophane tied with a bow of red ribbon. "A little something to say welcome."

A short silence as Lawrence racked his brain searching for an excuse why he couldn't open the door. Other than it was late and he didn't bloody want to, nothing came to mind.

"Don't worry, I can't stay," Wendy said, her tone disarming.

Lawrence adjusted the padding in his panties, slipped back into his heels and removed the chain. "Sorry, I was getting ready for bed."

Wendy held out the gift. "Welcome to our terrace. Full of wonderful friendly people."

"That's kind of you, Wendy," Lawrence said, studying the bottle. "I'd invite you in, but I've got a busy day tomorrow."

"Call in sick," the brunette said, producing a pistol from the back of her jeans.

Lawrence gazed at her with a puzzled expression. "If this is a prank, it's not funny."

"Inside," Wendy ordered, with a thrust of her compact Smith & Wesson.

Lawrence was in no position to argue. She didn't look like someone who would miss from that range. Hands held away from his body, he shuffled deeper into the flat.

"Now, don't you look like a prat?" Wendy said, back-heeling the door closed.

"You sure you've got the right address, lady?"

Silence, as Wendy glanced about the room.

"Can't think what you want from me," Lawrence said, inching closer to a set of kitchen knives standing on the bench next to the toaster. "Do I know you?" he added, studying her face.

Wendy raised her aim to Lawrence's head. "You think that'll work, freak? On the sofa, and put these on," she ordered, lobbing him two pairs of nylon zip-tie cuffs. "Feet first."

"Who the fuck are you?" Lawrence growled, seated on the edge of the sofa bed threading his feet through the nylon hoops. "Unless you're from the morality police, you've got the wrong man."

"I'm a party organiser, specialising in TVs, TGs and curious cross-dressers – isn't it obvious?"

Lawrence wished it was true, pulling the handcuff straps tight with his teeth.

"Lie face down."

He did.

"You familiar with autoerotic asphyxiation, Paul?" Wendy asked, removing a pair of latex gloves from her jeans pocket and slipping them on.

Lawrence strained his neck looking back over his shoulder. "Not my thing," he said, surprised he hadn't asked his tormentor to explain a thing or two. Like, what evil act had he perpetrated to justify such an end? Sure, he was a CIA operative investigating an international conspiracy, but he was pocket change. Why him?

"It's like bungee jumping. You must try it once before you die."

"I'll put it on my list," Lawrence said, regretting his cooperation. *What was I thinking?* A bullet between the eyes was a more honourable death than asphyxiation in a sex game gone wrong.

"Don't put off until tomorrow what you can do today," Wendy taunted, planting her knee into the small of Lawrence's back.

"Who sent you? Is that too much to ask? The Russians? The office?" Pause. "The goons from the safe house."

"Not bad. You got it in three."

"But why?"

"No idea. Perhaps a betrayal of trust. You'll need to ask your friend Rosenthal."

Slipping a clear plastic bag over his head, Wendy pulled the drawstring closed.

Lawrence bucked and rolled, trying to dislodge his mount. But with his hands and legs tied, she was too strong for him. With a dizzying head-rush, Lawrence felt a high before losing consciousness, then his life. The abstruse choking game had claimed another victim. Only this time it was murder.

Collapsed on Lawrence's back, Wendy lay momentarily catching her breath. The only sound she could hear was stale air leaking from the bottom of the plastic bag. Propping herself up, she felt Lawrence's neck for a pulse on the carotid artery. There was none.

The killer moved to the front door, listened, then stuck her head out. Clear. Scurrying to the stairwell, she retrieved a cotton tote bag containing props to complete the illusion and brought it inside.

From deep in her jeans pocket, Wendy removed a switchblade knife. She again checked Lawrence's pulse before cutting through the nylon ties and replacing them with bondage cuffs, the same brand used on Natasha.

Job done. No one the wiser. With champagne, knife and plastic ties stuffed inside the tote bag, she exited the flat onto the shimmering Chelsea streets that had been washed clean with rain.

41

"You know why they killed Chief James, don't you?" Cathy said, bent over her laptop at Rossi's desk studying the photographs she'd downloaded from her mobile phone.

"Because he disapproved of the White House's latest secret war." Rossi paused, then added, "And he knew too much. A deadly combination."

"An intolerable risk for those producing the show."

"So why are we still alive? We know just as much."

"There's a difference," Cathy said, turning in her chair to face Rossi, who was pulling on his blue pony-print pyjama pants.

"Do you mind?"

Cathy huffed. "Nothing I haven't seen before."

Rossi turned his back. "What's the difference?"

"That's your bum."

Rossi sneered as he tied a bow in his pyjama cord. "The difference between us and your dead colleague? Why are we still alive?"

"Perhaps the three wise men have underestimated us. Blinded by their own cleverness."

"How reassuring. I feel a lot better," Rossi said, hanging his jacket in the wardrobe, which Mrs Tarbottom had shifted next to the commode to make room for a metal-framed double bed.

"Convinced we're too stupid to work out what they're up to."

"If that's the case, why kill Morton? He presented no real threat."

"I'd like to think they panicked. It's possible we were getting too close to him for comfort."

"We? It was you doing the seducing, not me."

"If Morton's my fault, Natasha's yours."

Rossi's lips tightened and his head shrunk into his shoulders, as if he was hearing the unpleasant truth spoken for the first time.

Seeing Rossi's reaction, Cathy moved on. "How was your dinner with Bella? Baked beans on toast?"

"Absolutely superb. That woman knows how to please," Rossi said, opening the photo gallery on his phone. "A lovely creamy pasta with smoked salmon and asparagus."

"You're going to have to try harder than that, Enzo."

Rossi handed his phone to Cathy. "Look familiar?"

"Holy shit!" Cathy swung around in her chair. With a flutter of fingers, she found the photo of the golf set she'd snapped in Morton's room earlier that day.

"It's got to be the same," Rossi said, reaching over Cathy from behind and pointing to the enamel St Andrews bag tag visible in both images.

"This is from *Moon Shadow*, right?"

A nod. "Hidden in a storage locker under the stairs. No opportunity to open the headcover. But, by weight and sound, I suspect the bag was full of clubs – not that I know anything about golf."

Immediately, the golf set took on a new importance as they speculated who had shifted it from Bodley's Court to *Moon Shadow*.

"It's Percy's boat. Perhaps he stashed them there?"

A tut. "Why not Bella?"

"Only if she collected them before Morton flew out the window. Murder's not part of her repertoire."

"She's innocent, Your Honour," Cathy mocked. "Just look at the way she wiggles her arse."

"Oh. I almost forgot." Rossi opened the wardrobe and removed a photograph from his jacket. "I found this in the ball pocket of the golf bag."

"Thought you said—"

"Sticking my fingers inside the side pocket was a little easier than removing the headcover jammed under the stairs—"

"Got it already, Mr Rossi," Cathy said, studying the four-by-six-inch coloured photograph.

"Any ideas?"

"Stone bridge in a park." Cathy googled. "Too vague."

"Stone bridge on a golf course," Rossi suggested.

"Bingo." Cathy clicked on the image and read the description. "Swilcan Bridge, Scotland. Famous small stone bridge in St Andrews Links, Scotland, spanning the Swilcan Burn between the first and eighteenth fairways on the Old Course. Built 700 years ago as a crossing for shepherds and their animals."

"A souvenir?"

"Sad-looking souvenir. A bird's-eye-view of nobody."

Cathy opened Google Street View and clicked on a blue dot located south of the bridge. An image of the structure and the surrounding area filled the screen. In the background, the treeless course and St Andrews Bay. Cathy panned right. In the distance the Royal and Ancient Clubhouse. Further east, the famed eighteenth hole bordered by The Links – a quiet road lined with terraced housing.

"The photograph must have been shot from here," Rossi said, pointing to a three-storey brownstone Victorian house at the west end of The Links, with large bay windows and an uninterrupted view to Swilcan Bridge.

Cathy turned the photo over. Nothing on the back. "A golf set, the Royal and Ancient Golf Club, a photograph of Swilcan Bridge taken from the first or second storey of a large Victorian house 100 metres away. What does it mean?"

"The location of the next assassination?"

Cathy nodded. "Has merit. Along with a dozen other scenarios."

"Who and when?" Rossi said, as if he hadn't heard. "If we can work that out, we'll catch them in the act."

"You make it sound so easy."

"We need to put *Moon Shadow* and those golf clubs under surveillance." Rossi paused. "Can we trust Heroin Chic?"

"We've been through that already, Enzo. Besides, we're not exactly inundated with choice. Unless you'd prefer Lawrence, or to pitch a tent yourself on Jesus Green?"

"I *could* move in with Bella."

"What? In your grandpa pyjamas?" Cathy said, making light of the suggestion. "I don't see that."

Rossi looked down and straightened the waist. "Was there a diary or a calendar hanging on Morton's wall?"

"With a date circled in red and the words 'next assassination' written underneath?" Cathy shook her head. "Afraid not."

"So, what do we do – apart from checking the St Andrews site for upcoming events?"

"Be patient and stay put. We don't have enough information to do much more."

"We could fly up to Dundee on the off chance."

"The headless chook syndrome? No thanks."

Rossi glanced at his Tag Heuer as he set it on the bedside table. Midnight. "Shall we try out the bed?" he said, dropping onto the edge and bouncing on the unresponsive horsehair mattress.

Obscured by the wardrobe door, Cathy undressed. "Can't wait."

"Then hop in," Rossi said, flinging back the white duvet.

"As soon as I've arranged surveillance of *Moon Shadow* and barnacle-back Bella," Cathy said, parading to the desk in her scant nightdress, and dialling Heroin Chic on the pink burner phone.

"Self-control," Rossi mumbled to himself.

42

The pink burner vibrated on the bedside table. Cathy gently removed Rossi's arm from around her waist and reached for the phone.

"Hello," she whispered, eyes closed.

"Your ship has sailed."

Cathy sat up, wide awake. Holding Rossi's watch to the dull light permeating through the cheap curtains, she checked the time. They had been asleep for less than an hour.

"*Sailed?* Where the hell to?" she coughed softly, already standing by the commode pouring herself a glass of Evian.

"Don't know. It had gone by the time we got there."

"Bugger," Cathy said, ringing off.

Setting aside the water, Cathy poured herself a Scotch. She then opened the curtains and sat down at the desk. Peering out at the night sky, she couldn't help but feel

Rossi was right. A long sip as she checked the travel time to St Andrews. *Eight hours by car.*

Cathy continued knocking away at the keyboard for another ten minutes until she found a suitable hotel. Rummaging through her handbag, she removed Ashley Clarke's credit card and booked a room at the Rusacks Hotel on The Links – the same street as the Victorian house they gauged to be the assassin's lair. Well, more than a room – a feature suite with a bay window and views of the eighteenth hole and the old bridge. Four hundred pounds per night, including breakfast. *One must eat.* And dining out was not an option in a town the size of St Andrews. You never know who you might bump into.

Rossi woke with the noise. "Can't sleep?" he croaked, rolling over to face Cathy.

"Get dressed. We're going for a drive."

Propped up on one elbow, Rossi checked the time: 2:30 a.m. "Have the Martians landed?"

"Heroin Chic phoned. *Moon Shadow* has slipped her moorings and vanished without a trace."

"How's that possible?" Rossi asked, shaking off the sleep.

"Your Bella's not as innocent as you'd like to think. Sailed the instant you went ashore."

Brow furrowed, Rossi shook his head. "It wasn't Bella. She couldn't even find the tiller."

"Get your mind above your navel, Enzo. She's played you like an oversexed schoolboy."

"What's the plan?" Rossi asked, ignoring the sideswipe.

"Golf."

"Don't like the game."

"We can take Monsignor Baker's car. Mrs Tarbottom told me he's on a spiritual retreat in Perth."

"Australia?"

"She didn't say and I didn't ask."

"The Morris Minor? Looks like a snail, goes like a snail."

"You got a better option this time of morning?"

Silence.

***

"Fortune favours the brave," Rossi proclaimed, turning into the Rusacks Hotel driveway.

"Four hundred and three miles in ten hours – a British record for a sage-coloured 1953 Morris Minor with a defective demister," Cathy said, wringing out the cloth she'd used to defog the windscreen and laying it on the dashboard to dry.

"If it wasn't for the snow, and stopping to change the wiper blades, we could have been talking world records."

Rossi popped the car boot.

"May I take those for you, sir?" the hotel porter asked, stepping in front of Rossi and removing two travel bags.

From the back seat of the car, Cathy extracted a large aluminium flight case entrusted to her by Heroin Chic. Inside: a pair of high-powered, long-distance binoculars; a tripod; four CCTV cameras; a DVR; a split-screen computer monitor; and miscellaneous cables.

Rossi tossed the keys to the valet. "Don't scratch it."

"What? *The Morris*?" the valet said, laughing.

Cathy and Rossi followed the porter through the covered entrance and up a short flight of stairs.

The lobby of the Victorian hotel was light and spacious. Decor of reds and olive floral and patterned fabric. Sofas placed in a geometric pattern about the room. And a large montage painting of golfing greats hung over a ceramic fireplace.

"Booking for Ashley Clarke," Cathy said, resting her handbag on the black marble counter, foraging for her purse.

"Welcome, Ms Clarke," the receptionist said, checking the booking. "We have a lovely corner suite overlooking the Old Course for you, as requested."

Cathy handed her the credit card. "The converted Victorian house at the end of the street?" Cathy pointed west. "Is it a private residence?"

"It's a mix of owner occupants and short-term rentals."

"You don't happen to know the name of the agent managing the property?"

The receptionist pulled a gold embossed business card from under the counter and handed it to Cathy. "You can find him in the One Under pub any day of the week from lunch time until closing."

"Propping up the bar and boasting about his fictional golf handicap," the porter added.

Cathy read the card aloud. "Forrest Estate Agents. Robin Forrest: Owner, Managing Director." Pause. "A *big* firm?"

The porter sniggered. "A one-man operation, ma'am."

"The One Under pub – is it far?" Cathy asked.

"You'll find it down the hallway, Ms Clarke. Open until late," the receptionist said, tossing the porter the room key. "Room 111 on the third floor. Enjoy your stay."

The porter stood the suitcases next to the king-size mahogany sleigh bed, which was covered with fluffy white pillows and linen. A red, green and gold tartan coverlet from some long-forgotten clan was draped over the bottom half of the bed, reminding them once more they were in Scotland.

"Are you here for the golf, Ms Clarke?" the porter asked, drawing open the curtains.

"Don't play."

Rossi moved into the adjoining sitting room and stood in the bay window, gazing at the bleak terrain swathed in snow. The golf course was deserted. Not even a groundsman to be seen. Two hundred metres west, he discerned Swilcan Bridge, its stone parapet poking out above the fresh white powder. Beyond the course, the windswept beach and the Angus coastline. To the right, the Royal and Ancient Clubhouse.

"Looks like we've missed nothing."

"They reckon it will be playable by Friday," the porter said, looking Rossi up and down. "Are you celebrities? Should I know you? So many these days, it's hard to keep up."

Thinking the question odd, Rossi turned from the window. "Within certain circles – why?"

"No clubs. No golf. And with the big charity tournament starting on Friday. That leaves celebrities," the porter said, milling about in the entrance anteroom for a tip.

Rossi dug his hand in his pocket. "Big event, you say?"

"Ten thousand pounds entry fee. All proceeds to the Heart Foundation."

"Who's playing?" Rossi asked, pulling out twenty pounds.

"One or two pros, but by far the majority are well-to-do suits. All rotters, if you ask me." The porter smirked, glancing past Rossi into the £400-a-night off-season suite. "Not like you, sir," he clarified with a stutter.

Pressing the twenty-pound note into the porter's welcoming hand, Rossi continued to probe. "Is there a full list of players and tee times displayed somewhere?"

"At the end of this street." The porter pointed east. "There's a large hospitality marquee next to the Golf Shop. You can see it from the window."

"You seem to know a lot about what goes on in St Andrews," Rossi said.

"I'm a local, sir. Before I landed this job, I caddied at the course. Lots of my friends still work there."

"Leave the poor boy alone," Cathy said, slapping Rossi on the backside. "You're mine for the weekend. No time for celebrity spotting. We're not leaving the room."

"Aren't I the lucky one?" Rossi smiled. "It's our fifth wedding anniversary."

The porter, his hand on the doorknob, launched a mischievous grin. "I'll hang the 'Do Not Disturb' notice on the door, sir."

"Good idea," Cathy said, pulling Rossi into the bedroom as the porter exited and the door clicked closed.

"What a cheeky sod."

"Scottish."

"Nice bed," Rossi said, removing his jacket and kicking off his shoes. "We can make like John and Yoko until the weather breaks."

Cathy held up her hand, halting Rossi's advance. "Someone's goofed up. I ordered twin beds."

"You crazy?" Rossi shoved Cathy onto the bed and straddled her. "I just told the porter we're here on our anniversary. You don't want to make a liar of me."

"Stand down, soldier," Cathy said, sliding from under him. "Here's the deal. You're off to the hospitality tent, and I'm due in the bar."

"Shouldn't it be the other way around?"

"Who is better qualified to persuade Forrest to abandon his beer and to show his apartment? You or me?" Cathy asked, running her hands sensually down her body.

Rossi climbed from the bed and slipped back into his shoes and jacket. "You."

"Correct. So, get going while I take a shower."

"If I'm not needed here…"

"You're not."

Feigning defeat, Rossi slung his coat over his shoulder and headed for the door.

"That's your phone, Enzo," Cathy called out from the bedroom.

Rossi patted his pocket. "Not mine."

Cathy removed Rossi's Vatican phone from the pocket of his travel bag. "Ray Charles? Seven Spanish Angels?"

"Oops! I must have packed it by mistake," Rossi murmured, almost to himself as he studied the display. "Hello."

"Inspector General, this is Sabine Reich from the *Frankfurter Allgemeine*."

Rossi froze, not believing his own ears.

"Inspector General?" Sabine repeated.

"Who the hell gave you my number?"

"You of all people should appreciate the need to protect a confidential source."

"And how did you know it was me?"

"It wasn't that difficult. An Italian-accented man playing priest with a cocksure *Amerikanerin*. After Moscow, your name immediately sprung to mind. Couldn't sleep not knowing I was right. So early next morning I hauled myself back to the Grind espresso bar. For the price of a cortado and a ten-pound tip, the barista turned his back while I snuck a look at the café's security camera. Mystery solved. Either you and Ms Doherty are rank amateurs or you think I'm stupid." Pause. Rossi refused to fill the silence, so Reich added. "Perhaps a bit of both?"

Gaze locked on Cathy's saucer-sized eyes, Rossi laid the phone on the bed and put it on speaker. "How can I help you, Ms Reich?"

"I'd like to run something past you. Off the record—"

"Can't it wait? Over the phone is not the best idea."

Ignoring Rossi, Sabine continued. "You'll be pleased to hear my source has confirmed the killings are indeed extrajudicial. Not an anarchist in sight. Exactly as you said – a White House-sponsored enterprise contrived to counter Russian efforts to break up Europe and NATO."

"How reliable is this source?"

"Infallible. One hundred per cent."

"Well, let's give it a big tick then." Rossi hesitated. "You wanted to clarify something?"

"Something you didn't mention in Corpus Christi."

"Go on."

"According to the same source, the president, being a good Republican, has farmed out the hostilities to Burning Bush Consulting – a military contractor owned by the president's son-in-law."

"Keeping it in the family," Rossi quipped. "Has a long tradition in American politics."

"The operation is called Genesis," Ms Reich continued. "Their mission is to keep Europe white and Christian by using whatever means necessary. And, like most modern wars, the president plans to keep his military at home and watch the campaign unfold on Fox News."

"Fund, train and equip a transitory ally's army to do the dying."

"In this case, my source tells me, the foot soldiers are like-minded members of the European establishment." Pause. "How am I going so far?"

"You've passed with flying colours," Rossi said, his head nodding in unison with Cathy's.

"Goes without saying," Sabine added, "there's nothing written down, nothing recorded. Cash in large suitcases. All deniable."

***

Grinning wildly, Cathy opened her travel bag and laid her clothes on the bed. In front of the large mirror above the vanity table, she held a short blue floral dress against her body. A twirl. She liked it, but mid-afternoon alone in a bar? *Far too obvious*, she thought, tossing it aside.

Washing her hair under the shower, Cathy thought how best to conduct surveillance of the targeted house. No buildings or structures opposite. Only mowed lawns and a clear sky. A vehicle parked at street level had its limitations. *A small, silent drone with a camera*, she thought, blow-drying her hair in the bathroom mirror. *Heroin Chic's bound to have one.*

Seated at the writing desk in the sitting room dressed in skin-tight jeans, riding boots and a navy long-sleeve polo, Cathy studied an image of Robin Forrest on his website as she phoned Heroin Chic – burner to burner.

"Mum mentioned you got a drone for your birthday," Cathy said, in thick Scottish. "Come up and play."

"I'm on my way."

"But don't tell Dad. Best to avoid another family squabble."

Admiring her firm pear-shaped backside in the mirror, Cathy dabbed musk perfume on her neck and wrists. "Lucky man," she murmured, dropping the hotel key into her handbag as she exited the room.

The course closure meant the bar was busy. Cathy spotted Robin Forrest as she entered. Slouched on the bar, as the porter had promised. She scanned the room.

Too many nooks and crannies and backs of heads to feel safe. Perhaps the assassin was lurking amongst the crowd waiting to pounce.

Cathy glided to the bar and took a seat two stools down from Forrest.

"I'm Jimmy," the barman said, setting a coaster on the counter. "What can I bring you?"

"A double Laphroaig and a small bottle of Evian on the side," Cathy said, crossing her legs with a wiggling of her backside as she settled.

"Pity about the weather," Forrest said, fiddling with a large ring of keys with coloured rubber caps.

"But it's beautiful," Cathy responded, with a sunny expression. "Like a fairy tale."

Forrest, a stout man in his mid-fifties with unkempt red hair and the ruddy complexion of a heavy drinker, swung around on his stool to face Cathy. "You're a golf widow?"

"Don't you need a husband to be one of those?"

"Or the equivalent thereof," Forrest winked. "A beau?"

"I'm here alone. And, yes, I hate golf."

Forrest dropped from his seat and mounted the bar stool next to Cathy. "Forgive me for asking – then why are you here?"

The barman set the Laphroaig on the coaster and opened the Evian. Taking up the small glass bottle, Cathy added a dash to the Scotch.

"Cheers," Cathy said, holding up her glass.

"*Do dheagh shlàinte*," Forrest reciprocated.

Cathy took a long sip, not bothering to ask for a translation.

"You were explaining why you're here," Forrest continued.

"I didn't realise I needed a reason."

"In my experience, bonnie hens don't sit alone in bars unless…"

The barman picked up a cloth and polished the counter close-by Forrest. "Perhaps the lady wishes to be alone, Robin."

"Nonsense. Terms and conditions up front. Avoids any nastiness post factum," Forrest said, throwing Cathy a wink.

"Mr Forrest, the lady's a guest of the hotel. I don't—"

"He's fine, Jimmy." Cathy pushed her glass towards the barman. "Same again."

"Put it on my tab, Jimmy," Forrest slurred.

"Is that an apology?"

"If you think one's necessary."

"In America we have a word for men like you," Cathy smiled.

Forrest straightened his back and puffed out his chest. "Forthright?"

"Close – arsehole."

"Well, you're in Scotland now, lassie. Where men call a spade a spade. So, none of your feminist shit, please."

Tilting her head, Cathy leered at Forrest. "Let me guess, *Robin*. I can call you Robin, can't I?" Out of the corner of her eye, Cathy glimpsed Rossi standing at the end of the bar. He seemed to be laughing.

"I prefer you didn't."

"Are you always—"

Rossi approached, holding out his hand. "Mr Forrest?"

"At your service," Forrest said, shaking Rossi's hand.

"Trust I'm not interrupting, *signorina*," Rossi said, turning to Cathy as if she was a complete stranger.

"Not at all," Cathy said. "The bill please, Jimmy."

Rossi turned back towards Forrest. "The lady at the front desk suggested I speak to you. I'm in the market for a property along the eighteenth fairway. I think the street's called The Links."

"You've come to the right man. Take a seat. What are you drinking?"

"Scotch," Rossi said, pulling up a stool.

Forrest signalled to the barman. "Scotch for my friend, Jimmy." The barman nodded. "Are you buying or renting, Mr…?"

"Romano." A shake of the hands. "I'm looking for an investment. Something like the three-storey Victorian house at the end of this street." Rossi pointed west and added. "With a bay window overlooking Swilcan Bridge."

43

"The lock's a wee bit tricky," Forrest said, pulling hard on the stubborn front door and turning the key two full revolutions.

Stepping inside, Rossi glanced about as though he was expecting someone. The common entrance hall was small with grey striped wallpaper and a black-and-white tiled floor. On his left, a potted plant on a narrow entryway table standing next to a burgundy panelled door. In front of him, a dark-wood staircase with turned newel posts. Above hung a coloured leaded-glass hall lantern, throwing off insufficient light for the windowless space.

"The building was completely rewired last year," Forrest gushed in his salesman's voice, lifting the cover of a large fuse box cabinet attached to the wall.

"How many apartments in this building?"

"Four, including the semi-basement. But I can only show you the top floor today," Forrest said, leading Rossi up the stairs. "The others are occupied."

On the first-floor landing, Rossi stopped next to the door and pretended to check his phone. Above the sound of Forrest's laboured breathing and heavy footsteps, he heard classical piano. *Moonlight Sonata*, he thought. His trip to Melba House with Monsignor Baker listening to Beethoven on the Morris's eight-track stereo sprung to mind. *Coincidence?*

"Keep coming," Forrest wheezed from above.

Rossi jogged up and joined him. "No wheelchair access?"

"It was never considered, Mr Romano." A breath. "This grand old lady predates the invention of the wheel, let alone the wheelchair." Laughter and coughing.

Forrest's ring of colour-coded keys jingled as he unlocked the door. The flat was sparsely furnished, making it appear larger than it was. From the entrance anteroom, Rossi could see West Sands Beach and the dark wild sea of St Andrews Bay. As he moved through the dining area to the front parlour, the golf course blanketed in snow came into view. "*Magnifica vista*," Rossi said.

"That there's a million-pound view of St Andrews, Mr Romano," Forrest declared. "With front-row seats at the home of golf thrown in for free. You can never be built out. It's yours forever."

Rossi stood in the Bay window gazing down at Swilcan Bridge. The vantage point was higher than the photograph he had found in the golf bag on Bella's boat. "Very nice. But one floor down would be better."

"It's a question of personal taste," Forrest said, fully opening the red tartan plaid ceiling-to-floor curtains framing the bay window. "But I prefer, from an investment point of view, this one. It's bigger and has heaps more character. Sloping ceilings, dormer windows and a loft in the master bedroom. And no one living above you entertaining in high heels."

"No way I could sneak a look? Maybe we could knock on the door and ask?" Rossi said, although it was the last thing he wanted. *Bumping into the assassin wouldn't be clever.*

"Sorry, Mr Romano. It's just not done. My guests pay for their privacy."

"Are they staying long?" Rossi prodded. "I could extend my stay a day or two."

"Until Saturday."

"Do they drink at the One Under? I could introduce myself. What do they look like?"

"Never met them."

"How's that possible?" Rossi smiled.

"The lady insisted I send the key to Cambridge. A post box number, if I recall."

"A lady?"

"A wife, a secretary – can't remember. Why so much interest?"

"Reads like a thriller. That's all."

Forrest glanced at his watch. "Is that the time?"

Rossi followed Forrest towards the door. "Is the price negotiable?" he asked, concerned he had raised the property manager's suspicion.

"You can offer more if you like," Forrest said, with a hearty laugh.

Rossi passed a waitress pushing a service trolley as he bustled down the corridor. Three slow knocks on the door before entering with the spare room key. "Cathy," he called out, hanging his mackintosh on the coat rack in the entrance anteroom.

"In here," Cathy said, enshrouded in a red Queen Anne high-back chair facing out towards the yellow sun setting behind dark grey nimbus clouds. A glass of red wine in her hand, she craned her neck around the side of the chair. "Pull up a pew and help me eat this."

Picking up the green checked Sherlock chair standing in the middle of the room, Rossi heaved it over the glass-top coffee table and set it down next to Cathy.

"You'll need a glass," Cathy said, snatching a black olive from the antipasto platter laid out on the console table by her side.

Rossi poured himself a glass of wine and sat down. "I can see you've been busy while I've been putting myself in harm's way."

"Hobnobbing with celebrities in the hospitality marquee and viewing a flat with Redbeard's grandfather could hardly be described as perilous. From what I saw, Forrest is no match for you. Would have needed a Sherpa just to make it to the top floor."

"Granted. He *was* a little sluggish." Rossi fished his phone from his pocket, opened the photo gallery and handed it to Cathy. "The complete list of players and tee times. Check if you recognise anyone."

Cathy moaned and shook her head as she scrolled down the page.

"Good chance they're all crooks," Rossi said, filling in the silence.

"True. But we're only interested in crooks working to undermine the European Union." Pause. "Nothing jumps out at me. Most of the names I don't recognise."

"Then you'd better get googling while I watch the sunset. Because without a name, we're nowhere."

"What did you find out about Forrest's first-floor guest?"

"Likes Beethoven. Other than that, nothing. Redbeard claims to have never met her."

"Her?" Cathy scoffed. "Aren't you a lousy judge of character?"

"So what? A woman from Cambridge made the booking. Doesn't mean it was Bella. Besides, Bella despises classical music. Now, if it was electronic, you'd have a case."

Cathy blew out a sharp puff of air. "No one despises classical music, Enzo. You made that up." Pause. "Anyway, we'll find out soon enough. Heroin Chic's on her way up with a camera drone."

Rossi chewed on a piece of gorgonzola, then said, "We must be careful. It could just as easily have been Heroin Chic who booked the flat. Did you consider that?"

"The chief insisted she was one of us. So, get over it."

"This is the same chief who got himself tangled in an FSB honey trap in Moscow. What was the swallow's name? Albina? Yeah, he's a great judge of women."

Cathy topped up Rossi's glass. "Point taken. But she's the only person I know with a fully equipped CIA, Dodge surveillance van in the UK right now."

"We trust her until we don't?"

A shrug. "That's the idea."

"It might be all academic, anyway. Because, unless the weather improves, there'll be no golf in St Andrews this weekend. And no one to kill. Our best chance of catching the assassin may have gone."

"Jimmy told me in the bar they're expecting heavy rain tonight followed by bright sunshine tomorrow."

"I read the forecast too," Rossi scoffed. "Six degrees and sunny. That's not sunshine in my books."

Cathy took a long sip of her wine. "Our friend the porter assures me the snow cover will disappear with the rain, and we'll wake up to the sound of errant golf balls pinging against the bedroom window."

The sun had set and cloud had eclipsed whatever moon there was. Rossi put down his glass and rose from his chair. Staying out of view, he drew closed the curtains and retrieved the aluminium flight case from the bedroom. "Best to set things up before I get too comfortable," he said, laying the case on the three-seater sofa.

Unfolding the lightweight tripod, Rossi stood it in the alcove of the bay window and attached the binoculars. He then switched off the room lights and placed three floor-level CCTV cameras between the curtains and the glass. One focusing on Swilcan Bridge, another on the hospitality marquee, and the third on the stretch of road running past the target's Victorian house.

"All this activity is making me feel guilty."

"You need a conscience for that," Rossi said, as he hooked up the cameras to the DVR and the split-screen monitor, already standing on the sideboard obstructing the television.

"How's that?" Rossi said, standing by the sofa, chin in hand, watching with pride the feed from the three cameras on the monitor.

Cathy rose and handed Rossi his glass. "Pretty damn good, Enzo. Now sit down and eat."

44

The next morning Cathy and Rossi woke, not to the sound of wayward golf balls clanging against the windowpanes, rather to hail stones clattering on the roofs and bonnets of vehicles parked on the street.

Rossi sprung out of bed and drew the curtains, slowly at first as he checked for faces loitering below, then all the way. Blue sky on both sides of a towering cumulonimbus cloud rising from St Andrews Bay. The snow covering the course had melted, leaving puddles of icy water in the dips and hollows.

"The porter was right," Rossi smiled. "By tomorrow, the course will be playable, and there will be an assassin in our midst."

Cathy groaned, pulling the duvet over her head. While Rossi slept, she'd worked through the night scanning the internet for information on the players taking part in the thirty-six-hole tournament.

The doorbell chimed, followed by a loud knock on the door. "Room service," came a young lady's voice.

Dressed only in his pony-print pyjama pants, Rossi grabbed change from his jeans pocket and opened the door. "Just here will be fine," he said, blocking the waitress's advance beyond the anteroom. "My wife's still asleep." Five pounds in change and she was gone.

The pink burner rang. Cathy's hand shot out, snatched the phone from the bedside table and retreated back under the duvet like a moray eel with a catch. "Good morning," Cathy said in a raspy whisper.

"I'm at the airport," Heroin Chic said down the line. "High winds have grounded all flights."

"Visibility?"

"Slithers of light framing a curtain of dense fog."

"Got it," Cathy said, ringing off.

Rossi wheeled the trolley into the sitting room and set the breakfast on the coffee table. "You hungry?" he called out.

"Why are you shouting?"

"Sorry..." Rossi did a double take, finding Cathy already in the doorway with her arms stretched high above her head, dressed in panties and a tank top. "Late night?"

"Someone had to check the list. One hundred and twenty-one names. No wonder the economy's in the shit. Everyone's playing golf."

Rossi looked Cathy up and down. "Where's your Gina Lollobrigida number?"

"In the wash. Why? See something you don't like?"

"Not at all," Rossi beamed. "Naked is good – very good."

Cathy returned to the bedroom and slipped on the hotel's white cotton bathrobe.

"Any news from the front?" Rossi called out, manoeuvring between the surveillance equipment as he opened the bay window curtains.

"The drone's grounded for now. Strong winds," Cathy said, back in the doorway, brushing her tangled chestnut hair.

Rossi sliced a crispy bread roll in half and topped it with prosciutto di Parma. "Are the apartment curtains open?"

"Closed. But the lights are on so someone's in." Pause. "As much as I dislike it, we must show some patience. It's just a matter of time before our person of interest gets curious and pokes his beady eyes out."

"How did you go last night? Any luck with identifying the assassin's quarry?"

"Familiar names, but no one stuck out. All legitimate businessmen. Just be sure to bolt your doors and windows."

Rossi shot Cathy a puzzled look. "Is that a no?"

"A work in progress," Cathy smiled, buttering her toast.

"What?" Rossi said, catching the glint in her honey eyes. "You've got something. Out with it."

"If I'm not mistaken, two players have entered under *summer names*. Bloom and Mulligan."

"I think we can assume they're aliases."

A bite of toast and a sip of fresh orange juice. "And we know three others."

"Speed it up, Cathy. This isn't a game show."

"What's Monsignor Baker's Christian name?"

"Pass. Next question."

"Oliver."

"How the hell do you know that?"

"Point is, there's an Oliver Baker scheduled to tee off tomorrow morning at 9:45." Rossi's mouth opened but nothing came out, so Cathy continued. "His playing partners are Seabert Slack." Pause. "You asleep, Enzo? Professor Slack."

Rossi's face lit up. "Lord Percy's shooting instructor?"

"And the third is listed as a TBA. But I can guess who it is."

"Lord Percy?"

A smile and a nod as Cathy poured herself a coffee from the thermal carafe.

"That makes no sense at all. Why would they make themselves so obvious at the scene of an assassination? Serious Crimes would be straight on to them."

Coffee cradled in both hands, Cathy moved to the bay window and gazed out at the clearing sky. "That's what I thought. And there can be only one explanation—"

"None of them are the assassin," Rossi broke in.

"You'd think so," Cathy nodded. "But they're all known to him. And rather well, I suppose. My guess is our killer uses them to glean information about his target by overhearing casual conversations within their tight little circle of privilege."

"Prime suspects?"

"Natasha – dead; Robert Morton – dead. That leaves Bella. But she's too *beautiful* to be the killer."

"If you say so."

Cathy twisted towards the west-facing canted window. Something had caught her eye. "Christ almighty," she blurted out. "Is that who I think it is?"

Rossi raised his gaze to the split-screen monitor. He glimpsed the back of a man shuffling towards the sage-green bulbous beast. "Monsignor Baker!"

Dashing to the bedroom, Cathy returned with her phone. "We must neutralise him."

Rossi shot Cathy a concerned look as she scurried to the west window overlooking the car park. "In the CIA vernacular, doesn't that mean kill?"

"Most of the time." Laughter.

Rossi didn't get the joke. "What are you planning?"

"To tell him the truth," Cathy said, speed-dialling the monsignor. "Or part thereof."

"You thought this through?"

Still at the side window, Cathy watched as the monsignor checked his screen. "Why isn't he answering?"

Rossi grabbed his Vatican phone and dialled for himself.

"Good morning, Lorenzo," the monsignor answered, as he circled the Morris Minor with a muddled expression. "Not a chance call, I suspect."

"Have you eaten breakfast, Monsignor?"

"Two hours ago," the cleric said, looking up at the hotel through bushy eyebrows.

Cathy shot back from the window, pulling her bare-chested ex-fiancé with her. "Don't want to freak him out."

"Perhaps you can come up for coffee, Monsignor? Room 111."

A few minutes later came a rap on the door.

Barefoot, dressed in jeans and a white T-shirt, Rossi turned the handle. "I owe you an explanation, Monsignor," he said in a self-effacing tone.

"For hijacking my old friend?"

"Not only," Rossi replied, ushering his surprised visitor into the sitting room.

Monsignor Baker glanced about, then gestured with a nod of his head towards the surveillance equipment in the bay window alcove. "Didn't pick you as a voyeur, Lorenzo."

"Depends on your definition of a peeping Tom," Cathy said, standing behind him in the doorway, dressed in a grey sweater dress and black leggings, her long hair tied loosely in a bun.

"So, what do we have here? I'd heard the two of you had formed a warm bond."

"Has Mrs Tarbottom been talking out of school?" Cathy joked.

"That would be telling," the monsignor said, lowering himself onto the three-seater sofa facing the split-screen monitor. "Now, where's that coffee you promised me?"

Rossi picked up the hotel phone. "I'll order a fresh pot."

Pushing back in his seat, the monsignor made himself comfortable. "Well then, Cathy, what's this all about?"

Rossi shot the monsignor a look as he sat down. Had he misheard? "You mean Ashley."

"I might look dull, but I can assure you I'm not," the monsignor said in an amiable voice. "You're Lorenzo's fiancée – Catherine Doherty."

Rossi wasn't sure whether to deny it or to update the cleric on the status of their relationship. "How long have you known?"

"My dear friend Archbishop Joseph Esposito phoned me when you first arrived. He asked me to take special care of you. Told me about Moscow. How you planned to marry the CIA agent who helped recover the Concordat. And how things didn't work out."

Movement on the split-screen. A couple standing on Swilcan Bridge grabbed their attention. Tourists.

"Then when Cathy turned up," the monsignor continued. "It was clear you knew each other. I put two and two together and did a little snooping."

"You got me." Cathy shrugged. "Who else knows?"

"No idea. It's our little secret as far as I know. No one's heard it from me."

The doorbell chimed. "Room service."

"I'll get it," Cathy said, moving to the anteroom and returning a minute later carrying a fresh carafe of coffee and three cups on a tray.

"Leaving aside the small matter of my car, Lorenzo, perhaps you can explain to me what you're doing here in St Andrews." A nervous laugh. "The bishop hasn't sent you to spy on me?"

"Half an hour ago we thought you were in retreat."

"I am," the monsignor said, watching Cathy pour the coffee. "Or at least I was – at St Mary's Monastery, in Perth. Some twenty-five miles to the west. Finished up last night."

"Then you're on your way back to Cambridge?" Rossi suggested.

The monsignor's gaze dropped to the floor. "In a roundabout way. Lord Percy's taking part in the charity golf tournament tomorrow and Saturday. He invited me to join in. Can't pass up an opportunity like that, Lorenzo – I'm a keen golfer, you see."

"Lucky you," Cathy said, wandering over to the window.

"That's me," the monsignor continued. "What about the two of you? Why are you here? From what you've told me, Lorenzo, golf's not your thing."

"A romantic weekend," Rossi said, not expecting to be believed.

Monsignor Baker leant back and shook his head. "I don't think so."

A short silence before Rossi rose from the sofa with his coffee and joined Cathy in the bay window alcove. "He could prove useful…"

"But can we trust him?" Cathy said in a soft voice.

"What are we risking? He already knows enough to torpedo the mission."

A nod. "Then we reveal as little as possible. Enough to solicit his cooperation. No more."

"Are these croissants taken?" the monsignor asked, as Cathy sat down on the Sherlock chair to his left.

"Help yourself, Monsignor," Rossi said, resting his backside on the sideboard.

With everyone settled, Rossi turned to Cathy and gestured with a nod for her to start.

"Monsignor, you've heard of the circle-A killings?" Cathy said, studying his reaction.

"The *Forbes* list murders?" he said, throwing Rossi a glance. "I witnessed a killing first hand myself – at Melba House. A Russian oligarch called Zhukov."

"Lorenzo and I are investigating these murders."

"How exciting," the monsignor said, biting into his croissant.

"We've established a strong link back to Lord Percy."

Filling his lungs to proclaim Percy's innocence, the monsignor inhaled a mouthful of flaky pastry. Coughing and sputtering, he stared bug-eyed at the empty glasses on the coffee table, then at Rossi.

"Connected – not involved," Rossi said, pouring water into the cleric's glass.

"Lord Percy knew all the victims," Cathy continued, as she thumped the monsignor between the shoulder blades with the heel of her hand.

A sip of water. Then another. "In the circles he moves," the monsignor wheezed, "everyone knows each other. That doesn't mean he's the killer."

"We don't believe he's the killer either, Monsignor. But we suppose the assassin is well acquainted with Lord Percy and is using him to garner information about his targets."

"I'm not with you, Cathy."

"For instance, in casual conversation, Percy mentions to our assassin he's off to St Andrews for a weekend of golf with his latest business partners: Mr Filthy and Mr Rich."

"If you're an assassin, that's all you need," Rossi added.

"How close is this acquaintance?"

Cathy gave a faint shrug. "Someone he trusts with that sort of information."

"Not sure I agree," the monsignor said. "Percy likes to show off. A few drinks and he'll blurt out what the queen had for breakfast." Pause. "Could be anyone at the Fez Club." A cheeky smile. "Not that I've ever been there."

"Besides yourself and Professor Slack, who else has Percy invited to St Andrews?"

"Nobody that I know of. Mind you, I've only just arrived. Seen no one. Dropped my bag off at Lord Percy's cottage, grabbed a bite to eat, then went for a walk."

Not the answer they'd hoped for.

Rossi dragged over the Queen Anne chair from where they ate last night and sat down opposite Cathy, on the monsignor's right. He opened the list of players on his mobile phone. "Bloom and Mulligan. Do the names mean anything to you, Monsignor?"

"Other than *Ulysses*, no."

"They tee off in front of you tomorrow."

"Who's the third member of their group – Stephen Dedalus?" The monsignor chuckled.

Rossi checked his phone again. "Albert Toth."

The monsignor shook his head. "Sounds Hungarian. Perhaps I'll meet him later today. Percy's organised a fundraising lunch at his cottage."

"Which is where?" Cathy asked, sitting forward and topping up her orange juice.

"It's a big place on The Scores opposite the ruins of St Andrews castle with a haunting view of the sea." Monsignor Baker glanced out the window to get his bearings. "A mile east of here."

"That's a fair hike. What brought you all the way down here?" Cathy asked.

"The chance of snapping a selfie on Swilcan Bridge while the course is closed. It's my first time here."

45

Not long after Monsignor Baker departed, Cathy's pink burner rang. "Good news, I hope," she said to Rossi, who was peering through the binoculars at the comings and goings around the hospitality marquee.

Cathy snatched the phone from the sideboard. "Still grounded?"

"Afraid so. Zero visibility through a curtain of fog," Heroin Chic said, down the line. "No sign of it lifting."

Cathy moved to the window and gazed out at a family of seagulls standing one-legged in the last puddle on the eighteenth fairway under glorious sunshine.

"Could be like this all day," Heroin Chic said, breaking the silence. "Any ideas?"

"I'll get back to you," Cathy said, ringing off.

"Problem?" Rossi asked, straightening and arching his back.

"Who doesn't open their curtains on a day like today? Particularly if you're here to smack a little white ball around the most famous golf course in the world."

"Someone that's not here to play golf."

"We're running out of time, Enzo. We need to know who's behind the curtain."

"What if we're wrong?"

Cathy pursed her lips and shook her head. "We're not. I can feel it in my water."

"Poor you," Rossi said, following her to the bedroom.

"Get out while I change," Cathy commanded, pulling her jumper over her head.

Rossi didn't move. "Going somewhere?"

"I think I know how to persuade the gunman to let the sunshine in without freaking him out."

"By throwing pebbles at the window?" Rossi said, leering at Cathy's silky arched back. "It'll never work."

Folding one arm over her breasts, Cathy pushed Rossi towards the door. "We can cut off the electricity to the flat. The sniper can't sit there in the dark all day. He'll have to open the curtains."

"Or light some candles until an electrician shows up."

"Thanks to your fancy footwork, we know the fuse box is unlocked at the bottom of the stairs," Cathy went on, half to herself. "So, it's only a matter of getting inside."

"And how are you going to manage that?"

"With Redbeard's key," Cathy said, fossicking in her suitcase. "You didn't notice the colour of the key he used to show you the flat?"

Rossi smiled. "Pink. Definitely pink. No doubt about it. It reminded me of you. Well, at least of your lingerie." Pause. "And, come to think of it, he used the same key to open the flat door. Could have been a master."

"Good," Cathy said, fastening her pink bra. "Now go downstairs and see whether Forrest is in the bar."

"*Sì, Capo Supremo*," Rossi saluted.

"And check if his keys are lying there like before."

Cathy gazed about as she entered the One Under pub. With the improved weather the place was almost empty. Sitting at the far end of the bar, Heroin Chic glanced over but showed no familiarity. On the stool next to her was Robin Forrest; his cigarettes and keys abandoned six stools down. *Perfect*, Cathy thought, strutting across to where Redbeard had set up shop before trying his luck with the conservatively dressed Heroin Chic. *Lesson learnt.*

"Where's Jimmy?" Cathy asked, setting her bag on the bar next to Forrest's jumble of keys.

"Helping at the hospitality tent," the burly, square-jawed barman said, in indecipherable Scottish.

Cathy knitted her brow. "Sorry?"

"He's off today, madam," the Scot said, enunciating every word. "Now, what can I get you?"

"A large Laphroaig…" Cathy squinted at the row of bottles on the shelf. "The Triple Wood."

Forrest's head turned at the sound of Cathy's voice. "How's tricks, lassie?"

Not my name. Cathy looked straight ahead as if she hadn't heard.

"A double Triple Wood," the barman said, laying down a coaster and setting the glass on top. "Ma name's also Jimmy."

"Makes it easy."

"Here's to ye, lassie!" Redbeard said, holding up his beer.

This time Cathy reciprocated with a nod and a sip of Scotch.

With a touching of knees and a caressing of hands, it wasn't long before Heroin Chic regained Redbeard's undivided attention.

With an eye on Redbeard in the mirrored liquor shelf, Cathy unzipped her bag and laid the opening near the ring of colourful keys. Taking her cue, Heroin Chic pulled Redbeard close and whispered sweet nothings in his hairy ear. Cathy swooped, brushing the keys into her bag. Heaping her cardigan on the bar where the keys once laid, she dropped softly from the stool.

As Cathy flitted to the ladies', Redbeard glanced down at the bar in front of him, then back over his shoulder towards Cathy's cardigan.

With an alluring smile, Heroin Chic rested two fingers on Redbeard's chin and turned his gaze back to hers. "Have one of mine," she said, opening her clutch purse and producing a packet of cigarettes and a gold lighter. The same brand and kind smoked by the would-be real estate mogul, readied on Cathy's directive for just such a contingency. "But before we go outside finish your story."

Standing at the countertop handbasin nearest the door, Cathy coolly threaded the pink key off the heavy metal ring and squeezed it into her jeans pocket. Keys back in her bag, she returned quickly and softly to the bar and sat down.

A slight jingle as Cathy laid her open bag on top of her cardigan, slipped her fingers inside and gently coaxed Redbeard's keys onto the bar next to his cigarettes. An anxious glance in the mirror as Redbeard shifted his weight on the stool. Cathy needn't have worried. He was too mesmerised by Heroin Chic to pay her the slightest bit of attention.

"Bill please," Cathy said to Jimmy, who was filling peanut bowls nearby.

"Right away, miss," Jimmy said, moving to the cash register at the other end.

With the keys back on the counter, Cathy put on her cardigan, dropped twenty pounds on the bar, and headed to the reception.

"I'm expecting a delivery," Cathy said, scanning the room key boxes.

The receptionist reached under the counter and handed Cathy a sealed parcel. "Here you are, Ms Clarke. Enjoy what's left of your day."

Cathy peered out from the hotel window towards the surveillance van parked on a service road thirty metres past the Victorian house. A double flick of the headlights would indicate Heroin Chic had thrown off Redbeard and was now inside the Dodge Ram preparing the camera drone for its mission.

"That was the first signal," Rossi said, seated on the sofa in the dark, studying the split-screen monitor. "Your chance to shine."

Cathy slipped on her coat, tucked her hair under her fiddler cap, slung her tote bag over her shoulder and headed to the door. "Wish me luck."

"You don't need it." Rossi smiled, not taking his eyes off the screen.

Under a clear maritime twilight, Cathy strolled towards the Victorian house illuminated by bright streetlamps, biding her time until Heroin Chic signalled "good to go". A glance back at the Rusacks Hotel and the vague outline of Rossi silhouetted against the hazy blue glow from the CCTV monitor. She thought she could make out Rossi's reassuring smile but she wasn't sure.

A second flash of headlights and, if she listened hard enough, the buzzing of the CIA's best-in-class quadcopter mounted with a powerful twenty-megapixel one-inch sensor camera. Cathy walked the three sides of the corner block checking for light coming from behind the curtains. Other than the target's first-floor apartment, the house appeared empty.

"Here goes nothing," Cathy murmured to herself, marching up the steps. Pulling hard on the door, she turned the key then entered. Attached to the wall at the bottom of the stairs was the fuse cabinet, as promised. A smile of relief as she lifted the cover. Forrest had labelled the fuses for each floor.

Fishing in her bag, Cathy removed the kitchen butane blow torch Heroin Chic had delivered to the hotel reception. Testing it, she pulled the trigger. A short, fat, pale-blue flame shot out of the nozzle. "That'll work," Cathy mumbled to herself, flipping off the first-floor circuit breaker.

An angry scream from above brought a smirk to Cathy's face as she held the butane flame to the switch, melting it in the off position. With a lung full of air, Cathy extinguished the fire, then closed the fuse cabinet cover. As the front door clicked closed behind her, Cathy was sure she heard a heavy curtain being drawn open in the flat above.

46

It wasn't until dinnertime that Cathy received the drone images from her one-person surveillance team, accompanied by the godawful news: Lawrence had been found dead in his Chelsea flat, dressed as a woman with a plastic bag over his head.

Although Cathy had known Lawrence for less than three months, she felt nauseous, as though she'd been punched in the guts.

"They'll pay for this," Rossi said, his voice cold and calculating.

Cathy sat up straight on the sofa with her laptop balanced on her knees and opened the attachments. "But, for now, we stay focused."

"What the hell is that?" Rossi said, leaning into Cathy for a better view. "That's absurd."

"Unless you believe in ghosts," Cathy said, staring furrow-browed at a still photograph of Robert Morton drawing open the curtains, his face lit by the glow from the streetlamp standing outside his window.

"Does he have a brother?" Rossi offered.

"I didn't think to question it. We've been had," Cathy said, flicking through more images. "But by who?"

"Is it possible you misunderstood her? The two of you are always speaking gibberish."

Cathy sprung to her feet, grabbed the pink burner from the sideboard and speed-dialled. "Let's find out."

Heroin Chic picked up on the first ring.

"Am I seeing things?" Cathy asked.

"I can't explain it." Silence, so Heroin Chic continued. "I know what I heard. Someone took off. Though there was too much static on the line to be certain about the identity of the pilot. And, remember, I wasn't there for the landing. Too busy sweeping the room. By the time I arrived the plane was in the hanger. Pilot's name came courtesy of Ohio."

Cathy rang off.

"Are you sure it's Morton?" Rossi asked, stooped over Cathy's laptop. "You know him better than most."

"The images are too grainy for me to be one hundred per cent certain."

"How did Heroin Chic get it so wrong? She had ears in both rooms, for Christ's sake."

"She confirmed someone went out of the window. But she couldn't be sure from the audio it was Morton. Lieutenant Abbott – formerly known as Cleveland Jefferson – provided her with that information."

"Was her arse glued to her seat? Didn't she think of dashing downstairs and checking for herself?"

"Rattle's number one priority was to recover the audio bugs before the police sealed Morton's room." Cathy paused, waiting for a nod of agreement from Rossi. "By the time she got downstairs the victim was under a forensic tent."

A short silence as Cathy pulled the cork from yesterday's bottle of Scotch and poured two glasses.

"And you believe her?"

"We've been through that before, Enzo. We trust her until we don't."

"Have another look," Rossi said, turning the laptop screen towards Cathy. "Is it Morton or not?"

Cathy bit the meat of her index finger as she thought. "If Morton's still alive, it's him. If he's dead – it can't be."

The doorbell chimed. Cathy and Rossi locked eyes and held their breath. They hadn't ordered room service, and the "Do Not Disturb" notice was hanging in the corridor. Cathy tiptoed into the anteroom.

A light rap on the door. "Inspector General," a voice whispered.

Peering through the spyhole, Cathy turned the handle. "Come in."

"This is a surprise, Monsignor Baker," Rossi said, struggling to mask his annoyance. "Trust you weren't followed."

"No one knows I'm here," the monsignor said, pointing his staghorn walking stick at his muddy hiking boots. "Told Percy I was off to explore the ruins of the Church of St Mary on the Rocks."

Rossi shot him a sideways glance. "In the dark?"

"To be sure, Lorenzo. Church ruins at night are at their spiritual best."

"Scotch, Monsignor?" Cathy asked, readying another glass.

The cleric removed his fleece jacket and tossed it over the back of the Sherlock chair. "Don't mind if I do."

"How did your lunch go?" Rossi asked.

"Marvellous," the monsignor replied, holding up an approving thumb. "Haggis with neeps and tatties." Pause. "That's mashed potato and turnips, for the uninitiated. Washed down with a single malt."

Rossi rephrased the question. "Did you find out anything?"

"Bloom and Mulligan are Albert Tooth's bodyguards. Good golfers, from what I hear." A long sip of his Scotch. "They both play off scratch," the monsignor added in an impressed tone.

"And Albert Toth?"

"He's a duffer," the monsignor smirked, lowering his ample body onto the Sherlock chair.

Cathy frowned. "What's a duffer when it's at home?"

"Plays off twenty-six. Percy's worried he'll slow down play."

Rossi laughed. "But who is he? What does Toth do for a living?"

"He's a former Welsh rugby international who wants to save the world and get rich in the process. Manufactures solar panels in South Africa."

"He's British?" Rossi said. "Not Hungarian?"

"A typo, old boy. His name is Tooth. Two o's."

Cathy grabbed her laptop and sat down on the sofa next to Rossi. A flutter of fingers. "Is this Tooth?" she asked, turning the screen to the monsignor.

"That's him," the monsignor nodded.

"But he's nobody on the world stage. He couldn't be the target," Rossi protested, reading Tooth's profile on Wikipedia. "And why the bodyguards?"

"A nasty falling-out with his Chinese partner, according to Percy."

Rossi pushed back in the sofa, put his hands behind his head, and raised his gaze to the ceiling. "And then there were none."

"What are we missing?" Cathy asked.

A long thoughtful silence before Rossi lunged forward and snatched the bottle of Scotch. "A top-up?"

Monsignor Baker drained his glass and rose from his seat. "Better not, Lorenzo. Best I head back before Lord Percy dispatches a search party."

"Don't forget your walking stick," Cathy said, passing it to the monsignor, accompanying him to the door.

"What do you make of that?" Rossi asked, the instant the door clicked closed.

"I'm going out," Cathy said, already in the bedroom, clipping her holstered pistol inside the back of her jeans. "I need to speak with Heroin Chic."

Rossi followed her to the entrance. "Want company?"

"Not necessary." Cathy buttoned up her trench coat and draped a black scarf over her shoulders. "You stay here and monitor the screens."

Rubbing her back, Rossi turned the handle. "Be careful."

"I'll be fine," Cathy said, patting her pistol.

Switching off the lights, Rossi moved to the bay window and opened the curtains. Leaning against a vertical mullion, he watched Cathy stride onto the fairway and fade into the darkness. It wasn't until she was level with the target's house that Rossi again picked up her curves, lit up by the glare of the streetlamps on The Links. Binoculars trained on her back, Rossi followed her as she crossed Swilcan Bridge and veered left towards the CIA surveillance van, which had been moved further along the service road away from any ambient light.

"What's she doing?" Rossi murmured to himself. His heart raced as Cathy dived to the ground and, in a semi-crouch, scurried into a sand bunker protecting the front of the seventeenth green.

Rossi swung the binoculars onto the surveillance van. A vehicle, with headlights turned off, rolled to a stop, short of the Dodge. Rossi adjusted the focus. The interior light illuminated when the passenger side door opened. A short sharp breath as Rossi glimpsed a solid man with a short Afro fade climb from the saloon.

What's Cleveland Jefferson doing in St Andrews? Rossi couldn't help but wonder whether Chief James's schoolboy trust in attractive women had again compromised their mission.

Rossi scurried to the bedroom, grabbed his Heckler & Koch from under his pillow, slipped on his leather jacket and boots, and returned to his lookout.

"Moment of truth," he said, peering through his binoculars. The Green Beret waved at the Dodge Ram as he approached, seemingly aware he was being observed by the van's occupant. Peering through the driver's side window, Jefferson pulled on the door handle. Locked. He thumped his clenched fist against the panel.

The van's side door slid open and Heroin Chic jumped out. An embrace. From Rossi's vantage point, an amenable exchange. Rossi's heart sank. She's betrayed us. *Abort mission*, he thought. But where was Cathy?

Rossi refocused the binoculars on the bunker. He couldn't see her, which he took as good. Panning back to the Dodge, Rossi did a double take as he glimpsed Cathy in a commando crawl, scrambling towards the knee-high stone wall marking the course boundary.

"Get back, Cathy," he whined, focusing his binoculars back on the Dodge. "What are you doing?" He knew the answer. You didn't have to be lying on the damp grass behind the short boundary wall to understand what was happening. Heroin Chic had drawn her pistol and was motioning for Jefferson to back away. But Jefferson was having none of it, stepping forward and daring her to shoot. Rossi sensed she didn't have it in her. He was right. Heroin Chic was surveillance. Killing another human being was not part of her limited repertoire.

Holding Heroin Chic spellbound with his steely gaze, Jefferson seized the pistol from her shaking hand and tossed it to the ground. "I warned you to stay out of this, Rattle."

A short silence before Heroin Chic plucked up the courage to respond. "Out of what? Murder?"

Jefferson filled his lungs with fresh sea air as he looked around for potential witnesses. Left then right before wrapping his enormous hand around her throat and lifting her off the ground. Gasping for air, Heroin Chic smacked him open-palmed over both ears before landing a sharp kick to his testicles.

Jefferson didn't flinch. "Best you can do?" he mocked, tossing her like a rag doll into the back of the van.

"You'll never get away with this," Heroin Chic wheezed, her hand supporting her throat.

Reaching inside his jacket, Jefferson unholstered his silencer-fitted Beretta and trained it on Heroin Chic. "We're doing just fine, Rattle. A hundred years from now you'll read about us in the history books. How we saved Western civilisation and, with it, humanity."

Heroin Chic raised her gaze, challenging his authority. "Rich and poor. Believers and non-believers. Nothing in-between? Black and white. No melting pot for you?"

"You got it. It's the first rule of breeding, Rattle. Don't go corrupting royal blood lines with inferior breeds."

"To paraphrase Hitler?" Heroin Chic said, her voice building in courage.

Jefferson raised his pistol. "Didn't your mother teach you respect?"

"Who are you kidding? We both know you're not going to use that," Heroin Chic said, sliding forward. But Jefferson's chilling silence stopped her cold.

A long slow smile rolled across Jefferson's face as he pulled the trigger. A shot through the forehead and one to the chest. Slamming the side door, Jefferson jumped in the front and fired up the engine.

Rossi blinked, mouth open. *This is madness*, he thought, swinging the binoculars onto Cathy, praying she was not about to play hero.

He needn't have worried. No doubt realising there was nothing gained through daredevilry, Cathy laid hidden behind the wall until the surveillance van followed by the saloon drove off and merged with the traffic on the A91.

47

Rossi wasn't taking any chances. It was time to go before Jefferson lobbed a gas canister through the window. Frantically disassembling the surveillance equipment, Rossi heard someone standing in the corridor. He glanced about the room certain Cathy had taken a key. Holding his breath, he turned his ear to the anteroom. *The sound of a gun being unholstered.*

On autopilot, Rossi grabbed his Heckler & Koch from the sideboard, ejected the magazine, checked it, slapped it back into the butt, and racked the slide. Round chambered, he crept towards the entrance and waited.

A tap on the door with the barrel of a pistol. At least, that's how Rossi recalled it later. "Who's there?" he called out, standing clear of the door, not wanting to give Jefferson an easy target.

"Enzo, open up."

Gun in hand, muzzle pointing at the ceiling, Rossi peeked through the spyhole. "Whatever happened to three knocks?" he mumbled to himself, unlocking the door.

"Heroin Chic's dead," Cathy panted.

"I saw it from the window." Clicking on the safety, Rossi followed Cathy into the sitting room.

"Cold-blooded murder," Cathy declared, pulling the cork from the empty bottle of Laphroaig then flopping onto the chair. "This isn't good."

"You're right there," Rossi said, packing the CCTV cameras into the custom foam inserts of the flight case. "We need to go to ground."

Cathy drained the last drops from the bottle. "I meant, we're out of Scotch."

Rossi ejected the CD-ROM from the DVR and moved to the writing desk. "We'll grab a bottle from the bar on the way out." Fishing in his computer bag, Rossi pulled out a portable disk drive and attached it to his laptop.

"Where are you going?" Cathy asked, only now noticing what Rossi was doing.

"As soon as I've finished sending this CCTV footage to our journalist friend, we're getting the hell out of here."

Cathy rose and picked up the black push-button telephone on the writing desk. "Sit down for Heaven's sake, Enzo. We haven't eaten dinner yet."

Rossi shot her a concerned look. "Did you *see* what Jefferson just did? Head buried too far in the grass? Let me play it for you." Rossi loaded the disk.

"Good evening," Cathy said into the phone. "A bottle of Rioja Reserva, a bottle of Laphroaig, and the antipasto platter, please. Room 111."

"Have you lost your mind?" Rossi asked, his voice gaining a hard edge.

A smirk and a sideways tilt of the head. "Not last time I checked."

"Jefferson's on his way. Help me pack."

"Learn to relax, Enzo," Cathy said, sitting on the edge of the sofa and removing her shoes. "No one's coming for us – at least not tonight."

"You know something, don't you?"

A smirk. "As Jefferson held Heroin Chic's life in his hands, he bellyached about mothballing Project Genesis. Orders from above. Blamed it on some meddlesome German bitch."

"Well done, Sabine. Mission accomplished. We can go home."

"Doesn't it strike you as odd," Cathy continued, "Jefferson didn't ask about us."

"Not at all," Rossi snapped in frustration. "If he's been following Heroin Chic, he knows where to find us." Pause. "Why give him an easy target?"

"Yet here we are – the last two people on the planet pushing back on the White House's extrajudicial killings. Alive and kicking."

From their work in Moscow, Rossi knew Cathy had a brilliant analytical mind. *She's figured it out*, he thought, already standing by the minibar. "*Aperitivo* while we wait for room service – or Jefferson, whichever comes first."

"A Campara spritz would be nice."

Setting two high ball glasses on the counter, Rossi peeked in the refrigerator. "Let's see. We've got Campari, prosecco and soda – but no ice."

"You could dash down to the ice machine at the bottom of the stairwell."

"And run the risk of getting shot at. I don't think so."

"Chicken."

Rossi handed Cathy her cocktail and sat down next to her. "*Saluti*," he said, holding out his glass. A long sip. "Out with it."

"Out with what?"

"Whatever you're itching to tell me."

A rap on the door. "Room service," came a deep, unfamiliar voice.

Rossi set his glass on the coffee table and grabbed his gun.

Not taking any chances, Cathy did the same. Positioning herself against the sitting room entrance, she gestured with her hand for Rossi to advance.

Another rap on the door. "Room service," the man repeated.

"Just a minute," Rossi called out, stuffing his pistol into the back of his jeans. A roll of his shoulders and a flexing of his neck to ease the tightness before Rossi stepped forward and put an eye to the spyhole. A man with a military stance stood with his hands behind his back.

Rossi held open the door. Backside first, the waiter entered pulling the trolley.

"Good evening, sir. Where would you like it?"

"In here," Cathy answered for Rossi, who was busy checking the corridor.

The waiter set the platter on the coffee table. "Filmmakers?" he asked, motioning with his eyes at the flight case lying open on the floor.

"We're counting seabirds for the Scottish Ornithological Society," Cathy replied, closing the case lid. "Someone's got to do it."

The waiter glanced about as he pulled the cork and poured the wine. "From the room?"

"We've been testing the equipment," Rossi interjected, coercing the waiter towards the door with a ten-pound note.

Cathy sat down on the sofa and placed a napkin on her lap. "What do you make of him?"

"At a pinch. A displaced typewriter salesman being retrained at great expense to the Scottish taxpayer. Nothing to worry about." Laughter. "Now, your theory?"

"We're not as clever as we think."

"What do you mean – we? I've never considered myself smart. That would be arrogant."

Cathy drizzled honey onto a slice of Manchego cheese and popped it into her mouth. "They've tricked us into coming here. Led us by the nose. The golf bag, the Swilcan Bridge photograph, the Victorian house: all planted for us to find. They've played us for fools."

"It's possible, I guess." Rossi took a long sip of his wine. "But why?"

"We're theatre props. Extras. Hand-picked to help the three wise men tie a red, white and blue elephant bow around Project Genesis."

"We're *what*?"

"It mightn't have started that way. In fact, I'm sure in the beginning we were legitimate members of Langley's Bright Star team. Established by the real CIA to catch the assassin. But at this very juncture we're fall guys. Mugs the White House intend to frame for the extrajudicial killings."

"Good and well. But how are they going to prevent us from telling our story? And bringing down the president while we're at it."

"By killing us," Cathy said, munching on a grape.

A shrug as Rossi blew out a short breath. "Then we'd better hurry and send Sabine Reich everything we have."

"We will." A sip of wine. "But that won't make us any less dead."

"What have they got planned for us? A spray of bullets as we burst in on Morton?"

"Morton's dead."

"Again? Poor bastard. Twice in one week."

Cathy grabbed her laptop from the writing desk and sat back down on the sofa. "Look," she said, running the drone footage. "Morton's not wearing his ring."

"What ring?"

"A weighty gold ring with a ruby the size of a doorknob." Cathy made a fist. "A family heirloom he's worn since he was sixteen. Got caught in my hair when he tried to remove my bra."

"He took it off?"

"Not without sawing off his finger. Gets stuck on his bony knuckle."

"But why go to all that trouble?"

"They knew we wouldn't quit until we pegged the party in the flat." Pause. "So Jefferson showed us someone we recognised, even suspected at one point."

"A dead man?"

With a crooked smirk, Cathy raised her shoulders. "We bought it, didn't we? And, again, found ourselves questioning Heroin Chic's loyalty. Laughs all round."

"Let's say you're right," Rossi said, balancing a dollop of hummus on the end of a carrot stick. "How's it going to play out?"

"More or less as we tallied. A yet-to-be-identified target executed by a yet-to-be-identified assassin on or near Swilcan Bridge sometime tomorrow."

"That part is clear. It's what happens next that's got me worried."

"If I was the White House, I'd eliminate the shooter and anyone else without serious skin in the game." Cathy took a long sip of wine, staring into the middle distance as she thought. "It's the only way to ensure Congress or the press can't trace Genesis back to the president."

"Like Chief James, Lawrence, Heroin Chic, Natasha, Morton…"

"And you and me."

"How and when?"

"Imagine the eighteenth hole tomorrow, Enzo," Cathy said, putting down her glass. "Playing before a small but appreciative crowd, 'rich-bastard' number four is gunned down on Swilcan Bridge. Seconds later, three US special agents burst into the Victorian house and neutralise the assassin before heading upstairs and slaughtering the mastermind behind the circle-A murders: a gorgeous rogue CIA agent, Catherine Doherty, and her ageing Italian assistant, Lorenzo Rossi." More cheese and honey. "White House declares mission accomplished. No one left to dispute their version. Game over. World rescued." Laughter.

Rossi joined in then added, "The next day the president announces a trade war with Turkey and calls the Australian prime minister a gum nut. End of the news cycle."

"Dead or alive, we've still got Sabine Reich."

"Unless they kill her too."

Rossi and Cathy spent the next two hours drinking Scotch and dreaming up scenarios that would enable them to not only bring the president and his neoconservative crazies to justice but also prevent another killing. By midnight the only thing they had come up with was to give the three wise men enough rope to hang themselves.

"Not much of a plan," Rossi sighed.

"True. But under the circumstances what do you expect?"

"CIA backup."

"Afraid not, Enzo. This time we're on our own."

Rossi sat back, rested his bare feet on the arm of the Sherlock chair, and took a long, philosophical pull on his Scotch. "You know, the best military minds reckon no plan survives contact with the enemy."

"A plan's a waste of time? That's reassuring."

"Not quite what I meant, Cathy. We know what we have to do. No point in over-planning. In the end it comes down to who can think quickest on their feet. Adapt best to the changing battlefield. We have the assassin's vantage point, the intended victim's location, and we know the number of hired guns."

"And as soon as we've identified tomorrow's target, we'll know the time." Cathy rose from the sofa and collected her tote bag from the bedroom. "Let's pray Forrest doesn't change the locks in the meantime," Cathy said, fishing out the pink master key and bunging it to Rossi.

Rossi set the alarm on his phone. "I'll head over at four."

"Don't take any risks. If you're observed, abort. Come back and we'll figure out some other way of getting you inside."

Cathy moved to the bedroom, grabbed her last two burner phones and tossed one to Rossi. "My number's in memory. Now help me get rid of this."

Rossi lifted one end of the sofa as Cathy positioned the used pink phone under one of the solid wooden legs.

"Enough already, Enzo. It's late. You'll wake the whole hotel," Cathy said, as Rossi pounded the burner into tiny pieces.

"We'd better get a little sleep. Could be a long day," Rossi said, heading to the bathroom and turning on the shower.

Cathy stacked the plates, glasses and wine bottle onto the tray and left them out in the corridor.

"What *are* you doing?" Rossi asked, with a mouth full of toothpaste.

"If I die, I don't want anyone thinking I was a slob."

"Then perhaps I should shave?"

"Don't bother. The funeral director will look after that. Besides, who's likely to see you? The White House aren't planning to lie you in state."

Rossi undressed and stepped into the shower. "Jokes aside, Cathy, what's the probability we're killed tomorrow?"

"Fifty–fifty," Cathy said, standing in the bathroom doorway looking out.

"Then this might be our last night together. Our last chance for reconciliation – to make love."

Cathy tutted. "What was it you said in Moscow? You needed a better reason for making love than the physical pleasure? That sex was merely self-gratification?"

"You're misquoting me again. I said, without love, sex is self-gratifying and best avoided." A short pause as Rossi squirted shampoo into his hand then rubbed it into his hair. "And given, despite your denials, we love each other, I see no reason not to express our love tonight."

"How *persuasive* you are, Enzo," Cathy said, her hair veiling her face as she leant forward and peeled off her skin-tight jeans.

48

By the time Cathy's early breakfast arrived, Rossi was already safely ensconced inside the second-floor flat above the assassin. Cathy dipped her croissant into her coffee and took a bite, catching the drops running down her chin with the side of her index finger. *Girl's got to eat*, she thought, feeling a little guilty having packed Rossi off at 4 a.m. with nothing more than a Snickers and a packet of cashews from the minibar.

A chirp. Mail notification. Cathy glanced down at her laptop open on the sofa next to her. It was the response to an email she had sent Sabine Reich an hour ago, undertaking to provide material implicating the president of the United States in the *Forbes* list killings. But only on the condition Sabine and the *Frankfurter Allgemeine Zeitung* agreed not to disclose any of the information before 10 p.m. tonight. A smile came to Cathy's face as she read the one-word response. "Agreed."

Clicking "reply", Cathy wrote:

Attached are 8 files, hereafter collectively known as the White House Dossier.
Reminder: In order not to jeopardise life and the ongoing operation, it is paramount you abide by the agreed publication moratorium of 10 p.m.

She then attached the files and hit send.

Refreshing her coffee, Cathy moved to the bay window and peeped out between the curtains. It was pitch black, not even a hint of a horizon.

With a fruit skewer protruding from her mouth, Cathy sat back on the sofa and re-googled the players' names. Maybe there was something she'd missed. Although many were rich and moderately famous, nobody matched the assassin's target profile. Nothing popped out. No right-wing politicians, zero arms dealers, zilch Russian agents, zippo people smugglers, nothing.

Two hours later, a ray of low winter sun snuck through a gap between the curtains, striking Cathy in the eyes, and sending her to the window. Drawing open the curtains, Cathy peered into the distance. A crowd had gathered around the hospitality tent and, to the south, a dozen golfers warmed up on the practice green. Grabbing the binoculars from the flight case, Cathy focused on the faces. *Too far and too many*, she thought, glancing at her watch. Already eight-fifteen: time to go. Popping a strawberry in her mouth, she moved to the bedroom. Laid out on her unmade bed were her SIG-Sauer pistol, a spare twenty-two-round extension magazine, a bulletproof vest, and a stylish Ralph Lauren military jacket.

Dressed in black jeans, a long-sleeved navy-blue T-shirt and black boots, Cathy holstered her pistol and clipped it inside the back waistband of her jeans. She then donned the vest and slipped into the olive jacket. A check in the mirror. No bulges.

Not very golfy, she thought, adjusting her fiddler cap. *But damn sexy.*

Cathy put on her sunglasses as she stepped out onto The Links. Shading her eyes from the glare of the sun, Cathy scanned the Old Course boundary, half-expecting to see the three wise men staring back at her. *In the Dodge polishing their guns*, she thought, turning towards the hospitality tent.

Ambling along without looking back, Cathy felt alone. She was used to Rossi by her side. She couldn't help but wonder whether he was okay. Bumping about in the flat above a ruthless killer didn't seem safe. Not by a long stretch of the imagination. One out-of-place sound would be enough to alert the assassin of his proximity. A scraping of a chair on the wooden floor. The banging of old water pipes. *By the time I get there it could be all over*, she thought, fighting off the urge to send him a message.

The grassed area surrounding the hospitality marquee was roped off and a crowd had gathered on the pavement by the time Cathy arrived. A "Players Only" sign sent Cathy further along to the Links Golf Shop. She glanced at her watch as she entered: 8:45.

Obscured by racks of women's designer golf wear, Cathy peered out of the window at a group of backslapping old men moving towards the first tee.

"Excuse me, miss," came a familiar voice from behind, "you dropped these."

Cathy stiffened as she turned around slowly. She fought back a smile at the sight of Monsignor Baker wearing a cerise-coloured Kangol cap and holding out a packet of cigarettes. "Nice hat," she said, squeezing between racks.

"It's so nobody shoots me by mistake," the monsignor whispered through a cupped hand.

"Ingenious."

"There's been a development," the monsignor continued, his tone more serious. "Lord Melba arrived in St Andrews last night. He's planning to take Professor Slack's spot."

Cathy's eyes widened. "Any other changes?"

"I checked the field list again this morning. Nothing jumped out at me."

Cathy stuffed the cigarettes into her breast pocket. "Such a bad habit," she said, in full voice.

The monsignor turned to go, then stopped. "Remember, no shooting anywhere near the cerise cap," he said with a wink.

As Cathy threaded her way through the shop, her gaze following the monsignor through the window, one thought swirled in her head. Was Seabert Slack the assassin? British champion in the 300-metre rifle three positions. *Qualified.* But Cathy couldn't quite imagine the roly-poly professor bounding down stairways and climbing walls in pursuit of a better vantage point.

Already standing on the clubhouse side of the shop, Cathy peered between smartly dressed mannequins towards the first tee. A silly-looking man in plus fours and a tweed cap was addressing his ball. She glanced at her watch. Nine o'clock. *They're a punctual lot.*

Further towards the bay, Cathy spotted Lord Percy on the practice green stooped over his putter. The monsignor stood behind him, giving advice. On the pathway bordering the green, Cathy recognised the stick-like figure of Lord Melba chatting to a rough-looking man with a round face and brown hair. *Slavic*, Cathy thought, picking up a pair of golf shoes.

Then it struck her. *Perhaps Lord Melba's the target.* Cathy recalled reading his CIA file. Close ties to the Russians, shady associates, rumours of money laundering, and a major donor to the Brexit campaign that resulted in Britain leaving the European Union. *Why didn't I see it before? Lord Melba's the target*, she decided. Which meant the assassin was someone close? Someone who knew he was coming. Lord Percy and Slack sprang to mind. But the idea Lord Percy, the layabout from the Fez Club, would murder his own father was impossible to conceive.

It wasn't long before the tournament announcer invited the Cambridgeshire three onto the first tee. Cathy watched from the crowd as they teed off. As she turned to head back to the hotel, Cathy did a double take. Lord Melba was handing his driver to his caddy: Professor Slack. *How could that be?* she wondered. Slack can't be the assassin, unless he's prepared to be caught. He would need to abandon the group before Swilcan Bridge, take up a position in the flat, hit his target, then make it back to the course without being missed. *Absurd.*

49

Kneeling on the sitting room floor listening to Carl Orff's "O Fortuna" drifting up from the flat below, Rossi tied together the ends of four king-size sheets he'd found in the linen closet. *That'll hold*, he thought, tugging at the knots.

Rossi looked up anxiously, his sea-green eyes squinting in the half-darkness at a tiny flashing red light emanating from the sofa. Stretching out his long arm, he scooped up the burner Cathy had given him late last night.

"Hello," Rossi said, in a grim whisper, fearing bad news.

"The lord of the manor has put in an appearance. Taken the professor's spot in Group 4. In all probability, he's today's target."

Rossi, puzzled by Cathy's directness, asked, "Are we okay to speak?"

"We have little choice. Besides, I'd be amazed if the Washington crazies hadn't already cut the three wise men loose. Distancing themselves from what happens next."

"You mean they're on their own? Zero backup, like us?"

"That's what I'm counting on. An even playing field."

A short silence as Rossi mulled over the news. "Your target assessment makes sense. But who's the shooter? The professor?"

"Unlikely. He's caddying for the old man. Unless he's quicker and nimbler than his flabby body suggests." Pause. "You hear music?"

"Someone's knocking about below. The shooter, I'd assumed."

"How did you go making the screen?"

"Linen to spare."

"Good. Now relax and keep out of sight. My best estimate is they'll be putting out on the seventeenth around one." A pause. "Oh! I almost forgot. Our favourite landlord is wearing a cerise-coloured Kangol cap. He's asked if we can refrain from shooting him." A chuckle.

"I'll bear that in mind, though it's not up to me," Rossi said, wanting to tell her he loved her. But, before he could speak, she'd rung off.

Rossi rolled up the makeshift screen and set it down in front of the bay window. Peeking through a three-inch gap between the heavy curtains, he saw small groups of spectators trailing the players on the front nine. Then, without warning, the scraping sound of metal on metal. Inside or out? He wasn't sure. Rossi leant his ear closer to the window and held his breath. A smirk of recognition. In the flat below, the assassin had twisted open the window lock and pushed up the single-hung sash. Rossi glanced at his watch: 11:25. *Why so early?* he thought, scanning the area around Swilcan Bridge. Deserted, other than a pair of brown hares standing in the long grass near the service road.

Suddenly, silence. For the first time since daybreak the music had stopped. Rossi went to the window and again peeked out. He couldn't help but think he and Cathy had missed something. It was as though the assassin was ready. But the assumed target was an hour and a half away. A cold shiver ran up his spine. Maybe they plan to kill Cathy first? After all, it didn't matter. They could tell their story a thousand ways.

Rossi massaged his temples, trying to clear his mind. A Scotch would come in handy, but he settled for the small bottle of Evian Cathy had packed.

Then came the slamming of a door in the stairway and a short time later, music. He prayed for Tchaikovsky's "1812 Overture" and the climactic cannon shots to mask the sound of him opening the window. Instead, he got electronic music. *Changing of the guard*, he thought. He raced to the second bedroom overlooking the entrance and peered down onto the street. The back of a man wearing a coat and a hat. The military gait removed any doubt. It was Ethan Rosenthal, or, more correctly, Colonel Beasley, US Army Special Forces, heading towards the Rusacks Hotel.

Rossi ripped the burner from his pocket to warn Cathy. As he did, fettuccini with asparagus and smoked salmon popped into his mind. "Bella," he said, listening to the music. "*Eleganz und Dekadenz, Europa Endloss…*" Rossi's heart sank. *Kraftwerk. Bella's favourite.* It had to be more than a coincidence. Could Percy's cousin be the assassin?

Rossi dialled. "Cathy, Rosenthal's on his way to the hotel."

"Yes, I know. I saw him leave. I'm up a tree across the street."

"And it's possible it's Bella one floor down."

"I'm coming up."

"Too risky. They'll see you."

"I doubt that very much. Jefferson and Riccardo are in the university library swotting for exams, and Rosenthal's gone looking for me at the Rusacks."

"And Bella?"

"If she's the shooter, she'll be too busy staring out at the course to notice. Besides, she's never met me. I could be her neighbour for all she knows."

From the bedroom window, Rossi watched Cathy appear from behind a tall stone wall, a bulky rucksack slung over her shoulder. By the time Cathy reached the building entrance, Rossi had already released the magnetic lock.

At the bottom of the stairs, Cathy removed her boots. Ascending on tiptoes, Rossi greeted her with a smile from the doorway as she approached. The door closed without a sound. An embrace. It reminded Rossi of the grotto in Kazakhstan where fear had brought them so close. Seemed like a lifetime ago.

"I wasn't expecting visitors," Rossi whispered. "What did you do with Jefferson and Riccardo?"

"Wasn't keen on being a sitting duck. So, I decided to flush them out."

"And it worked?"

"I led them on a merry dance around the university precinct." Cathy fished about in the pockets of her olive jacket and pulled out two miniature bottles of Johnnie Walker and handed one to Rossi.

"Where are they now?"

"I dropped them in the library. They might be fearless soldiers, but they've got lousy tradecraft. And another thing: as we suspected, they appear to be working alone. No backup, no high tech. Just beef and brawn."

"We're in with a chance then."

"Too right," Cathy said, breaking the seal on the Scotch bottle and draining it.

The music grew louder. "Kraftwerk," Rossi said, motioning towards the floor with a nod of the head. "Bella's favourite."

"You mean 'Bella the Butcher'. You make her sound so sweet." Cathy opened her rucksack, removed a CCTV camera she'd taken from the hotel, and moved to the second bedroom window, overlooking the entrance. Stacking three hardback books on the sill, Cathy balanced the camera and focused it on the front steps.

Back in the sitting room, Cathy connected the feed to her laptop and set it on the arm of the sofa. "Is there only one entrance?"

"If you exclude climbing down the chimney."

"Let's."

Standing before the double front bay window, Rossi slipped his hand behind the curtains and slowly turned both sash locks. An audible scrape, but impossible to hear over Kraftwerk from the floor below.

"The first group is on the seventeenth fairway," Cathy said, peering out through the edge of the curtains with the binoculars. "We're down to thirty minutes."

"Anyone below?"

Cathy peeked down at the street. "It's clear."

Staying out of sight, Rossi reached between curtains and raised both window sashes six inches. He glanced down at the roll of bedsheets at his feet and then to Cathy. "Enough?"

A firm nod. "Now all we have to do is wait for Lord Melba to come into range, catch the three wise men in the act, and stop Bella from inadvertently shooting Monsignor Baker in his incandescent cap."

"That's if it *is* Bella," Rossi said. "All we're going by is an old Kraftwerk album."

"And the St Andrews golf set and the Swilcan Bridge photograph. Not to mention, Bella's one of a handful of people who could have known Lord Melba was playing today."

Rossi puffed out his cheeks and shrugged. "If you're so sure, I'll invite her up for tea."

"Bloody good idea. Just don't get yourself killed. I'm too young to be a widow bride."

"We're getting *married*?" Rossi smiled. "I thought you'd ditched me."

"Never," Cathy said, throwing her arms around Rossi's neck and kissing him. "I've been testing you. Making sure you love me after Moscow. It's easy to get all emotional in the face of death and make commitments you regret. Thought I'd give you a chance to back out."

Rossi's head shot back. "Jesus, I've never heard such bullshit."

Through the open window came the noise of the crowd. Cathy peered out. "The first group of players are approaching the stone bridge. You'd better put on your vest."

50

Colonel Beasley screeched the grey Chrysler saloon to a halt on North Street in front of the University Library and Lieutenant Abbott and Sergeant Tripi, waiting on the pavement, jumped in.

"How the hell did you lose that floozy?" the colonel barked.

Abbott, sitting in the front, seemingly felt a sudden urge to check his phone, leaving the not-so-bright Sergeant Tripi to fill the silence.

"Agent Doherty is CIA-trained, sir. She was on to us from the get-go. Spotted us as she was leaving the golf."

"You being insolent, son?" Beasley growled. "You're US Army Special Forces, God dammit. And you let a moppet outfox you?"

"What now, Colonel?" Abbott said, as Beasley took a breath.

The colonel checked his watch, made a U-turn, and planted his foot on the accelerator pedal. "We take up surveillance and wait."

"And if Doherty and Rossi don't show? Without a bag of bones, the evidence is thin."

"They'll show all right. Those two liberal do-gooders would rescue the Devil himself if they thought he was being unlawfully deprived of his liberty."

Abbott conceded with a grunt.

"My guess is they're already inside laying a trap. Planning an ambush like Robin Hood."

"They could come at us from behind," the sergeant said.

"If they did that, Rossi's new girlfriend would be dead by the time they got up the stairs," Lieutenant Abbott said. "They wouldn't risk it. Besides, I'll be watching the street until Balls hands over the sniper rifle. I'll have your back, Sergeant."

The colonel drove at the speed limit through the City Road roundabout then swung into the driveway of John Burnet Hall. Steering with one hand, he pulled up between parked vehicles, thirty metres from the front entrance of the Victorian house.

"Which way's the wind blowing, Lieutenant?" the colonel asked, lowering his window. "We need to hear the starter's gun."

At that moment, a man wearing an army-green backpack appeared from the direction of the golf course. A gust of wind picked up his boonie bush hat and blew it onto the road.

"There's your answer, Colonel," Abbott smiled. "Due east – directly over the sniper's position."

A screech of tyres as the man dodged traffic, chasing his boonie.

"If I'm not mistaken, that nitwit is our shooter," the sergeant said, tapping the window with his index finger.

None of the three wise men had ever met Slack. Deniability demanded it. All communication had been by encrypted text messages.

They stayed put and watched until the portly academic entered the adjoining building and the door closed behind him.

"Athletic-looking dude." Abbott laughed. "I hear he goes queasy at the sight of blood."

"He gets the job done," the colonel said, popping the boot.

Sergeant Tripi jumped out, grabbed a ranger-green tactical carry bag from the back, and set it on the seat. The saloon rocked as the Green Berets slipped into their bulletproof vests.

"What's the drill if Doherty and Rossi aren't inside?" Sergeant Tripi asked, checking the chamber of his Glock.

"Have faith, son," the colonel said. "They're inside okay." Pause. "They mightn't be where we expect them to be but we can deal with that. Shock and awe. That's what we do best."

"But you said it yourself, sir. We'll be walking into an ambush. Two against two. Not good odds under the circumstances."

"For mercy's sake, Sergeant. Stop your whinning," Lieutenant Abbott interjected, working the action of his pistol. "I'll be right behind you mopping up. But if you do your job properly, it'll all be over by the time I get there."

"You can count on me, Lieutenant."

51

Below him, Rossi was sure he heard laughter. He pulled back the rug, got down on all fours and put his ear to the boards. Quietening his breath, Rossi listened. Bella had turned down the music and was speaking on the phone. "Something's not right," he said, looking up at Cathy. "That's not the focused mind of a female assassin bracing herself to shoot Lord Melba between the eyes."

Cathy lay on the floor next to him. "We've been set up. She's speaking to her mom."

Back at the window with the high-powered binoculars, Cathy focused on the sixteenth tee. "Still no sign of the target's group." Pause. "Does the pink key open the assassin's flat?"

"I haven't tried."

A pensive silence before Cathy spoke. "Go get Bella. Use the key. If it doesn't work, knock on the door. She'll be over the moon to see you, anyway. Just bring her here."

"Then what?"

"By then I should have come up with something."

Rossi slipped his jacket over his ballistic vest then crept down the stairs to the first-floor landing. With his ear to the glossy black door, a faint static voice confirmed Bella was deep inside, probably in the sitting room. Unholstering his pistol, Rossi inserted the key in the door then stopped. What if it's chained? Don't want to panic her. Rossi withdrew the key, holstered his gun, and rapped. Nothing. He rapped again, only louder. Footsteps. Then a face peeked out from behind the door.

"Lorenzo," Bella screamed, removing the chain. "I wasn't expecting you."

Rossi pushed her inside, smothering her mouth with his huge hand. "Your life's in danger," he said in an anxious whisper.

Eyes as big as saucers, Bella stood frozen in place, too frightened to protest or ask for an explanation.

With a firm grip of Bella's hand, Rossi moved from room to room, slinging closed the curtains, looking for any hint of what the three wise men intended. Tossed on the sofa in the sitting room, a Robert Morton latex mask. Empty bottles of expensive wine stood on the kitchen floor next to an overflowing bin.

"Whose are those?" Rossi asked, gesturing at the bondage mittens and cuffs and a black leather gimp mask lying on a long-hair sheepskin rug in the master bedroom.

Bella winced. "Not mine."

Rossi's thoughts turned to Natasha, and how he'd found her on *Moon Shadow*, hands and feet hogtied behind her back. Revenge flashed to mind as he raced through the apartment.

"You need to come with me," Rossi said, turning off the music then dragging Bella out onto the landing.

"Enzo, you're hurting me."

"Be quiet," Rossi ordered testing the pink key in the lock. It turned. "Upstairs. Now."

Hearing Rossi's heavy footsteps ascending the stairs, Cathy opened the door. "Get in," she growled, looking Bella up and down.

Bella glared angrily back and dug in her heels. "Lorenzo, what's going on? And who is she?"

"Did Lord Percy invite you for the weekend?" Rossi asked, shoving Bella inside then locking the door.

"More or less."

"Then why aren't you staying with the others at the cottage?"

A blush of embarrassment. "My uncle's there. He doesn't approve of me carrying on with Seabert."

"You mean Professor Slack?" Rossi said, his tone damning. "Nor would I."

"Such a fascinating guy, Enzo," Bella said, her tone defensive. "Most of the time we talk philosophy and politics. The kinky stuff is a small price to pay for access to such a brilliant mind."

"Not if you end up at the bottom of the River Cam."

Bella shot Rossi a puzzled look. "Meaning?"

"Did you ever discuss the circle-A killings with Slack?" Cathy asked impatiently.

"Only within the context of the Russian conspiracy,"

Bella said, gazing innocently at Cathy, "and what Seabert considers a legitimate counter to the Kremlin's long-term strategic goal."

Cathy, one of the CIA's leading experts on Russia and the former Soviet Union, couldn't help but smirk. "And what strategic goal is that, Bella?"

"Seabert reckons the Kremlin are working towards re-establishing its Soviet era sphere of influence—"

A scoff. "Nothing new there."

"He says they plan to win back lost territories by creating global chaos and destroying the European project."

"And *you* agree with Professor Slack? The Russians should be stopped?"

"Why, of course."

Cathy picked up the binoculars and wandered over to the bay window. "So, what did the good professor suggest we do about it?"

"Not just the professor. We're all of the same mind."

A lull as Cathy scanned the sixteenth. "Where's Slack at this very moment, Bella?"

"Caddying for Lord Melba."

"And if he's not?"

Cathy handed the binoculars to Rossi, who was already by her side. "The sixteenth tee. Can you see Slack?"

Rossi studied the group as they teed off. Percy went first: a long drive straight down the middle. The monsignor in the cerise-coloured cap played next: a fade to the right. Lord Melba completing the threesome played last: a wicked hook to the left, landing in the long grass.

It wasn't until the players were striding down the

fairway that Rossi got a good look at Lord Melba and his caddy. "I know that guy," Rossi said, handing Cathy back the glasses. "He's the gamekeeper at Melba House."

Cathy swung around to confront Bella. "Where the hell is Professor Slack?"

"I don't know."

"What did he ask you to do today? Meet him here at the flat?"

A nervous nod. "What's this all about, Lorenzo?"

"What time?" Cathy continued.

"Twelve-thirty. Said he might be late."

Cathy looked Bella up and down. "Did Slack tell you to dress like that?"

"Seabert likes to play out his sexual fantasies. When he called earlier, he begged me to dress as a cat burglar. At such short notice, the best I could come up with was this black tracksuit and the beanie hat."

"The bondage gear in the bedroom downstairs," Rossi asked. "Is it yours?"

Cathy frowned at Rossi but kept silent.

"Seabert brought them with him. As I told you – he's weird."

"That would explain your fat lip and painful walk," Cathy said, her voice spiked with sarcasm.

"Lorenzo, you're scaring me. What's going on? What's with the bulletproof vests and guns?"

Drawing a sharp breath through his nose, Rossi glanced at Cathy, then back at Bella as he considered how much to reveal. "We figure Slack is the circle-A killer, working for rogue elements within the US government."

A peek at his watch. "And if we're right, in a handful of minutes, the mad professor will attempt to assassinate your favourite uncle, Lord Melba. And, when he's done, three American Green Berets will burst through the door to lynch you, me and Cathy."

Pale and faint, Bella grabbed Rossi's arm. "But why? I don't understand."

"To frame us for the circle-A killings."

Above their heads, a prolonged sound. Like a pebble or a piece of broken tile rolling down the steep sloping slate roof.

"Slack," Cathy said, picking up the binoculars and scurrying to the bay window. "Lord Melba will be in range in ten minutes."

Rossi pushed Bella onto the sofa. "Stay here and don't move. Keep away from the windows and don't open the door."

Bella sat back, drew her knees to her chest and wrapped her arms around them. "I'm sorry, Lorenzo. I couldn't have imagined…" she said, starting to sob.

"How do we get to the roof?" Cathy asked, checking her pistol.

Rossi led Cathy down the short hallway and into the spacious master bedroom. At the far end, built halfway up the vaulted ceiling under the flat roofed dormer, an open loft.

In stockinged feet, they climbed the ladder stairs and gently drew open the curtains. Through the triple pane window, an uninterrupted view of the back nine.

Rossi grinned, pointing above his head. The dormer ceiling creaked under Slack's shifting weight.

"Give me your iPhone, Enzo," Cathy whispered.

"You told me not to bring it," Rossi said, extracting it from its signal-blocking pouch.

A tut. "Do you ever do what you're told? Now open the window without getting caught."

Rossi lifted the well-balanced middle sash a few inches, unheard by Slack above the gusting sea breeze and the serendipitous roar of spectators on the seventeenth green.

Switching the camera to selfie mode, Cathy stuck the iPhone out of the opening and tilted it towards the dormer gutter. On the tiny screen she could see the suppressor of a sniper rifle protruding over the edge.

"Where's Lord Melba?" Cathy asked.

"Out of range," Rossi said, focusing the binoculars on the seventeenth tee. "Can you see Slack?"

"Just the barrel."

Rossi put down the binoculars and raised the sash on the right. Twisting his torso, he stuck his head and shoulders out of the window and checked the alignment of the rifle.

"What the hell are you doing?" Cathy said, pulling him back inside by his trouser belt.

With the dynamism of a professional, Rossi reached back, drew his gun, and attached the silencer from his jacket pocket. "Slack left or right-handed?"

Cathy thought. "Right."

Aiming his pistol at the dormer ceiling, Rossi drew an imaginary line where he judged Slack was lying prostrate, eye resting up against the scope. "Stand aside," he said, picking his spot. "Could get dusty."

Cathy did.

Then three shots. *Pht – pht – pht!* "That's for Natasha."

The way Professor Slack's body flopped onto the dormer roof suggested the first shot had done the job. But Rossi wasn't taking any chances. As he discharged the second bullet into what he visualised was the chest, it surprised him how easy it was to kill a man in cold blood when not looking him in the eye. Drones and aerial bombing popped to mind.

"What next?" Rossi asked. "The three wise men won't be as easy."

Picking pieces of ceiling plaster from her hair, Cathy unveiled her plan.

"If that's your least-worst option," Rossi scoffed. "Then God help us."

"So we are in agreement. Excellent."

Cathy climbed out onto the steep sloping slate roof and clambered up onto the flat loft extension. "It's Slack, all right," she called down, snapping evidential photos to send to Sabine Reich. "Cocky prick. He's already painted circle-A #68 on the roof."

By the time Cathy clambered back inside with Professor Slack's mobile phone and rifle, Rossi was already on the ground floor, switching off the power to Bella's dungeon of pain.

"Pull yourself together, Bella," Cathy said, returning to the sitting room. "And help me cover the first-floor window with the linen."

Hanging one end of the two-metre-long bolt over the sill, Cathy fed it through to Bella, who was pulling from the adjoining window. Each holding a corner, they tugged the cloth taut then unfurled it, blocking the direct line of sight from the first-floor flat to Swilcan Bridge.

Cathy poked her head out and checked. "That'll work," she said, slamming the sash shut to hold it in place.

"Power's off," Rossi called out, as he burst through the front door.

Cathy drew her pistol as she pivoted around, then shook it angrily toward the noise. "Christ, Enzo. You aiming to get yourself killed?"

"What are you doing? How's that going to help?" Rossi motioned with a flick of his head towards the window. "Slack's dead. Sniper no more."

"Insurance," Cathy said, ignoring Bella's gasp. "Just in case one of our American heroes decides to have a pop at His Lordship on their way out. Besides, you went to all that trouble. Be a shame not to use it."

Rossi peered out of the window. "Lord Melba's approaching the green."

"Then I'd better go up and fire the starting gun."

"I just had a horrible thought. What if one of the Green Berets is on the course waiting for Lord Melba to drop?"

Cathy narrowed her eyes as she thought. "Unlikely. They're too thin on the ground to be following the old man. They need all hands on deck to deal with us. Without us in body bags their plan fails. Besides, they'd trust Slack to do his job."

Rossi stood with Bella watching the street entrance on the laptop as Cathy bustled from the room and back up to the loft.

***

The distinctive crack of Slack's sniper rifle sent Colonel Beasley and Sergeant Tripi scurrying across the road to the Victorian house. Under normal circumstances, Lieutenant Abbott would have joined them but someone had to collect the discharged weapon from Balls for planting on Bella's body. As luck would have it, he drew the short straw.

Abbott's gaze flashed from one building entrance to the next. "Where is he?" the lieutenant murmured to himself as he scanned the column of windows providing natural light to the internal staircase used by Slack to gain access to the roof.

***

"That didn't take long," Rossi said, squinting at the screen. "But Abbott's missing."

The house rumbled as Beasley and Tripi, wearing North Face jackets over bulletproof vests, ascended the staircase two steps at a time.

"Who are they, Enzo?" Bella asked, her watery red eyes locked on the apartment's entrance.

"They're Professor Slack's peace-loving comrades in arms."

"We're on, lover boy," Cathy said, returning from the loft.

Treading as softly as his bulk allowed, Rossi led Cathy through to the entrance hall and opened the door. Below, they heard the clicking of bullets being chambered and a key turning in the lock.

"Where are the fucking lights, Sergeant?" the colonel barked.

Tripi pulled a torch from his jacket and shone the beam on the door frame. "Power's out, sir," he said, flicking the light switch up and down.

"Hello, Bella," the colonel called out, advancing, gun drawn. "I've a message for you from Professor Slack. He's running late."

Rossi and Cathy descended the stairs as the colonel spoke. Tucked in next to the door, Cathy counted down from five with her fingers. Pistols raised, they entered and took up positions on either side of the entrance hall. Cathy jammed in tight on the right, squinting down the long dark corridor. Rossi tucked away on the left, peering through the elliptical archway opening to the sitting room.

The flat had fallen silent. Nothing other than the smell of testosterone and an atmosphere thick with reckless danger. Shining his torch beam down the corridor, Rossi shuffled forward. Cathy held up her hand. The door at the end was ajar, emitting a soft natural light. Someone had drawn open the curtains.

Rossi held his hand over his head, signalling Cathy to cover him. Fist up and a nod, Cathy gestured she'd understood.

In a crouch, Rossi scurried across the corridor opening and took up a position hard against the right wall behind the engaged column of the sitting room archway. Torch held high, Rossi ran the beam from one side of the room to the other. Empty.

Then, without warning. *Pht – Pht*. Followed by the thud of a body hitting the floor. Rossi swung round, imagining the worst. But he needn't have worried. Framed in the front doorway, Cathy gave him the thumbs up as she moved down the corridor and checked Tripi's carotid artery. "He's dead."

"Colonel Beasley, do you also want to die fighting one of the president's clandestine wars?" Rossi didn't wait for an answer. "Is this the hill you want to die on? There's no glory in it. No white cross in Arlington Cemetery like your father and grandfather before you. They'll ship you home in a body bag marked loser."

"You're too fucking simple to grasp the gravity of the threat," the colonel barked from beyond the sitting room. *The kitchen*, Rossi thought.

Cathy joined Rossi, sheltering behind the decorative column on the opposite side of the archway. "Where is he?"

"Hiding like a little baby," Rossi taunted.

"Yellow belly not Green Beret," Cathy added, searching for Beasley's reflection in the large baroque mirror hanging on the wall.

Outside, Lieutenant Abbott had grown tired of waiting. Slack was long overdue. Something was wrong. He pushed on the front door as if he expected it to open. It did. Tripi had jammed a cork in the latch strike plate to stop it locking. Listening from the main foyer, he heard voices coming from upstairs. "That's not shock and awe," he murmured to himself, chambering a bullet as he ascended one step at a time.

On the first-floor landing, Abbott positioned himself hard against the wall, then shuffled towards the open door. A faint smell of gunpowder hung in the air. Staying out of sight, he stood in the dim light waiting for his eyes to adjust to the darkness. Then gun raised, he peeked inside. Two combatants standing each side of an archway as if they were holding up the ceiling. He aimed his pistol at the back of Cathy's head.

"Don't move," Bella said, descending the stairs.

Abbott raised his gaze as he turned slowly to face her. "I was looking for that."

"Drop your weapon," she said, aiming Slack's sniper rifle at the lieutenant's barrel chest.

"Bella, get back inside," Cathy shouted. "We've got this under control."

For a split second Bella's gaze shifted to Cathy's voice coming from the open door. Abbott stepped away from the wall and fired. Two shots to the body. Bella collapsed forward, rolling head over heels onto the landing.

Cathy gasped. "Bella!" But it didn't stop her discharging a single shot into the back of Abbott's oversized head.

"That leaves you, Colonel," Rossi called out.

"What you say we call it a draw?" Beasley offered.

"I'm happy to explain to the authorities what *I've* been up to. Are you, Colonel? Could get messy. British PM demanding answers from the US president – or his son-in-law – or whoever's running the bloody country these days."

"Liberals like you don't understand until it's too late. We're in the midst of a cultural war. Christian Europe has become demographically unrecognisable. America too.

Soon we'll be dreaming of a white Ramadan instead of a white Christmas. Why should we just sit back and let it happen?" Despite his fiery rhetoric, Beasley's voice had a tone of doomed inevitability about it.

"Spare me the crystal ball, Colonel," Cathy said, watching Beasley in the mirror straighten his back and salute. "You're no hero. You killed your own. That makes you a murderer in my books."

"I was protecting my president."

"By killing Chief James and Special Agent Lawrence?"

"James was a loud-mouthed womaniser. And Lawrence? Well, you can blame yourself for his death."

"How do you figure that?"

"Involving that German journalist. Stirring up the White House press corps. Causing the president to close down Crusade and cancel Genesis. It became too risky to have non-aligned outsiders like Lawrence running free. Ticking like a time bomb. Willing to spill their guts for the promise of a new dress."

"Lawrence gave his life in the service of his country. He was an American hero. We'll carve a star into the marble of the CIA Memorial Wall in his honour. Not yours."

"He was a faggot."

"A heterosexual cross-dresser," Cathy said, her tone angry.

"Is there a difference? They're all queers, and there's no place for them in the United States Intelligence Community. They risk being compromised. Blackmailed. Turned. You can never trust them one hundred per cent."

"It seems it was you rather than Lawrence who betrayed his country and the constitution."

A short silence.

Cathy leant her head forward, searching for the colonel's bully gaze in the mirror. As their eyes met, Beasley raised his pistol to the side of his head and pulled the trigger.

"Christ," Cathy said, looking away as the bullet exited in a spray of blood and brain tissue, hitting a copper pot hanging above the kitchen worktop with a clang like it was the end of a round.

Rossi locked eyes with Cathy. "What was that?"

"Beasley throwing in the towel."

As Cathy snapped photos of the carnage, Rossi searched the pockets of the departed for phones and documents that would help support their version of the story.

"They've got a vehicle nearby. Wouldn't mind a look inside," Rossi said, examining the Fobik key in the faint light of the stairway. "A Chrysler. Shouldn't be difficult to find in this part of the world."

"I'm sure they won't object to us borrowing it. But let's check there are no bodies in the boot before we set off for Heathrow."

Cathy stepped over Bella and jogged up the stairs. Rossi followed.

"Heathrow?" Rossi questioned. "Shouldn't we stay and explain this mess to someone?"

"Best done with a home-court advantage. Unless you fancy arguing your case from inside Belmarsh Prison."

"I don't mind, as long as we're together."

"Men's only club, that one."

"Homeward bound it is then," Rossi said, slipping into his coat. "But my passport's back at the hotel."

Cathy picked up her rucksack and patted the bottom pocket. "Already taken care of, Mr Rossi."

"Then what are we waiting for?"

EPILOGUE

Homeward bound, Rossi thought sadly, as the British Airways flight barrelled down the runway and lifted off into the late-night sky. Gazing down at the terminal, as the plane banked south, Rossi was sure he glimpsed from his aisle seat the United Airlines tail logo of Cathy's flight to Washington reversing from the gate.

When Cathy suggested they away home without delay to save being caught up in the dazzling blue lights of the Scottish constabulary, he assumed she meant Rome. Apparently not. Without question, she was right. But it hurt all the same. It was Washington's mess, and that's where she needed to be. Well, at least a few miles up the Potomac River at CIA headquarters in Langley.

Although Cathy promised to visit him the moment she had put the Agency straight and cleared her name, he wasn't buying it. *Visit?* What sort of word is that?

My parents visit, he grumbled to himself, wishing he'd smuggled a large hip flask of Scotch on board for the two-and-a-half-hour flight to Rome.

During their run down from St Andrews, Cathy's voice had turned distant and cold. Not dissimilar to the tone she'd selected for their reunion at the Cambridge Hilton two weeks ago. But why? Perhaps the recent reconciliation was more to do with the smell of death and a sense of her own mortality than true love. Like a boy soldier smoking for the first time before heading to the front line. Why worry about lung cancer when you could be blown to smithereens tomorrow?

Even farewelling Cathy at the airport post office before heading to his gate in Terminal 5, there was no tearful goodbye. Just a hug and a good luck peck on the cheek. *What was that?* he thought, sensing it was the last time he'd see her.

"Miss," Rossi said, holding out his hand to a flight attendant bustling through economy pushing a meal trolley, "I suppose a Scotch is out of the question?"

"You can buy a wine after the captain extinguishes the seat belt sign," the attendant said, not bothering to stop.

From bad to worse. Why am I being punished? Feeling sorry for himself, Rossi tried to sink in his seat but his knees, already jammed against the fold-down table, had nowhere to go. A wry smile as he recalled his last assignment: returning from Russia with Cathy and Chief James in a customised Boeing 737 business jet all to themselves.

Exhaling a breath of wariness, Rossi closed his heavy eyes. Vivid images of the St Andrews golf massacre scrolled across his mind. Professor Slack, Bella, Heroin Chic, and the three wise men. What was it for? East versus West. A Sisyphean struggle.

Chief James, Lawrence and Natasha: will the world change for a handful of the newly dead? Were the European Union, NATO or any of the other global institutions put in place to prevent war any safer? Rossi doubted it.

Was it right to have stopped them? Rossi pondered. Had he acted out of moral duty or rather a dislike of a narcissistic US president who lacked basic humanity? Was he any better? After all, he and Cathy had killed four adversaries, posing as judge and jury.

Rossi shifted in his seat as beads of sweat formed on his temples. He stripped down to his T-shirt, opened the overhead vent and took a gulp of water from the bottle stored in the seat pocket at his knees. Closing his eyes, he tried to sleep but his mind continued to race.

Had he made a big mistake? Perhaps Project Genesis was for the greater good?

Sure, it was a high-stakes game of money, power and politics. Nothing to do with little people like himself. Rich greedy arseholes setting the rules to protect what they have and to take more of what they don't need. A bloody good revolution, that's what's required. Rid the world of its paternalistic systems and bring freedom and equality to all. But where's the tipping point? The uprising is fifty years away. Rossi smirked, realising he was sounding more like an anarchist every day. A twinge of sadness as an image of Natasha sprung to mind.

A hand resting on Rossi's forearm woke him from his reverie. Rossi's eyes, ringed with tiredness, shot open, finding an alluring brunette smiling down at him. "Was I snoring?" he asked, glancing about at the other sleepy faces.

"Compliments of the captain, Inspector General," the flight attendant said, unfolding his table and setting down four fingers of peated Scotch whisky on a paper napkin.

Inspector General? Did I hear her right? Rossi thought. "How on God's earth…"

"We have our methods, Mr Rossi," she said with a wink, turning and leaving like a model on a catwalk.

Leaning out into the aisle on one elbow, Rossi's eyes widened as he gazed at the flight attendant prancing back to first class. *Life goes on, my friend*, Rossi thought, taking a long sip, his mood lifting. *Time to let go.*